# Belonging

# Other Works by Catherine Kos

Novels
*The Huntress and the Hound*

Novellas
*Them Summers Boys*

# Belonging

Catherine Kos

Copyright© 2018 Catherine Kos

All rights reserved.

This book is a work of fiction. Names, characters, places, and incidents are used fictitiously. Any resemblance to persons, living or dead, or local is entirely coincidental.

For Mom. For everything you've done. And for all the people who have felt that they do not belong. You'll find your place one day, and you will love it.

## Prologue

She runs through the woods; branches snatch at her hair, her breath coming in short pants. She hears the sounds of paws on the ground ahead of her, and she runs as fast as she can, trying to catch up. Branches cut into her, marking her skin red as she continues on, but she doesn't even notice. She doesn't feel anything other than the need for blood. She can hear the white hare running fast ahead, as its predator hunts it. The urge for the hunt has kicked her into overdrive and she is moving at the speed of light, a blur to anyone who should glance in her direction. She follows as close as possible, and when they reach the clearing, which turns to a cliff, she slides to a stop. The small hare stands at the edge of it and she can smell the fear coming from it. Its predator stands between the girl and it, bowing its head, it's dark brown fur standing up on end. She inches closer, and her foot lands on a twig, snapping it, making her presence known. The dark animal turns around. His yellow eyes gleam at her. His teeth are barred as he growls at her. Fear strikes clear through her gut.

"Wait," She says to the wolf, sticking her hands out in front of her. It inches closer to her and she inches back. She knows what is going to happen, and she cannot stop it.

"Wait, I'm one of you," she stammers, struggling to keep composure. Desperate, she throws her arms out in front of her.

The wolf comes closer.

"I'm one of you!" She shouts. To the wolf. To herself. To the world.

The wolf pounces.

Her scream echoes through the woods.

## Chapter One

I wake up with a gasp, my body jolting me forward into an upright position. Perspiration covers my body, causing my hair to stick to my neck and forehead. Something about the dream… it felt so real. The ending of the dream keeps flashing through my mind. The wolf's eyes staring deep into mine. A shiver runs through my body. I do a little shimmy to shake the feeling from my body. As I take a deep breath, there is an impatient knock at the door. Oh right, a knock on the door is what woke me up. Well, best not to keep whomever it is waiting.

Judging from the amount of light that is *not* streaming through the window, I can assume that it is still sometime in the middle of the night. What could this possibly be about?

Throwing the covers off my body, I stride to the door, unlocking it, and pulling it open a few inches. Through the darkness, I can see Franklin, Marcus' second in command standing just outside my door. He stares at me with distaste written on his face, as if summoning me is a serious chore.

"Yes?" I ask, irritated.

A smile forms on his face. As if he is telling a joke.

"Your father wants you in his office," he says.

"Okay, I will be there in a moment," I say, beginning to close the door, but he sticks his foot out, stopping me.

"Now," he growls as I look up at him. Without waiting for me to move on my own, Franklin yanks my arm dragging me down the hall towards Marcus' office.

Franklin is a short man with dirty blonde hair that goes down past his ears, and beady little black eyes. He is shorter that I am, but right now he is stronger than me, and his hand digs into my arm.

There is no light in the hallway, but after all we don't require light to see. The closer we get to Marcus' office, the heavier my stomach feels. Dread fills my body, my usual sensation when I am in Marcus' presence. But this time… it feels substantially worse. This can't be good. Why would he wake me in the middle of the night? What could be the reason? I've been in my room the last few days. I've done nothing to make him mad.

As we reach the door, Franklin reaches in front of me to open the door. With a hand at my back, he forcibly shoves me into the room, making me stumble. I glare at him over my shoulder but he just smiles, and closes the door sealing me inside. Alone with *him*.

Marcus' office is a large room with one large window in the wall across from the door. In front of his window is a massive oak desk that faces the door. Marcus is standing between the window and the desk, staring out the window with his hands behind his back. I don't need to see his face to know that there is a scowl forming on it.

"How is it that I ended up with a daughter that struggles to simply walk into a room?" He says.

I could tell him that Franklin shoved me, but he would never take my side. He never has before.

Marcus turns around to face me, the features of his face displaying his disgust for me. When I was younger I would have flinched. Now, I just stare in return, waiting patiently for the next hurtful thing he comes up with. He steps around the desk, and leans back against it, crossing his legs at the ankles, and he studies me.

He is not a tall man, nor would he be considered a large man. The only powerful thing about him is the position he holds, yet compared to other packs, he is barely a blip on the radar. He craves the power he doesn't have. Observing the two of us, there is no one on this green earth that would ever think of us as father and daughter. I stand at nearly six feet tall, whereas Marcus is around five foot five. He has greasy brown hair that hangs in limp waves across his face, and I have stark white hair that flows down my back. He has a small round face with beady brown eyes that are always filled with rage, yet mine are large, bright, and a rare violet color. His head hangs on his shoulders as if he is talking down to every person he meets. And let's face it, he *is* talking down to them. He knows his status of power, and that he is low on the food chain, and yet he still believes himself to the best. Almost as if he has some secret that no one else knows.

After a moment of silence, he orders, "I need you to go to your room and pack all your belongings."

His face remains a neutral disgust, showing no additional emotion at all. Hope blooms in my chest, but I squash the silly feeling down. This has to be a trick. There is a catch somewhere. This is a joke and I am just waiting for the punch line. There is no way he would let me go, just like that.

My voice is quiet when I ask, "Why?"

I feel the growl before I hear it. He doesn't like to be questioned, most of all by me. Still, he answers me.

"An opportunity arose. And I took it."

"What opportunity?" I can hear the irritation in my voice, but I can't help it. I don't like his games.

"Careful," he says in warning. I bristle. "I have made a deal with another Alpha. His son is coming into his powers. He is getting ready for the change. But he doesn't have a mate. You are to go with the Alpha, and you will be married to his son."

Most of the time, when someone wants to be an Alpha, they have to fight the current Alpha for the position, to prove that they are strong enough. Other times the Alpha position is inherited. If an Alpha wills away his powers to someone else, then that other wolf gets all of the Alpha's powers.

He stares at me. He stares as if he expects me to be okay with this. I stare at him, waiting for him to tell me that he is joking. But I've never seen him make a joke.

"You cannot be serious," I nearly yell, completely outraged. When he doesn't respond, I retreat. "No, I won't do it. No-"

Before I can finish, he is in front of me, and his hand is gripping my chin, bringing my face so close to his, I can smell his fowl breath.

"You. Will. Do as I say," he growls. His fingers dig in, and I cry out. "Do you understand?"

"Yes," I seethe from both pain and anger.

He releases me, but he does not back away.

"What pack?" I whisper.

"Blackheart."

Growing up, the one thing I knew was that Marcus did not like the Blackhearts. He despised them. They seemed to be the exact opposite of Marcus. They seemed good.

From the stories that I have heard, the Blackhearts are people who take care of each other. They treat each other with respect, and as equals. Marcus' pack mainly contains men because they see women as only needed for certain things. They are not allowed positions in the pack, because the men feel women are only servants. The Blackhearts welcome people who are different, and don't expect the woman to cook, and clean, and have babies, just because they are woman. They take care of everyone because every single person in the pack is essential to making the pack last and be larger than life. Marcus' pack is so small because he has pushed so many people away with his hateful and callous attitude. In Marcus' eyes the Blackhearts are weak because they do not turn people away. They don't discern the weak from the strong. In Marcus' eyes if you are in any way weak, you do not belong in his pack.

"What did you get out of this? Why is this so important to you?" I ask.

The fist hits me before I can even react. A loud crack fills the air, and pain erupts in the side of my face. I fall to the floor from the impact of the hit, clutching my jaw in pain.

"Never question me!" He screams, his round face red with rage, his teeth sharp and lengthening, spit flying all over.

His anger must have triggered his change. He rushes towards me, grabs me by my forearms, pushing me into a wall with his fingernails digging into my arms. He relinquishes his hold on my arms to grip my jaw once more and lift me completely off the floor. I gasp as his nails cut the sore skin around my face. My face burns and all I want to do is scream. He forces me to look at him. His eyes have changed color to a dark yellow. Just like the wolf in my dream.

"You will go to your room, and you will pack. In exactly one hour, you will come downstairs and you will go with Damon Blackheart. You will join their pack, and you will not embarrass me. Do you understand?"

I nod the best I can.

"Speak," he orders.

"Yes," I breathe.

"Yes, what?" His grip tightens.

"Yes. Alpha," I spit the last word out with disgust.

When he finally relinquishes his grip, I breathe a sigh of relief.

The door to the office opens, and Franklin steps in, grabs my forearm, and drags me out of the room. My hand cradles my chin, I gently slide a hand over my face to judge the damage during the walk back to my room. I can feel something jutting out just slightly on the right side of my face. As I touch it I nearly cry out from the pain.

We get to my room, and Franklin throws the door open, then shoves me into the room. I can't get my feet safely under me, causing me to fall, and part of my body hits the side of my bed. At least it was the bed this time. The door slams closed and I am left alone in the dark. I grab at the mattress and pull myself up. When I'm standing I walk into my private bathroom in the corner of the room and turn on the light. I look in the mirror and I am not at all shocked by what I see. My jaw is hanging low to the right side of my face. My cheek is starting to swell, making everything appear worse.

Okay, I just need to pop it back into place. If I do that it will start to heal. I do a little dance, shaking out my hands and arms, while taking in a deep breath. I can do this! It will be okay! I've got this! Placing my bent elbows on the countertop of the sink, I place my jaw into the palm of my right hand, with my fingers spider webbing over my mouth. I wrap my left hand around my right, and take a deep breath.

One.

Two.

I press my chin into my hands. My jaw shifts, there is a pop, and it locks back into place. I jump up and down. Once. Twice, shaking out the pain.

"Fuck," I drag out the word in a ragged pain filled breath.

After a second the pain slowly begins to fade. I take another look in the mirror. The swelling on my face visibly starts to go down, and now the marks from his nails are clearer. Little red half moon marks are scattered along my chin and lower cheeks. Wetting a towel, I bring it to my chin, and wipe away the little bits of blood. The marks are noticeable but they will fade in a day. Not a big deal. My chin will be sore for the next couple of days, and it will probably bruise, but it should be fine by the end of the week. I don't heal as fast as others like me, but I heal faster than the average human.

Compared to others, I'm different in every way, not just with healing. I'm stuck somewhere in the middle. I am a disgrace to my kind, but I am

Godlike to humans. And, I don't mean that in an egotistical way. I mean that in the literal way. Humans have worshiped my kind for centuries; we were once considered Gods.

I am a werewolf. Well… I'm not technically there yet. But, I come from a long line of werewolves. The man who shares his DNA with me is the Alpha of the Beaumont Pack. It's a small pack, but he is the Alpha nonetheless. He is not a good one, but I still have to do what he says. I am his subordinate. Every pack has an Alpha, along with a long list of other members with job titles, some more important than others. But the most important one is the Alpha. Each Alpha has an Alpha Voice. They summon it from deep within them, and they can make any wolf in their pack, even those with the strongest wills, do as there are told. Most Alphas do not use the Alpha Voice, as a show of respect for their subordinates. Marcus knows nothing of respect. He uses his Alpha Voice every time he talks to me. He's never been a father to me. Always an Alpha.

Speaking of Alphas.

I walk back into my room, and I grab a duffel bag from under my bed, and start filling it with clothes from my dresser.

Part of me cannot pack fast enough. A chance to get out of this house? A chance to get away from Marcus? I will take it. Maybe, when we are on the road, I can break away. Jump out of the car or something. Run away, and become a rogue. A rogue. Do I really want to do that? I have no idea what Damon Blackheart is going to be like. What if he is like Marcus? What if he is worse? What if he hates me just as much as Marcus does because I cannot shift?

That's right! I cannot shift. And what kind a wolf cannot shift? Me. Aurora Beaumont. Though no one calls me that. Rory. That's who I am to everyone. When I was little, I had a father, and a mother, and a brother. We were a normal family to say the least. I always knew that my father favored my brother over me. But, when he was angry he never bothered me, so I never minded that he didn't like me that much. Then, I turned fourteen and it all changed. My brother and my mother are gone, and since then I am the one that he takes his anger out on. His anger that I am the one he is stuck with, and that my brother is gone. All that and the fact that I cannot shift.

Normally, my kind shift for the first time somewhere in their teens. It is like the werewolf version of puberty. It can happen anytime but for most it commonly happens around fifteen. It is very rare for a twenty-year-old wolf to have not shifted completely. And when I say completely, I mean that every month on the full moon, my change is triggered, and my body begins to change. *But*, the pain is too much, and I end up passing out from it. When I wake up the next day, I'm naked and in my human form. The first change is always the hardest, or so I have been told. It hurts the worst. Eventually your body starts getting used to the pain. Kind of like when you work out for the first time, your body hurts really bad the next day but the more you do it the less it hurts. It is all about conditioning your body. But, me, my body hasn't fully made it through the change, so it hasn't been able to be conditioned.

There have been numerous stories told about werewolves throughout the years, but the truth is that werewolves can shift whenever they want but they forcibly shift whenever the moon is full. On the days before the full moon, we get kind of testy. Tensions rise. Feelings are enhanced. We get very PMS-y if you know what I mean.

Now, you're probably thinking why would I still be with my father if I were twenty? Shouldn't I have been able to move out? Well, my human friend, that is not how my life works or how pack life works. We have rules. Laws. And when you are a part of a pack, you *live* with the pack. Sometimes not in the same house, but very near each other. If you don't have a pack, you are considered a rogue, and rogues cannot live within pack territories. They are nomads. To be a rogue, you don't have an allegiance to any pack. They don't have an official home. They travel from place to place and they are not allowed to settle down. Rogues are not allowed inside the territories of other packs. If they step foot onto someone's territory, they don't usually make it out. Rogues are practically forbidden. Our kind is not meant to be alone. We survive in the comfort of others. These laws were put into place to assured that everyone has a place in a pack. Of course, that logic is flawed because sometimes your place in a pack can be the worst place to be. It is because of these laws that I am still with Marcus. Actually, that is not true. I came to peace with the idea of becoming a rogue a long time ago. And, I tried to escape numerous times. Each time I was caught, the consequence was worse with each attempt at escape. Eventually, Marcus locked me in this room; hence the reason for my own personal bathroom.

Now, I finally get to leave.

We live on a small piece of land in the western region of the United States. From what I have heard over the years, the Blackheart Pack is based in the South East Region. It is quite a ways away. If I can break away from the Blackhearts halfway on this trip, I should be free and clear. Because did they seriously think I am going to participate in an arranged marriage? I mean, do our kind even *do* arranged marriages anymore? Sure, centuries ago there were arranged marriages so packs could get stronger, as well as land, but come on! Nowadays we just kill each other for those things.

Kidding.

Kind of.

Nowadays, if someone wants to become Alpha or take over another pack, the Alpha steps down, forfeiting, or the challenger and Alpha of said pack fight to the death. Winner becomes Alpha.

Loser… well dies. It is barbaric, but it doesn't happen that often. And after all, we are part animal.

## Chapter Two

It is still dark out when Franklin comes to get me. I'm sitting on my bed, staring at the basically empty room, just staring, feeling dubious. Am I grateful for a chance to leave this place? A real chance. Not some half-wit attempt at running away. No, this time I will be crossing out of the packs territory, and it will be all Marcus' idea. Or am I sad because I am leaving the place that I've lived for the past twenty years? Yeah, like I could ever be sad about leaving here.

Grateful. Definitely grateful. I scoff. It is not even a question. A part of me even feels hopeful. That things could be better from here on out. But I hate to be hopeful. It is just an emotion that leads to sadness.

There is a curt knock on the door. It opens a second later.

"It's time," Franklin says.

Grabbing my bag off the bed, I take a deep breath and step out of the room. I follow Franklin down the hallway, and down the steps. As I move down the stairway, with each step I get a clear view of three men standing in the foyer. One man is Marcus. The other two I do not know. One is tall, with jet black hair, and a clean-shaven face. He is the Alpha. I don't need them to tell me. Not only does he have the essence of an Alpha, it is also the way he stands. Without a care in the world, yet he is totally prepared for anything.

Most Alphas have this sort of... pull about them. Whenever they are near another wolf, the power of the Alpha is felt. The control that they have is felt by anyone near and the stronger the Alpha, the stronger the pull. And this Alpha's power is abundantly strong.

The man next to the Alpha is a few inches shorter with short brown hair. He has a face set in stone as if he can't believe he is here, whereas the Alpha's face is soft, almost as if he is amused.

"Gentleman, this is my daughter, Aurora," Marcus says, turning to look at me with a pleasant smile on his face. Almost like he is proud to have me as a daughter. Both men turn their eyes up at me, and something in the Alpha's eyes doesn't reach the small smile on his face. I watch as he assesses me, and his eyes linger on my hair. I don't hide or shy away; I raise my chin even though it might be trembling.

"Rory, this is Damen Blackheart. He is the Alpha of the Blackheart Pack. And his Beta, Darius."

Beta's are an Alpha's second in command. If something were to happen to Damen, then Darius would be the interim Alpha until another has been found. In theory, Darius could become Alpha if Damen and Darius were to spar, and Darius won, or if Damen were to willingly give Darius his powers.

"Nice to meet you," Damen says.

I don't respond.

We're quiet for a moment.

Marcus turns to me, wrapping his arms around me. I don't move, except the fist that tightens around the strap of my duffel. A small part of me feels bad that they have to watch this poor display of a father and daughter relationship. When it has been too many seconds, I forcefully take a step back.

"We should be going," Damen says, and I glance at him.

He sounds almost as if he doesn't want to be here anymore than I do.

"Yes, of course. Please take good care of my daughter," Marcus says to Damen.

Damen looks briefly at him, and responds with a stiff nod.

His features are softer when he returns his gaze to me.

"Let me take that from you," he says, and reaches for my bag, taking it from my hands. He places his other hand at the small of my back, and leads me out of the house. There is a black Cadillac Escalade parked outside the house in the front yard. Damen walks me to the car, and he opens the passenger door for me. I climb in, eager to leave this place and never come back. Darius takes my bag from his Alpha's hands, and he places it in the trunk while the Alpha rounds the car and climbs into the drivers seat. I take one last look at the ramshackled house in front of me. The place where I have lived for twenty years. The place that I am finally free of.

Marcus stands in the doorway, a pleasant smile on his face.

"Daughter," he says in goodbye.

I may not be able to shift, but I can hear like any other of my kind.

"Marcus."

Then Damen puts the car in reverse, and within seconds the house is behind us.

We've been driving for a few moments when Damen speaks.

"Aurora, did - "

"Please don't call me that. It's Rory. Just Rory."

He casts a glance at me, and then nods.

"Did he do that to you?" He asks. "Your jaw?"

For a moment I think about not responding.

"It's fine now. I popped it back in," I finally reply, looking out the window.

"You popped it back in?" Darius asks from the backseat, completely astounded. "By yourself?"

I shrug. "Not the first time."

A muscle tightens in Damen's jaw.

"Well it is going to be the last time you ever have to do that," he says.

Yeah, because I am getting out of here the first chance I get. But he doesn't need to know that.

"Just sit back and relax. We have a long way to go. And trust me when I say, no one in my pack is going to hurt you."

I hold in a loud laugh. Sure, you won't hurt me, but I just have to marry your son. Either way, I sit back and relax, and wait for my chance to run.

## Chapter Three

"Bathroom break," Damen announces, pulling up to one of those road side gas station and fast food places. We're in the middle of nowhere. I take a look around looking for a place to escape. There is a bus stop to the right of the gas station. Bingo.

"Pick up anything you want," Damen says. "We'll meet you at the front."

He casts me a smile as he steps out of the car. Hesitantly, I follow. They walk into the store in front of me, and I silently slow, and come to a stop in the doorway. They both continue farther into the store, and I take a step back. The door closes, and now is my chance. Sneaking to the side, I creep along the side of the store, and charge across the street to the bus station. On the other side of the street, I take a quick look over my shoulder, and the two men are still inside the store. I slip inside the bus station.

Instantly, I back against the door, overwhelmed. Thankfully the doors only opens one way, so I don't fall backwards.

People are everywhere. There are so many of them. Way more than I've been around in a long time. There's an abundance of sounds; an abundance of smells. Sensory overload. Fear shoots through my system, and for a moment I'm frozen, not sure what to do.

Humans don't know about us. It's another one of those rules that we have. If we shift we are to be very careful. Humans are not to know about are kind. About what we really are. Because of this, I feel myself slipping, something I have never really felt before. It is almost like my wolf. So, reaching behind me, I fumble to find the door handle, because I *have* to get out of here. My hand grasps it and I pull it open, slipping out into the fresh air. I take deep breaths of air. Looking around, I see an empty bench. Numb, I walk to it, and take a seat, wrapping my arms around myself. My mind starts to race, and I realize how idiotic I am. How could I think I could really do this? I have no money. No idea where to go. No idea how to live a normal life. I run my hands through my hair, exasperated, with shaking heads.

A car pulls up in front of me, and the window rolls down. I glance up, and see Damen staring at me through dark sunglasses.

"Doesn't look like there's going to be a bus anytime soon," he says to me.

I cross my arms, and lean back, facing away from him.

"The lady inside said there's one coming in five minutes."

"Is that so?"

I nod.

"Is going rogue really what you want to do?"

I shrug and he sighs.

"You don't trust me."

"Don't take it personally, I don't trust anyone."

"Look, there's nothing I can say at this moment to make you trust me, but let's make a deal."

I scoff.

"A deal?"

"Yes. You come back with me, and spend four months in our pack. No one will touch you, and no one will bother you. After four months you can decide whether or not you want to stay or go. If you chose to go, we won't stop you, and your father won't find out about it either."

"What's the catch?"

"Well, you'll have to get a job. And enroll in school, which we will have taken care of. You won't have to marry my son. You won't have to do anything that you don't want too."

"Why would you do all of this for me?" I ask him.

"You remind me of someone I used to know," he says simply.

When I don't say anything, he checks his watch.

"Two minutes until your bus comes, Rory. Decide fast."

Seeming that as of right now, I am out of options, I reluctantly stand up.

"Just to be clear, I am not marrying anyone," I say, opening the car door, and sliding into the passenger seat.

Damen chuckles. "Understood. The smoke signals you're letting off say that marriage is definitely out of the question."

"Glad you noticed."

He smiles as he puts the car into drive, and we're are back on the road.

"Can I ask, when he did that to you?" Damen asks, and I look over at him, confused. "Your jaw," he clarifies.

"Just a few hours before you showed up."

He casts me a sidelong glance. "And it hasn't healed yet? The bruise looks like it is just beginning to form."

"I don't heal as fast as I should," I say with a shrug, unsure of what else to say.

He doesn't reply, but something in his jaw ticks. It makes me wonder whether he's mad at me or at Marcus.

"You can sleep if you like. We've got a long drive ahead of us."

Nodding, I curl up against the door, my head against my arm and my arm against the window. I close my eyes, grateful when sleep grips me in its claws.

## Chapter Four

Our kind runs on power. We judge who is the strongest by who has the most power. The most followers. The most land.

Most of our powers come from the Moon Goddess, the things that we received at birth. Our strength our natural abilities. When one of us is killed by another wolf, that other wolf gets these powers.

Years ago, there was a family with an Alpha, who was close to being considered a King. They were beloved and they were the strongest. Everyone looked up to the Alpha. He had the most land. The most followers, and all the powers that Moon Goddess bestowed upon him were told to be extraordinary. The pack was so big and powerful that stories were lore told to children. One couldn't tell if the stories were true or false. His son was told to be something much like his father, but he wasn't as careful. He fell in love with a girl. A human girl; one that proved to cause trouble for his pack, like his father dreamt would happen. The father disapproved, but the son wouldn't give the girl up. When it was time for the son to take over the pack, the father wasn't sure if it was right, but he believed he taught his son well. A few months after the son's takeover, a man showed up to the son's door. He had a proposition. The son didn't want it, so he sent the stranger away. That same night, the pack was attacked, and some of the strongest members were killed. A week later, they were attacked again, by a pack of Hunters. Even the son couldn't fend them off. With the pack wounded, most everyone died except for the son. He disappeared into the night, and the story goes that no one has heard from him since that night. After the death of the pack, our kind needed someone else to look up to. And so they turned to the Blackheart Pack.

My mother used to tell me this story when I was a child, along with stories of the father's powers. It was hard to discern what was true and what were fables. Growing up with Marcus, what I knew to be true is that the Blackhearts are the biggest and most powerful pack. That is why Marcus hates Damen Blackheart. Once upon a time, Marcus had a large following, but the wolves chose Damen over Marcus. Slowly, people left Marcus' pack as they realized that he wasn't a good leader, and he wasn't going to get them anywhere. Jealousy fuels the anger. Now, this is what's left; Marcus with nothing, and Damen with everything.

There is a slam that shakes the car, causing me to jolt awake.

"Sorry," Damen says. "That's just Darius getting gas."

"It's fine," I say, and I give myself a stretch. Looking around, I see nothing but trees. We're at a small gas station with only two pumps. We're the only car. We're the only people in sight.

After a few minutes Darius gets back in the car, and then we're back on the road. It's only been a few miles when we pass a sign reading *'Welcome to Skarletbach. Population 7,500.'*

"Skarletbach?" I ask, turning to Damen.

He nods. "It's an anagram. For Blackheart. My ancestors founded this town. They built everything from the ground up, including the college. That is why you'll be getting in for free. As far as they know, you're a relative of ours."

"So, the town is a part of your land?"

Damen smiles. "Yes, and everything surrounding it. Fifty miles out to the east and west; one hundred miles out to the north and south."

I keep my jaw from hitting the floor. Turning in my seat, I face the front and let that digest. 100 miles. That's a long way to go if I try to run away.

He must have read my mind. "My pack can run a mile in under three minutes. It's not that long in the scheme of things."

After a few more miles we start to pass houses and I start to see people. Slowly, we navigate through the town. Once we hit what seems to be Main Street, we stop at a red light, and Damen points to buildings that peak out over the trees.

"That is S.U. Skarletbach University. The pack members that decide to go here get in for a discounted rate. Unfortunately, I can't let everyone in for free. But, for my immediate family, I can. That will include you."

"All of this... it is a lot to do for someone you don't even know."

He glances over at me, before driving again.

"You are probably not used to people doing things for you, huh?"

"Not without reason."

"Well, it is time to try something new, don't you think?"

Rather than speak, I shift my gaze out the window.

*Everything's so fucking green.*

It is mid-September, and the trees are all colorful from fall changes, and it looks amazing. I kind of like it. The weather is a little cooler out but we don't really need coats around this time of year. We run really hot, even in our human form. We will wear light jackets to fit in with the normal humans, but we don't wear thick jackets until the snow begins to fall.

The car twists and turns, going past so many trees; I'm not sure how I'm every going to remember the route. Finally, Damen makes one last turn. He slows down, before coming to a stop in front of two big metal gates that stand over ten feet tall that connect to stone walls. On the front of the gates are two giant letters. 'B.M.'

"'B.M.'?"

"This is Blackheart Manor. My pack lives scattered throughout the territory but if something happens, if anyone needs a safe place, they come here. Here we are protected. The man who founded the pack centuries ago, was named Jackson Blackheart. He built this place in hopes that it would be a sort of, a safe haven for wolves. This is our pack house."

A buzz sounds, and then the gates slowly open. Damen presses on the gas, and we move forward. We travel through what has to be another two miles of trees before there is a clearing. A few hundred yards ahead is the manor.

"When the moon is out, we go running as a pack, that is the only time we go running outside of these gates in our wolf form without a reason. Otherwise, we run inside the walls. That is why there is so much space within the compound." Darius pitches in from the backseat.

"Why?" I ask, amazed at, well… everything.

"Many years ago, Hunters were a large issue. We haven't been bothered in a long time, and I like to think it is because of the rules that we keep here. It is safest for us."

Damen pulls the escalade into the front of the mansion.

"Welcome to Blackheart Manor."

I get out, staring up in awe at the building. It is a beautiful building made from red brick. It is in the shape of a 'U', and in the very center are two double doors. There are three stone steps, each one stretching out three feet, to where the bottom step meets the gravel of the driveway. Most of the walls are covered with vines, and the building has to stand at least three stories high. On the left side of the mansion there is a pathway that leads into a garden. On the right side there is a tall hedge maze.

At the very center of the house, are two doors, connecting to each other. They are solid oak with brass handles, and small windows at the top. The windows are small and round and there is a sort of crest carved into both.

"My ancestors founded this pack, and throughout the centuries it continued to grow. Everyone has a place here. We're one of the biggest packs around, and we pretty much run the town. We are a family here. Everyone pitches in, everyone helps."

"It's beautiful."

"Everyone has a place here. We all work together to keep this place safe and clean."

I nod in understanding, and turn in a circle, taking everything in. When facing the house again, Damen smiles at me.

"Ready?" He asks.

"Can I really say no?"

Damen chuckles, making me smile in response.

"Come on," he says, "Darius will take your things to your room. Let's take you to get your jaw checked out."

With a hand at my back, he leads me into the house.

Past the front doors is a beautiful rustic interior. The foyer is wide and open with two sets of stairs along the far wall. They are both are exact replicas of each other on opposite sides of the room. To the right there is a large doorway that leads into a dining room. There is a huge oak dining table in the center of the room; with one glance it seats at least twenty people. To the left there is a sitting room. It has a large flat screen TV on the wall, two couches, and two chairs centered in front of it. Behind the TV, and a little over to the right is a set of French doors. Four glass panes, all brown to match the interior, with red curtains that are currently spread to the sides, letting the morning sun shine through, covering the room in a hazy golden glow.

My attention turns back to Damen who stands behind me and is is looking at me, waiting patiently. I go to speak but my eyes lift up, and my jaw drops. Above the doors, there is a replica of the crests on the door. The crest is large and beautifully carved. A howling wolf rests in the crest, and ribbons of blue and yellow swirl around the carving. A shield with a solid plate in the center rests next to the wolf.

"That is our crest. The crest of the school, and the crest of our pack. Our motto is 'It is with loyalty and honor that we stand ahead of the rest'. The blue represents loyalty, and the yellow represents generosity. The shield represents honor," Damen says, and I nod in awe. I've never seen anything like it before. Certainly not in Marcus' pack.

"Most parents send their teens to live here to get used to working together in a pack. This is where they train so that they can have a high place in the pack if they want one. My blood family lives here. My son is training to become Alpha, and his sister is training to be his Sentinel. You will stay here with them. Bond with them; maybe you'll find a place if you want one. But, more important than training, this is a sanctuary for those in need. This is where we come together as pack. Where we live and bleed. No matter where we are, this is our true home. That is why we take care of it so."

"I understand," I reply.

This place is sacred.

"For the teens of the pack, dinner is mandatory, but breakfast and lunch are optional. All meals are served in the dining room," he says, motioning to the room to the right. "You can also have your food delivered to your room, just let the cooks know ahead of time."

"When we have pack meetings, they are held here," he says motioning around the house itself. "When we run together on the full moon, we start here and then we run together outside of the wall. That is the only time you can run in wolf form outside of the wall. If you need to stretch your legs at all, you are to do it within the walls, unless told otherwise."

Again, I nod, but I decide not to tell him that my shifting is not something I really need to worry about at this moment. He doesn't need to know that yet.

Damen turns and begins walking up the stairs, and I slowly follow.

"There are five floors, not including the main one. The first three house the other teens from the pack. There are fourteen teens at the moment. My daughter and one of my sons live on the fourth floor. I don't live here. My home is close, and I am here frequently, but if I am not around, my son will help you with anything you need."

As Damen walks up the stairs, I take a moment to really assess him. He is tall and clearly strong. I have a feeling I don't want to see him when he is mad. His hair is dark brown that reaches his ears. A five o'clock shadow graces Damen's chin, making him look scruffy, and tired. There are specs of grey in his hair, but I have a feeling that it is from stress rather than age. We, werewolves, age differently from humans. We grow what some might call normally until the age of eighteen when our bodies are fully grown, and then our aging process slows dramatically. Damen could be over a hundred years and I really wouldn't know it.

When we reach the top of the first flight of stairs, we walk down the wide hallways where we pass one door on either side of us. There is a second door on the right which Damen walks up to and opens. He holds it for me to walk through, and I step into a white, sterile room. The walls are half windows, and there are seven beds placed against the walls. In the far right corner is a small office. Damen walks to the door, and I dutifully follow, to see a petite woman sitting at a desk. Above the desk there is a cabinet full of medicine, and next to her there is an adjustable, cushioned table with paper on it.

The woman has long brown hair that is twisted high on her head in a bun. Her back was to us, but she turned when we approached the door. She has to be in her mid thirties, with fair skin and well-defined cheekbones. Freckles scatter across her nose and cheeks, and she has light brown eyes to match. There are red glasses placed high up on her head, and matching lipstick stretches across her face as she smiles at us.

"Good morning, Alpha," she says with a sweet smile. Her chocolate eyes fall upon me, and I watch as they look me over, lingering for a moment around my head. "And you must be Rory. Good morning, Rory."

"Good morning," I reply, my voice hoarse all of a sudden. I clear it, and her smile seems to grow.

"I'm guessing you don't talk much do you?" She asks, her smile turning wry, making me shift uncomfortably, and shrug.

"That's okay," she says, her voice sweet. Caring. "Why don't you have a seat?" The Doctor motions to the table, before she turns her gaze on the Alpha.

"Sorry, Alpha, but I'm going to have to ask you to wait outside."

Damen nods. "I'll see you in a few minutes."

He steps out of the room while I take a seat, and the Doctor closes the door. She grabs her chair and sits in front of me.

"Alpha's and their manners," she chortles. "My name is Lucy, and I am the pack doctor. It is very nice to meet you."

"You too," I say, feeling surprisingly calm.

"Now, the Alpha has told me that you recently had your jaw dislocated. Do you mind if I check it?"

Slowly, I shake my head.

Lucy pulls her glasses down from her head to her eyes, and pulls rubber gloves over her hands, before slowly reaching for my chin. Lightly, she applies pressure.

"Does this hurt?"

"Not really." The skin is still slightly tender, but I don't flinch as she touches it.

"And you popped it back in yourself?"

"Yes."

She pulls back. "Well, it seems okay, but I do find it odd that you haven't healed yet from it. If something like this happens again, do not pop it back in okay? Come straight to me. Understood?"

I nod. "Yes."

"Good. Now," she says as she grabs a clipboard from her desktop. "I'm going to ask you a few questions, okay? I want you to answer them honestly. These will stay between us."

"Okay," I say, feeling a little uneasy.

"First, what is your daily diet usually like?"

I shrug.

"You can do better than that," she says with a sweet smile.

"The usual, I guess."

"That is a little better. What is the usual?"

"Scraps. Whatever I could get."

Doc doesn't seem surprised by this.

"Who dislocated your jaw and gave you those cuts along your cheek?"

My fingers graze along my cheek, feeling the little half moons imprinted in my skin. I didn't realize they were still there.

"Your father? The Alpha?" She asks, when I don't answer.

Nodding, I look away.

"How often did things like this happen?"

Scoffing, I answer, "Often."

"Have you ever healed instantly?"

"Yes. When I was fourteen."

"Why only then do you think?"

"Because my mother and brother were still alive. My brother was Marcus' favorite. When he was there, Marcus never paid attention to me."

"Have you ever shifted?"

I shake my head. "No. My body starts to. I can feel the pain, but I pass out before I can actually change. When I wake up, I'm in my human form, naked."

"Can you feel your wolf?"

"Sometimes, when I feel an emotion really strongly. Like, if I'm really angry I can feel that she is there. Most of the time she is dormant though."

Lucy pushes her glasses up high on her head, and smiles at me, reassuringly. "Well, the not shifting or healing has to be because of you malnourishment. It does concern me, but I think that if we get you eating right, we can have you shifting within a couple of months. We will get you through this, Rory. We will get you healthy."

When I am about to respond there is a knock on the office door. It opens to reveal a young man, around the age of twenty with short fiery red hair. His hair fades from the bottom up, with the longer hair on top, combed back. He has a beard spreading across his jaw, and dimples show on his cheeks as he smiles at me. He towers over me, and I am not even sitting low, and he seems so muscular and massive, he fills out the doorframe.

"Hey, Doc," he says, smiling to Lucy. When he looks back at me, I see that he has vibrant blue eyes. He reaches out his hand out to me. "Hey, I'm Kyle. I'm training to be the Beta."

I tentatively take his hand.

"I'm here to take you to get something to eat, and then we will take the grand tour, once you are done with the Doc."

"I actually have to go talk to the Alpha for a few moments. Why don't you two talk for a moment?"

Before we can respond, Lucy is out of the room. She leaves the door open, and I hear her start talking to the Alpha.

Kyle begins to say something, but suddenly an alluring smell fills the air, and I can't think about anything but it. It is a mouthwatering scent, and I start sniffing the air, trying to figure out where it is coming from. It's smells like trees, and that moment just after a heavy rain, when everything is wet, and the air smells so clean and fresh. Yeah, it smells like that and more. Something deep within me begins stirring. My wolf.

"What..." I stand up, sniffing the air as the scent grows stronger. I've never had a strong sense of smell before, but suddenly this particular scent is overwhelming. It feels... like it is meant for me. I breathe it in and it fills my whole body with a sort of tingling feeling.

"You okay?" I vaguely hear Kyle ask me.

Outside the door, a new voice floats through the air.

"Dad?" The deep, masculine voice calls out, sounding like music to my ears.

"Ren. Good you are here," Damen replies.

"What –" The new voice, Ren, begins but he stops, and a low growl fills the air.

My teeth elongate, and a growl erupts from my throat. Suddenly, I have no control over my body.

"Hey, guys. You might want to come in here," Kyle calls out. Clearly, he is confused about what is going on. Glad I am not the only one.

Footsteps echo in the air and the delicious scent gets closer. My body begins to shake as my wolf tries to break free.

Damen appears in the doorway, stepping in with Lucy following him. A boy – a man comes last. When he sees me, when our eyes meet, he stops in his tracks. He is tall and built like a mountain, filling in the doorframe. His stance is ready, prepared like he is ready for anything. His eyes are hard, but there is something… different in them. Something I've never seen before. He has jet black hair, with a matching scruff covering his face. I see a flash of bright green before his eyes turn a golden color, as his wolf takes over. His mouth opens an inch and I can see his fangs sticking out. Another growl comes from his throat.

"Mate," he growls out, low and deep.

*Mine*! My wolf howls.

My wolf breaks through the surface, but I fall before she can truly escape. My eyes roll in the back of my head, and the lights go out.

## Chapter Five

The only thing more important than power to our kind, are mates. The truest honor of our kind is to find our true mate that the Moon Goddess has sent to us. A mate is your true love. The person you are meant to be with. Let's be honest, it sounds like a total myth. A fairytale told to young girls to get their hopes up. To me, that is exactly what I thought it was. Despite it's sounding totally unreal; growing up with my father is what made me doubt it. At first, I had the girlie daydream about my *mate* finding me and taking me away, saving me from my father. I let go of that pipe dream real quick and decided that finding a mate was not in my future. Mainly because I would probably never be able to escape my father long enough to meet someone else. Also, because I decided that if I'm going to be saved, it was going to be by my own hands rather than someone else's.

In short, the last few hours have been a tad bit surprising.

You know that dream, where you are falling and right before you hit the ground, you wake up, gasping for air, wondering where the hell you are? Well, I have that dream. Except in mine it's always a wolf hunting me, and right when it jumps at me, I wake up. That is what happened today. This time the wolf was golden rather than the dark brown of Marcus' wolf. And when I woke up, I thought I was back in Marcus' house, back in my room. But the paint on the walls is not cracking and old, and the room I am in is much bigger than my 'room' at the pack house.

Suddenly, everything comes back to me. Damen. His pack. His son. My *mate.*

Holy – I found my mate.

Great, I find my mate, and I totally wipe out in front of him. Classy.

I can feel the bed underneath me, and I remember seeing the gurney in the infirmary. That's where I am. They must have put me here when I fell. Wait. Where is everyone?

Then I feel the hum. The soft, warm feeling running across my skin, and I know, some how I *know* that he is still in the room. I lift myself up on my forearms, and there he is. Standing across the room, leaning against the wall. Hiking boots stick out from under his dark blue faded jeans. A black hoodie shows underneath a gray commander jacket. Black wavy hair cascades over his ears, but it is not long enough to pull back. He's just missed a few cuttings. Short whiskers cover his face, giving him a very manly look. Deep forest green eyes stare down at me. They flicker to my hair, and I watch as they move around my face before coming back to rest on my eyes.

"I caught you before you fell," he says, his voice soft and lyrical.

I don't respond. What am I supposed to say 'Thank you for doing the right thing and not letting me hit the floor'? Yeah, no.

"Are you alright? Can you speak?" The words are kind, but his voice is not.

"Yes."

"Good. I will show you around."

Hesitantly, I stand, and when I know for sure I won't fall, I move towards the young man. He holds open the door to the infirmary, and lets me walk through. He leads me to the end of the hallway towards the front of the house. He points to a door on the right.

"Lucy's son lives there. Don't bother him."

We continue to the stairs. Up, and up we go, stopping on each floor. He points out the rooms on each floor in a gruff voice, and then we move to the next one. At the top, he points to his room, and then mine, where he informs me that we will be sharing the same bathroom. He seems ecstatic about it. And when I say ecstatic, I mean, he is the farthest thing from ecstatic as possible.

When he quiets, I turn away, and look out the windows at the miles of land before me. The trees seem to go on forever.

There is a touch of a hand on my arm before he pulls me, and pushes me up against the wall next to the window, and crowds my space. I look up into forest green eyes, that stare down at me with a harsh gaze.

My pulse begins to race, but I think its from excitement rather than fear. Stupid mate bond.

"Did you know I was your mate before you came here?" He asks, his voice low in warning.

"How was I supposed to know that?" I ask, irritated. Is this how this whole 'mate' things is to go?

He growls out at the disobedience. Oh, someone doesn't like not getting his way.

"You are Marcus Beaumont's daughter," he scoffs. "He always has an angle to play-"

"I am nothing like that man," I snarl, and give him a shove. He doesn't move or seem to get the hint that I want him off of me. "He is not my father."

He releases my arm and grasps my chin. He pulls it the side so he can examine the bruise on my face.

"Marcus did this to you?" His gruff voice asks. "Why?"

"He's not kind, is all you need to know." I pull my face from his grasp. "Do you want me to leave?"

Doren doesn't say anything.

"Just say the word, and I am gone. I am grateful to be gone from that place. Anything is better than there, but I won't be locked away again. You don't trust me, fine. I don't trust you, either. I tried to run in the car, but your father made me a good deal. If that doesn't work for you, then I will go. As long as I am far from *him*, that is all that matters."

"And what of us being mates?" He asks, peering down at me from his too tall height.

"I never thought I would meet my mate. I never thought of what would happen," I say, looking away, suddenly completely uncomfortable.

"Neither did I," he says. "I hoped… I hoped I wouldn't meet my mate." His words make me look at him. "The life I have chosen has no room for a mate. I cannot have one in my life. I have too many loyalties. Too many promises to keep, and I cannot, I will not make any promises to you. You can stay here. You can live here, and you will be safe, but you and I will not… be."

"Okay," I say, because what can I say? What can I do? My wolf lets out an anguished howl, but I do my best to ignore her. I'm not going to get on my knees and beg. Moon Goddess be damned.

He starts to turn away.

"What do I call you?" I ask, quickly, remembering that we were never actually introduced.

"My name is Doren. You can call me Ren."

Then, he disappears into his office across the hall from my room.

Walking into my new room, I hold in a gasp. I glance around the room, amazed at the size. It's almost three times as big as my old room. The wall across from the door is a wall of windows. The bed rests under the middle window, and there are blue curtains on each side of the bed. There is a bedside table next to the bed with a lamp on it. On the other side there is a wooden bench seat under the window. I turn around and see an armoire with a large TV in it and empty bookshelves. At the very bottom there are cabinets. I open them and find a DVD player. On the left wall there is a door, and on the wall to the right there's a set of double doors.

I open the double doors first and find a large walk in closet. I don't even have that many clothes. I walk across the room and open the last door. It's the bathroom. I'm assuming the door on the other side of the bathroom leads to Ren's room. I close the door to the bathroom and turn on the bedside lamp. Then I lean across the bench and look out the windows. I can see the trees and the pathways that are on this side of the house.

Farther away, I can see the tall brick walls. It's so beautiful here. For miles all I can see is the colorful foliage of the fall. Oranges and reds, mixed in with different shades of green that scatter the forest surrounding the home and the small town. I wonder what winter will look like here. I wonder if I'll be here long enough to know.

Backing away from the window, I go back to my bags, and start unpacking. I hang up all of my clothes, which isn't much: a couple tops, mostly t-shirts, some jeans, a jean jacket, a pair of combat boots, and flip flops. Every once in a while my father let me go shopping with Franklin. And, let me tell you that was so much fun. I was lucky if

Franklin actually let me out of his sight to look for something I needed. Most of the time he made me made me follow him, barking orders at me, or threating to tell my father I was being insubordinate. So, of course, I could only get a few things whenever I went out. Plus, I didn't really have anyone to impress.

I wasn't allowed to do much, so for the most part I read and watch movies. Anything I know about the world, I mainly learned from books.

Once my belongings are all put away, I lie down on my bed, and look around. Everything here is vastly different from Marcus' pack life. Just the feeling of the place is even different. This place... it is a home. This is a home for people. Marcus' was nothing like that. It is completely different here. A good different. A welcomed different.

For a moment, my thoughts go to Doren. I always thought we had it easy, us wolves. All we must do is find our mate, and bam, there is no thought, no questions as they are the person we are supposed to spend our lives for. We don't have to worry. But then, just like humans it not always easy. Doren is my mate but he is the one that I am supposed to spend my life with? It is no secret that mates get rejected, that people think they know better than the moon goddess who chose our mates for us. They want someone else, so they cause terrible pain for their 'meant to be'. So, is that what Doren is doing? But after all, he didn't actually reject me.

All these scattered thoughts run across my mind. Slowly, my eyes start to drift, and it is not long before I am out like a light.

## Chapter Six

The feeling of a body landing on mine jolts me from sleep. I let out a loud yelp at the impact, and there is a giggle in response. A hand covers my mouth, and when I wrench my eyes open, they meet bright green ones. Ren's face pops into my mind, but I know it is not him. I search the face, but I don't recognize it. The girl on top of me is stunning. With perfect red lips, and long black hair, she reminds me of snow white in a way.

The door to the bathroom swings open, banging into the wall, and Ren storms in on high alert. His gaze swings to the girl, and his shoulders instantly drop, and he lets out a sigh, while running a hand through his hair.

"Dahlia, it is six in the morning," he complains, his voice laced with sleep.

"But, Dory," the girl on top of me says. At first, I am confused by her name for him, but then realized it must be a pet name. "I didn't get to meet her yesterday, and someone had to wake her for school."

"Again, Lee, it's six. We do not have class until ten. Remember?" Lee? It must be his nickname for her.

The girl, Dahlia, rolls her eyes and looks down at me with a grin on her face.

"Boys, they will never understand what it takes for a girl to get ready in the morning. I am Dahlia, by the way. I'm this idiots twin sister." She jerks her head towards Ren, who is rolling her eyes at her. Now it makes sense. Looking at them together, they look almost exactly alike.

"I'm Rory," I say with a hesitant laugh. "Sorry, I didn't mean to sleep through dinner."

"It's fine," Dahlia replies. "We figured you were tired so we let you sleep. You will meet everyone this morning, either way. But I wanted to make sure you got up on time. Breakfast is at seven-thirty. I'll let you get ready."

Dahlia crawls off of me, and stands up at the edge of the bed. Ren clears his throat, and I look over at him.

"Um, well. Since I'm up, I'll just get ready. You can shower first if you would like."

"Okay," I tell him.

He nods, and then leaves the way he came.

"Don't mind him. He grows on you eventually, kind of like a fungus."

I let out a laugh.

Dahlia shrugs. "Yeah, but I've called him worse. But on another subject, I'm so excited you're here! Finally, another girl!"

"There aren't any other girls here?"

"There are, but most of them spend all of their time with their mates. Plus, I'm usually with Ren and Kyle. But you will be welcomed into out little group. And on the plus side you seem much cooler than I thought you would be."

"Thanks, I guess?" I ask, with a little laugh.

She waves a dismissive hand through the air. "Don't take it personally. Most people – mainly girls – hang out with my brother in hopes of becoming the next female Alpha to the strongest pack in the world. I wasn't sure if you would be like that or not."

"And now you know that I'm not like that?" I question, raising an eyebrow.

"Well, of course I don't really know just yet, but you're his mate. It kind of… changes my perspective, if you know what I mean."

I nod. "I think I do."

She claps her hands together. "Good, we're on the same page. I'm just really excited, not only did my brother find his mate, but now we've got another girl."

"Well, I'm glad I can help," I say, smiling at her. Genuinely smiling.

"So are you ready for tomorrow?" She asks.

"Tomorrow?" I question, not entirely sure what it is she is talking about.

"Did my father tell you about school?"

"Ah, yes. He did say that I would be enrolling."

She nods. "Yes, it is his rule. That we at least try a few classes in college, to see if we like it. He thought since you are going to be staying here that you try to get in the habit of doing some of the things that we do. He has you enrolled in the classes that we are in; that way, you will at least be around someone you 'sort-of' know. So, are you excited?"

"No. I – I haven't been to school in a long time," I say, scoffing.

"Really? Why?" She stops herself, and her cheeks turn a little pink. "I mean, you don't have to tell me. I'm just a curious wolf."

"It's fine," I say, reassuring her. "From what I've heard, most people know about the kind of man Marcus is. I do not mind telling you. It was my sophomore year of high school when a teacher saw some bruises. She asked questions, and I wouldn't answer. She called my father, and then the police. He took me out of school after that. He gave me workbooks and textbooks and I had to teach myself. I haven't been to school since."

She touches my arm gently, and it is such an odd sensation, being comforted.

"Well, you are here now, and it will be better. And I -" She lowers her voice to a whisper. "I know my brothers stance on mates. I've always known it, but it is different now that you are here. He'll change his mind. He just needs time."

I don't really know what to say to that. I wasn't expecting any of this, but then a little over twenty-four hours ago, I was told I was arranged to marry a young soon-to-be Alpha. I moved in with said Alpha and his family, while finding out that he was not only my soon-to-be husband, but my mate as well. Then, said mate told me that he could not in fact be my mate. Then said mate's sister tells me, that he will be my mate, I just need to give him time because he has issues.

It hasn't even been thirty-six hours yet.

"Have you found your mate?" I ask.

She shakes her head.

"Do you mind if I come back and talk to you when you are out of the shower? I want to get to know you, but I also don't want to scare you away."

"I also know that I am new here and this is your home. You have to make sure I am not in league with my father."

A sheepish look falls upon her face, but I wave a hand.

"Don't worry about it. I understand. If I were in your place I wouldn't trust me either. But just know… I would never help him. I hate him more than I thought I could ever hate a person."

She watches me for a moment. "I believe you."

I nod. "I should shower. I'll be out in a jiff."

"I'll be here," she says, and I walk into the bathroom.

The bathroom is a large room, maybe half the size of the bedroom. Along one wall there is a shower with a gray curtain covering half of the wall. Next to the shower, covering the rest of the wall, is a long, oval shaped tub. Four people could probably fit into it. Opposite the shower and bath tub, there is a large counter top with two sinks right next to each other set in the middle of the wall with about four feet of space between the sides of the room. There is a large rectangular mirror covering almost the whole length of the upper wall. The counter rests atop two cabinet doors, which I open to find towels and extra toiletries. On the left side of the counter, the toilet seat sits with the paper roll nailed to the edge of the cabinet. On the right side of the cabinet there is a tall heater. On the counter there is a bottle of hand soap, and a toothbrush holder with one brush in it.

Reaching out, I lock the door to Ren's room. Better safe then sorry. It is not like I automatically trust them either. Then, I strip and step into the shower. It doesn't take long before I am stepping out of the shower, wrapping a towel around my body. I start to leave the room, before remembering Ren is locked out. I quickly unlock his door before stepping into my new room.

Dahlia is lying on the bed, but now dressed in leggings, a red flowing shirt, and a jean jacket.

"So, I have a serious question, that I hope you don't get offended by my asking," Dahlia says as I walk towards the closet.

"Your hair… is it dyed?"

Ah, I was wondering when that question would get asked. Turning a little, I catch a glimpse of myself in a mirror hanging in the center of the wall. The reason why everyone stares when they first see me is for two reasons. Stark white hair that goes down my back, and violet eyes. Odd combination, but something I was born with.

"No," I say. "My hair is real."

"Does your mom have white hair, too?"

I shake my head even though she can't see me. "Uh, no. My mom and brother had brown hair, same as my dad. I was their odd child with my white hair and violet eyes."

She doesn't ask about my use of *had*, which I am thankful for.

"So tell me about the pack," I say, as I pull on some undergarments, jeans and a t-shirt.

"Well, we're the strongest, and we have the largest territory. You probably aren't going to meet any of the wolves in ranking for my father besides his beta. They're pretty scarce since nothing much happens here, and if anything does, like an unknown crossing the territory, my father leaves it to Ren and Kyle to take care of it. He's teaching them how to handle everything. That's pretty much everyone's focus, trying to prepare them for the future. I'm my brothers sentinel by the way."

A sentinel is sort of like an Alpha's third in command. Normally, there are two Sentinels and it's a mated pair, but I guess that's not a law or anything. Basically, Sentinels have no power unless the Alpha allows it, or unless something happens to both the Beta and the Alpha.

"We don't have many kids in the pack, but a large group of teens, and then the rest is part of my dad's era, but they all live in town amongst their families and the elders. A lot of the town is run by elders, but we still have a large number of humans. Wolves are common around here, but we still have to be careful because there are some hunting families that live within the town's limits. Thankfully, they don't suspect anything. Some of the faculty members at school are wolves as well so don't like freak out when you get there."

"There's so many of you. I'm not used to that."

"Yeah, there are homes for everyone all along the territory. When they all come over, the house fills up. Our territories north side ends right on the edge of the school grounds, and it's the only one for miles. There's a small pack near our territory, and a lot of the young wolves go to our school."

"Do the packs get along?"

"Um, for the most part."

I start brushing my hair.

"That's good that the packs get along. You don't see that happen often."

"Yeah, it's mainly because of the Alpha's. Since there is not much to do around here, usually we go to parties on the weekends. Sometimes we throw them on our territory. Other times, the other pack throws them. Also, I work at a clothing store in town, which you will be working at too. Other than that, we party with the people from school."

"So, you guys have a lot of parties?"

"Well, the other college students are always throwing parties. I always want to go, but I usually have to drag the guys with. Especially Ren. But personally, I think he has to have some fun, since he's going to become Alpha soon, I think he should spend some time being not so serious. Anyways, I really hope you like it here. I already like you and I know the others do too."

"Really?" I ask, stepping out of the closet.

"Trust me, I know," she says, tapping her forehead. She must be referring to the pack's mind link. I won't be a part of that, until I'm officially a member of the pack. I never had the link with my father's pack. They all blocked me out.

"You should be warned though at school, some of the wolves from the other pack… some are cool. Some… aren't so much."

I let out a small chuckle. "Good to know."

"I like your t-shirt," she says. "That band is great."

Looking down at my 'F.O.B.' shirt, I smile. "Thanks. This is from my punk rock phase. T-shirts are all that I really have."

"You weren't even allowed to go shopping?" She asks, almost outraged.

I shake my head. "I've barely seen sunlight in the past three years," I scoff. "I got to go shopping every once in a while but it was really only quick stops, not actual going in to try things on."

When I look at her, she smiles at me warmly. "Well, if you ever want to borrow some clothes I have a lot of clothes that I don't mind sharing."

"Thanks. I… I appreciate that."

She just smiles. "Ready for some food?"

"Yep," I say, hearing my stomach growl.
"Alright, let's go," she says, and I follow her out of the room.

## Chapter Seven

When we walk into the dining room, there are two young men already scarfing down food at the table. I recognize the redhead instantly; he is Ren's Beta, Kyle.

"Morning, Ladies." Kyle says with a smile.

I feel my lips stretch before I even think about it.

The other boy looks at me with wide eyes but doesn't say anything. He's got shaggy brown hair, and brown eyes. Dahlia sits across the table from the boy I have not yet met, and I sit next to her in front of Kyle.

"Rory, this is Hunter. He's the Peacekeeper. Hunter, this is Rory," Dahlia introduces us.

"Hey," I say to him.

"Hi," he replies with a smile.

At the center of the table are large platters of food. There are pancakes, sausage, bacon, waffles, and eggs. I take some eggs, and two pancakes. As I cut into my pancakes, the chair next to me is pulled out, and I look up to see Ren sit next to me. When I look at him, he stops and peers at me from the corner of his eye. He gives a small nod before looking away, and reaching for the food.

"You're pretty," a voice says, and I, along with everyone else at the table turn to look at Hunter who is staring at me. He's talking to me? I look around and everyone is glaring at Hunter.

"Sorry," Hunter says sheepishly, looking around at everyone. He gulps when he looks at Ren. "I just had to say it." He turns to Dahlia. "Lia, you look breathtaking as usual."

Dahlia laughs. "Suck up."

"So," I say, trying to ease the tension. "Anything I should know about before going to school tomorrow?"

Ren doesn't respond but Kyle, Hunter, and Dahlia go into detail about things I should stay away from. Dahlia assures me that she was able to arrange it so that I have every class with at least one of the four teens I'm sitting with today. I pretty much follow their schedule, or at least Dahlia's; three classes on Mondays and Wednesdays, and one class on Tuesday and Thursdays. She works at a small boutique on Tuesdays, Thursdays, and Fridays. They all eat lunch together most days. Dahlia tells me about people who are cool even though she really only hangs out with the guys at the table. Kyle tells me the guys to stay away from, which is mainly a bunch of guys on the football team for some reason. Hunter warns me to stay away from a girl named Tess, which he looks at Ren when he says her name, his face turning red. Ren's jaw tenses, but he doesn't take his eyes off of his food.

Throughout breakfast a couple more people trickle in. I meet Trevor who is the Lead Hunter, and his mate Mary who is a Warrior. Alice is a Hunter, and Lauren is the Lead Scout. Corinne and

Kevin are Warriors. There was another person in the pack, Jeffrey the Assassin, but he doesn't show up at breakfast.

It's around eight when Ren stands up, and says, "We should get going."

The others stand up and head to the foyer, but when I stand up, Ren grabs my arm.

"I - we noticed that you didn't have a phone, so my dad got you this. All our numbers are already in there," he says, and hands me a box for a new iPhone.

"I – I really don't need it. And I can't pay-"

"Don't worry about the money. And we want you to have it that way we can always be in contact with you if need be."

"Okay… Thanks."

Dahlia appears in the doorway. "We are going to go. We should be back around four-ish. Feel free to wander around, get to know the place. You can call us if you need anything."

I nod thanks.

Ren leaves the room, and Dahlia peers at me.

"You going to be okay?"

I nod. "Don't worry about me, I'm used to be being alone. I will find something to do."

"We'll see you later," she smiles, before stepping away from the room, and leaving the house. I go to the front window and watch as the pile into a yellow jeep with its top down, and they drive off.

I look around the foyer, wondering what it is I could do, and I think about what Dahlia said, and decide to walk around, and get used to the house. Starting at the top, I wander through the house, getting used to the arrangement of everything. After going through the halls, I step down at the bottom of the steps, and walk into the living room. Behind the wall of the TV, photos cover the walls. Some black and white, some in color. Slowly, I go through looking at each one, seeing the familiar faces, and seeing ones that I do not and probably will never recognize.

At the end of the room, there is a door, and I push through that to a small library. The room is not huge, maybe ten feet by ten feet, and there is a window, with a bench seat, and cushions.

"These have been collected for years. Some of them are hundreds of years old," a voice says, making me jump. Damen stands in the doorway, leaning against the frame.

We are quiet for a moment as I continue looking around, scanning the spines of the books.

"Your son seems to think that I am working in some way with my father, and that you are all in danger," I say to Damen.

"Mm, he is very cautious. I would be lying if I say that he doesn't have reason."

"You mean you know the kind of man that Marcus really is? Shocker," I say with a chuckle. "Of course Ren he has reasons. I'm cautious all on my own. I don't even know why I am here."

"I've told you-"

"Yes, I know. I remind you of someone. You are doing a good deed. Where I come from though, good deeds don't exist and everyone has a game plan in mind."

"My game plan was to save your life," he says, and I finally look at him, trying to read him. "It is as simple as that."

"But, how did he agree to it? Marcus' goal in life seemed to be to make mine as unbearable as possible. Why he would just let me go like that? How did you make the deal?"

He sighs. "Your father crossed into my territory."

"He is not my father. He may be the reason why I am here on earth, but that man is no father." I say nastily. "And so what he just said, 'here you go, my favorite punching bag, you can have her?'"

Damen watches me for a moment. "Marcus crossed into territory with a hunter. A known killer of our kind. As an Alpha that people look up to, I needed to know why. With my pack behind me, we went to his house. He made up some story about how he didn't know who the man was but that was a lie. The Hunter that he was with? He has killed many of us. Many from this pack. He has had a warrant on his head for years. If Marcus found him, he was obligated to bring him to me, so I could give him the sentence he deserves. Marcus let him go, and he wouldn't tell me where he was. Marcus, like the pathetic man that he is, begged me to let him live for what he had done. He knew he was in trouble. His time was coming, and so he tried to bargain. He knew about my son and that he did not have a mate, so he offered you, as a mate for my son. I made a choice."

"I don't believe you."

"That's a shame. We've given you an opportunity, Rory. Don't ruin it by asking questions."

He walks away, and all I can do is stare after him. There are so many thoughts rushing through my head. Marcus is consorting with Hunters. Damen - there is something that he is not telling me. He doesn't trust Marcus, so there is no way he wouldn't just welcome me into his home without question. I run my hands through my hair in frustration, because I don't know what I am doing here. They do not trust me and I do not trust them, but - I look around the house – this place is better than going Rogue. I close my eyes, making a promise to myself. Any sign of trouble, and I will go. I will run far away, from them and from Marcus.

I wander to the left side of the house, into the large garden. The walls of the compound can barely been seen. They are covered in green moss and vines, making them blend in with the tall trees. There is a winding path that filters out along the walls, which leads me to a large weeping willow near the very far left corner of the compound. The tree towers over me, seeming to be over ten feet tall, with a width of the same amount. The branches hang down almost touching the ground. There is a stone bench underneath all of the branches, near the trunk.

The back of my neck begins to tingle, and before I can even think about what might be causing it, a voice asks, "What are you doing?"

It makes me a jump.

When I look over my shoulder, I see Ren staring at me, no warmth anywhere in his gaze.

"How is there a weeping willow here? I thought they grew near water."

"There is a small lake nearby."

"Mm. I like trees." I can't believe – did I just say *'I like trees'*? In my mind, I am shaking my head in shame at myself.

"Did you know your father was in contact with Hunters?" Ren asks, obviously paying no attention to my silliness.

"No," I say, shock filling me, and I turning around to facing him. "I had no idea."

I look at the ground.

"Did you ever see any Hunters around your packs territory?"

"How do I even know if someone is a Hunter?"

He scoffs, and asks in an annoyed voice, "Did you ever see any bipeds?"

For a moment, I'm stunned silent. What the hell are those? "Bipeds?"

Ren rolls his eyes. "You know – people with two feet? The normal humans?"

"I've never – I've never heard them be called that before."

"Well, now you have. Did you see any?" He questions, impatience high in his voice.

"You know, I don't think I really had time with all the being locked in my room all the time," I snap, annoyed at his tone.

"You mean to tell me that you *never* left your room?" The doubt is clear in his voice.

Something about his tone hits me the wrong way, and suddenly I cannot control my mouth.

"No, you are right. I did leave my room. Let's see, there were the times that I would go to go to the mall, about once every couple of months. Or the times that he would actually let me eat dinner with them, but trust me, those times I'd have rather been in my room. Then, there were also the times that I got sent to his office were he would punish me because I was 'too loud' or I 'spoke to that person in the wrong tone'. Also, lets not forget about the times that I tried to run away, but every time, just when I thought I was going to make it, he somehow found me. Yeah, you are right, I left the room all the time. And no, I never saw any *bipeds*. Now, do you have any more questions?"

When I look at him, his eyes are dark and unreadable. He doesn't say anything. I turn to face the tree again, my back to him.

"Hunters have a symbol. A tattoo on their person; it is usually somewhere visible to others. It is a green plus sign in a circle. It is Celtic for Purity. That is how you know a Hunter from a regular biped."

His voice is surprisingly soft. I glance over my shoulder to see his back as he walks away.

I'm staring up at the large hedge maze when Dahlia finds me.

"It's time for training."

When I look over at her, she continues. "We blindfold the wolf, and give them a scent that they have to follow. We time them to see how soon they can find the scent."

Well, isn't that handy.

"Are you hungry?" She asks, changing the subject, I think for both of our sakes.

"No," I say, shaking my head. "I'm still full of breakfast."

She gives me an odd look. After all, breakfast was hours ago. I shrug.

"I don't really eat much."

"Well," she says when understanding fills her eyes. "Dinner is soon. Want to at least sit with us?"

"Of course," I say, and we walk back into the house.

Dinner is more like a welcoming party. It is packed with people, all introducing themselves to me. The room is filled with laughter and talking for what seems like hours. For most of the time, Ren sat at the other side of the table, watching me. Some moments I could ignore him, other times I watched him back, with a raised eyebrow. At one point, he nods at me, in what I can only understand as 'touché', and then he rises from the table, and leaves. Ignoring his absence, I pay attention to the people around me. *Friends.* That's what they are called. Friends. That has a comforting ring to it.

## Chapter Eight

"Wake up, Sleeping Beauty," a voice says.

Opening my eyes, I see Lia, as she has asked me to call her, standing at the foot of my bed, smiling down at me.

"What time is it?" I ask, sitting up. In a way I am grateful she woke me up. I was dreaming the same dream as always. I had reached the cliff right when called out to me.

"Like eight-thirty-ish. We should get ready for school."

I nod, and run a hand through my hair.

"Ren says you can have the shower first," she says, tapping her head again. "I'll be back in a jiff, I'm going to go change."

Her hair twirls as she practically runs out of the room. Pulling myself out of the bed, I shuffle into the bathroom, and quickly wrap my hair in a bun before stepping into the shower.

After a few minutes of scrubbing, I step onto the tiled floor of the bathroom, wrapping a towel around my body. Going to the sink, I scrub my face with some face wash, and then I begin brushing my teeth, while pulling my hair out of its bun to reveal loose waves.

Mid brush, I hear a yell from Ren's side of the bathroom. "No, Jas!" He yells.

Before I know it, his door to the bathroom opens and a little boy runs through. He skids to a stop in front of me. He's got short curly blonde hair, and bright baby blue eyes. He has to be around five years old. Ren follows closely behind him, and lets out a frustrated groan. "Jasper."

The boy, Jasper, ignores him. "Wow, your eyes are cool!" He exclaims.

Ren drags a hand over his eyes, and squats down, turning the boy so that they're facing each other.

"You could've at least waited until she was-" He chooses that moment to look up at me. I see his gaze slowly go up my body, which is still wrapped only in a towel. His eyes widen. I then realize I still have my toothbrush in my mouth, and I probably have toothpaste covering my mouth, making me look like I have rabies. I turn to the sink, and rinse my mouth while I hear Ren clear his throat and finish his sentence.

"Ready to go."

I wipe my mouth with a blue hand towel that is hanging on the wall above the sink, and then I turn back to them. Ren is standing with the boy's hand in his.

"Jas, this is Rory," Ren says to the boy.

"Hi," I say, looking down at the pretty blue eyes.

Jas launches himself at me, probably going for a hug, with a wide smile on his face. With his wolf reflexes, Ren catches Jas before he can reach me. Ren picks him up, and holds him up with one arm, and the boy wraps his legs around Ren's waist.

"Wait until she's ready for school. You can hug her at breakfast," Ren says to the boy sternly. Then he turns to me with an apologetic look on his face. "Sorry, he's a hugger. And sorry, for barging in, I tried to stop him."

I wrap my arms around myself, and laugh. "It's okay," I say, and Jas grins at that.

"She likes me better than you," he says to Ren, sticking his tongue out at him. Ren ruffles the boy's hair, and I chuckle. Ren turns to me smiling a real smile, and I think it's the first time I've seen it.

The smiles fades, and he opens his mouth to say something, but then Dahlia opens the door behind me. She stops when she sees all of us.

"Doren seriously, you couldn't wait until she was dressed," she scowls.

"It was the kid!" Ren exclaims, motioning to the boy in his arms.

Jas puts on an innocent face, "Don't blame me."

I laugh at how convincing he is, and Ren starts tickling Jas.

"Ren, you should get ready," Dahlia says.

Ren sobers up, and hands the boy over to his sister. "Can you get him dressed?"

She nods.

I look over at Ren. "It's all yours in here," I say, motioning to the bathroom.

He nods. "Thanks."

The three of us walk into my room, closing the door to the bathroom. Looking at Dahlia, I notice her outfit. She's wearing a black maxi dress with a red bodice. She looks stunning.

"You look amazing," I say to her and she smiles.

"Thanks."

"I'll be right back," I say, and head into my closet, closing the doors behind me. I take off my towel, and grab a pair of underwear and a bra, putting them on. Next, I pull on a pair of light blue skinny jeans, a t-shirt that says 'Creepin' it Real', and a jean jacket over that. I slip on my flip-flops, and grab my practically empty backpack up off the floor, before walking out.

"I'm ready," I say.

"You look great. You've got an 'I don't really care' look. I wish I could pull that off. When I try, I look like a bear who just rolled out of bed."

I laugh. "I doubt that, but thanks."

Dahlia laughs. "You want to go with me to get him ready?"

I nod, and I follow her out of the room.

In the hallway, Dahlia puts him on the ground. "Go pick out some clothes," she says and he takes off running.

"So, he is he your brother, too?" I ask, Dahlia as we walk slowly behind him.

A ghost of a frown forms on her face. "We consider him as one, but no, not by blood. His... his parents were killed by Hunters about a year and a half ago. He had no other living relatives, just the pack. So dad adopted him. For the most part he stays with my father, but last night was date night for him and Lucy, so he spent the night here?"

"Wait, Damen and Lucy?"

She chuckles. "Yeah, my mom passed away a long time ago, and Lucy came to the pack a few years ago."

"I'm sorry about your mother," I say to her.

"Thank you. Anyways, Jas and Ren have a really strong bond. Ever since Jas' parents passed, he's been even more afraid of the dark, and he sometimes has really bad nightmares. That's why he was in Ren's room this morning. You know how a kid crawls into their parents bed when they're afraid?" She asks, and I nod, but in reality, I don't really know. I never had that kind of relationship with the people I share my blood. "Well, he crawls into Ren's. Ren protects him from the monsters."

"Wow, looking at Ren, you wouldn't think he has that kind of soft side to him."

"Yeah," she says, sadly. She places a hand on my arm. "Rory, listen. I know that this is sudden and new, and I know that Ren isn't making this transition easy. I trust you, and I know he will too, and vice versa with you. But, all I can ask is that you give him a chance. He's going to be a dick at times, trust me, but there is a reason for why he is the way he is. He's had a hard past, much like you. Just trust me when I say that he will come around. He is worth knowing."

I give her a hesitant nod. "I trust you."

She pulls me into a hug, which I awkwardly reciprocate. When she pulls away, she gives me a sheepish grin.

"You're not really a hugger are you?" She asks me.

"I'm just... not used to all the touching," I respond.

She gives me a warm smile. "I understand. Just know, Jas and I will probably be hugging you. A lot. We're huggers."

"That's okay," I say. "Bring on the hugs. I'll get used to it."

She laughs at my serious enthusiasm.

Then, suddenly, a dragged out "Dahlia!" pierces through the air. "Rory!"

"We're coming, Jas!" Dahlia yells back with a laugh.

We both laugh and I follow her down a flight of stairs, and into the first door on the right. Jas holds a pair of superman undies, a pair of jeans, and a black shirt that says 'I'm Batman'.

"I love Batman," I say to Jas.

"So do I! He's the best."

I giggle. "Yeah, he is."

Do you want me to help you change or can you do it?" Dahlia asks him.

"I can do it!" He explains, and runs into the bathroom.

Dahlia and I wait just outside the room, and then moments later, Jasper bursts into the hallway.

"I'm hungry!" He exclaims.

"Well, then let's go, silly." Dahlia replies to him.

We walk to the kitchen to find Kyle, and Hunter eating already. We sit and chat and eat. Eventually, Ren comes in and has a quick bite before announcing that it is time to go.

Ren looks at me. "You have your phone?"

I freeze, and mentally check my pockets.

"No, I left it in my room." I stand up. "I'll go get it."

He shakes his head, and nods at Kyle, who takes off running out of the room.

"Lets go," Ren says, and we all stand up, following him out of the house, and onto the gravel driveway, where there is a yellow jeep parked.

"Is Jas coming with us?" I ask, when I realize he is not with us.

Ren shakes his head. "No, my Dad will take him in to daycare when the time comes."

Kyle appears, and hands my phone to Ren, who turns to me, holding out.

"You need anything, or get separated, call."

I nod, and take the phone, slipping it into my back pocket.

He walks to the driver's side of the car, but stops when Hunter asks, "Uh, how is this going to work?"

Ren stops and looks at all of us, then at the car. It's a five-seated car, and there are five of us. He looks at Hunter. "You ride shotgun," he says. Ren and Dahlia share a look, and Dahlia nods.

Okay. Then Dahlia sits in the back of the car, in the middle, with Kyle and I on her sides. Her brother gets into the drivers seat, and then we're off.

## Chapter Nine

It's all trees the whole way to the school. Literally, for miles and miles it's all trees. It must have rained last night. The air is foggy, and smells fresh, and the air is cool feeling against my skin. I settle comfortably in my seat, and welcome in the smell and the feel. October is coming soon, and then snow. I love the look of untouched snow and on the trees it will look great. I pull out my new phone from my pocket and take a few photos of the trees. I see Ren glancing at me from the corner of my eye, but I ignore him and continue on taking shots. Ren has the top of the car down, so the wind goes through our hair.

When we get to school, Ren pulls into two parking spaces. He literally parks on an angle, taking up two parking spaces. I stand up, putting my hand on the headrest of the passenger seat about to jump down, when Ren appears his hand raised in the air, palm open and facing up. After a moment's hesitation, I place my hand in his, warmth spreading through my body as his fingers close. I put my weight on him, and jump to the ground. He immediately lets go of my hand, without looking at me; he goes to the back end of the car. He reaches in, and pulls out two notebooks, handing me one. I take it.

"Thanks."

He nods, his eyes finally meeting mine. For a moment, we just stay still. Feeling like something needs to be said to break the stare, I say, "Nice park job."

I know I said the right thing when a corner of his mouth lifts up into a smirk.

"I don't want it to get scratched."

We both turn at the same time. Skarletbach University is a small school. The buildings are no higher then three floors, even what looks to be dormitories. People are everywhere, piling out of their cars, walking out of buildings, going to other buildings.

My hand goes to the strap of my backpack, wrapping around it tightly. I take a deep breath as Lia steps up to my side.

"Are you okay?" She asks.

I give her a smile, and nod. "Yeah."

Ren stands ahead of us, his head cocked towards us. When I say 'yeah' he nods slightly, and starts walking. The rest of us follow.

When we get close to the front doors of the building, we pass a group of girls standing next to a green Volkswagen bug. One of them, the one with red hair stands out from the rest. She's a wolf; I can smell her from here. And, she also happens to be glaring at me, too.

"Ren," she snaps, and suddenly my wolf is awake, wanting to growl. *No one talks to our mate like that*. I push that thought out of my mind. We may be mates, but he is not mine.

Ren doesn't pay any attention to the redhead, but he stops and snaps his head to Lia and they stare at each other. It goes on for a full minute, and it is obvious that they are having a conversation in their minds.

Here we are, stopped in the middle of the parking lot. My eyes wander to the girl who called Ren. I can tell she is definitely something else. She has a black leather skirt, and a bright red tank top on. She has a 'trying too hard to look badass' about her.

Looking her over, I try to see what Ren might see in her. She looks... unpleasant to be around. Has Ren done things with her? Is he still doing things with her, or no because he has found his mate? But, he doesn't want me. I cast a look over at him. Does having a mate mean anything to him?

Suddenly, Ren speaks.

"Fine, Lee, don't believe me. Jesus, what kind of guy do you think I am?"

Regret instantly crosses Lia's features. "Ren-"

"No, I'll go handle the situation all over again," he says.

He doesn't look at me as he brushes past, and walks towards the fire crotch. My hands squeeze the straps of my backpack but then I take a deep breath, and relax my body. I have no reason to be upset. We aren't anything.

My wolf howls inside. She definitely doesn't agree with that.

Lia links her arm with mine and pulls me inside a tall, dark building that has Smith Hall on a plaque above the door. It is a small building with two floors. On the first floor there are six rooms, each right next to each other. On the wall to the left is a big painted version of the crest that is placed inside of the Blackheart Manor.

We find Alice, a Hunter in the Blackheart Pack, standing outside a room on the first floor, texting on her phone. She looks up when she senses us, and we all greet each other.

"You have English 201 with Alice and I first," Lia says.

Alice fills me in on what the teacher and the homework are like, and the other students in the class.

I'm nodding along to Alice's rant when the hallway gets oddly quiet. I turn towards the front doors where everyone parts. The guys walk in. Ren, Kyle, and Hunter, with Ren at the head of the pack. He has a smirk playing on his lips. I check out his outfit for the first time today. He's got on a pair of dark blue acid wash jeans, a long sleeved black shirt, and a blue commanders twill jacket. On his wrist he has a black leather band with a red stone centered in it. He doesn't have a book bag, just a lone notebook under his arm, and the other two are dressed very much like Doren. From the scared look on some of the students faces, and the smug looks on the boys' faces, well I can tell that if I were to stereotype, I would classify them as the bad boys of the school. But of course, I wouldn't do that. Plus, we are in college after all. This isn't high school.

I'm distracted from them when a tall boy with shaggy blonde hair and a blue and yellow letterman jacket stands in the view of them. He has a pair of sparkly blue eyes, and most would say that he is cute but personally, I wish I were staring into a pair of dark, forest green ones. God, I need to get a grip on reality.

"Hey," the boy says, smiling down at me, showing dimples.

"Uh, hi," I reply, crossing my arms.

"So, you're the new addition to the Blackheart family. I'm Colin," he says, sticking his hand out. I just look at his hand. He opens his mouth to say something but he's cut off when a shadow falls over us, and a throat is cleared. I know who it is; I can feel him from here without having to look. I'm surprised when Colin knows who it is, too.

"Can I help you, Blackheart?"

"Yeah, you can move," Ren says.

Colin throws him a look, and then looks back at me, smirking.

"So, the rumors are true." Colin asks.

"You could say that," Ren says in a cool tone. I look at Ren, my eyebrows raised. He doesn't look at me.

"You move fast, don't you?" Colin asks with a chuckle.

My eyebrows get even higher, eyes still pinned on Ren.

Ren doesn't answer, but his jaw clenches. Colin turns back to me.

"Well, I guess I should go. It was nice to meet you... What did you say your name was?"

"I didn't," I say, smiling sardonically at him.

He grins. "Well, be careful with this one," he says, jerking his chin in Ren's direction. "There's a reason why his name is Blackheart. I'll see you around, new girl."

Colin walks away, shoving past Ren on the way. Ren clucks his tongue, and then chuckles. He and his other two wolf sidekicks walk away. I turn and look at Lia who is staring at me with wide eyes.

"It is going to be a hell of a day," she says with a wolfish grin.

It is not until the end of the second class of the day that I realize what exactly she is talking about. We are sitting in a classroom; Lia and I near the back of the room. The professor lets the class out, and he is out of the door before we even put our books away.

The students, who were quiet, start talking amongst themselves, chatting loudly, as they begin to pack up and leave the room. Lia starts speaking, but I can't help but overhear two girls behind me. They are talking about a guy - a guy who left a girl because he started sleeping with another girl.

"Oh, go fuck yourself," Lia whirls around, snarling at the girls behind us.

I look at her, shocked, having yet to see such anger from her before. First time for everything, I guess.

Following Lia's gaze, I see the redhead that was in the parking lot earlier. Next to her is a brunette, who happens to be staring at me. I look between the two of them and Lia.

The fire crotch leans forward in her seat, a coy smile on her lips. She ignores Lia and her comment, and asks me, "So, what did you do? Sleep with him?"

"Excuse me?"

"Just know, he'll come running back to me, so don't get attached."

"Oh, shut up, Tess. He was never actually your boyfriend," Lia says. She takes my arm in her hand and nearly drags me out of the room. Once in the hallway, I see that Tess and her friend follow us, of course, because they don't seem like they have anything better to do.

"Dahlia, why don't you hop off your brothers dick already?"

I whirl around to say something, but the words die in my throat when a body shoves its way in front of Lia and I.

"Don't talk to either of them like that. Ever," Ren threatens in a low growl.

"Aren't you cute? Coming to save them," Tess says, smiling in a sickly sweet way that makes me want to puke.

Sure, it's cute, but I don't need him to come to our rescue. Not when I can handle it. I push my way around Ren until I'm staring at Tess straight in the face. I've got two inches on her, and I use it to my advantage, stepping close to her.

"Look, it's my first day, and I'm not looking for any problems, but you talk to her like that again, and we will definitely have one."

A grin forms on fire-crotch's face. "You have no idea who I am," she chuckles.

"You know," giving a small chuckle of my own, I say, "I really don't give a shit."

"Watch your back," she says, leaning in slightly.

"Originality is lost on you, huh?"

She gives me a fingered wave, and then walks past me.

A large group of people stand, staring at me.

"Leave," Doren says in a booming voice, and they all scamper away.

Then it's just Ren, Lia, and I.

"You need to be careful with her," Ren says. I don't look at him. Something about this whole situation doesn't sit right to me. For some reason I can feel anger rising in me.

"She doesn't scare me," I say to him.

"She should. She is an Alphas daughter."

"So am I," I say, raising my chin.

"Yes, but you're weak-"

"Just because my bones are easily broken, does not mean that the word weak should be associated with me."

"Rory -"

"No need to be ashamed of it, in a month, I'll be just as good as her," I say, throwing my chin in the direction that Tess went.

Ren seems shocked by what I've said. He takes a deep breath, and raises his hand, which makes me flinch without even thinking about it.

"Doren," Lia warns, watching me.

He looks at her in confusion, then back to me, and then to his hand. He runs it through his hair.

"Jesus, I would never," he says.

I just nod, not sure how to respond.

Suddenly, a bell rings. Lia comes to my side. "Come on. We'll go eat, and then class."

"We still have classes left?" I ask, trying to make joke.

"Yes," Lia laughs. "But only one more! Come on, we'll go get some food, relax, and then one more class.

I look over my shoulder, and see Ren in the same spot, watching me with an odd expression on his face.

This day needs to be over soon.

## Chapter Ten

By the afternoon, I'm ready to go back to the manor and take a long nap. Being near people is far more exhausting than I thought it would be. But, I cannot take a nap. Instead, I have to go to lunch.

Lia and I walk into the cafeteria with our food.

I have a fruit salad, and Lia has two slices of pizza, a burger, fries, and a salad. Wolf genes; we are always hungry.

She leads me to a table where Kyle and Hunter already sit. Lia sits in front of Kyle, with me on her right. Hunter's on Kyle's right as well. Kyle smirks at me as I sit down.

"I could've sworn Hunter told you this morning to stay away from Tess. But… I have to say. I'm kind of glad you didn't," he says.

"I didn't do anything," I reply with a laugh.

"You could've played nice," Hunter responds.

I shrug. "Nice isn't really my thing."

He doesn't say anything just gives me a humorous smile.

I look around the cafeteria, and I notice some people are staring.

Turning to my new friends, I ask, "Is it just me or are people staring over here?"

Lia grins at me. "Not over here; at you. There's a rumor going around."

"Seriously, it hasn't even been a day, yet," I say with a groan.

"Well, apparently, there's a new bad girl in school, and she has the bad boy settling down." Lia says, her grin growing.

"What does that have to do with me?" I ask, confused.

Kyle smirks. "You are now the bad girl. Anyone with the balls to tell off Tess Bailey will be considered a 'bad girl'. Now you're right there with Lia," he explains.

I look over at Lia with my eyebrows raised and she just smiles at me. "I never liked the bitch. No matter how many times she was screwing - " She stops herself.

"So, I'm guessing that the bad boy in rumor is Ren?"

All three of them nod.

"And the settling down thing?" I ask.

"Ren's never had a girlfriend. Just hook-ups," Kyle says simply.

Lia glares at him.

"Oh, please, Lia. Like she's not going to find out anyways."

"Then why did Tess call him her boyfriend?" I ask.

"Because she's a clingy bitch who wants to become Luna of our pack," Lia says bitterly.

I look at her with wide eyes, surprised by Lia's words, not Tess. It doesn't surprise me if she is after the Luna spot. Everyone wants power.

"Remind me not to make you mad," I say.

She laughs. "Sorry, I just really don't like her."

"So why did he cut her off?" I ask.

Kyle casts me a curious glance. "You're not dense are you? 'Cause of you my beautiful future Luna. The moment he found out he would have a future... bride, he cut her off."

A Luna is an Alpha's mate. She is the queen to the king. But, if we were mated, and Marcus were to will me his power, then I would be an Alpha as well. We would be equals in every way.

"Really? He couldn't have actually thought that we were going to get married?"

Kyle and Lia share a look. "No. He went along with his fathers plan," Kyle says. "But he was not planning on actually marrying you. When he found out that you were his mate. That was a different story."

"But... we're not even in a relationship. He basically rejected me."

Kyle ignores me. "Ren's got... Look, despite what he has said to you, he doesn't want to hurt you. With your bond, being with another person and being so close to you, it won't be fun for you. Ren can certainly be a dick when he wants to be, but he's not that bad. He will treat a girl right, when she means something to him. And despite the fact that you only met him yesterday, trust me when I say you mean something to him. You're just going to have to give him some time."

I'm quiet as I mull over his words.

"Speaking of girls he cares about, you need to apologize to him," Kyle says, pointing a finger at Lia.

"Me? Why?" She scoffs.

"Because you accused him of being someone he's not. I saw the texts, Lia. He ended it with Tess the day he found out about Rory being his mate. Today, Tess just saw him with Rory, and got all jealous and shit like she usually does."

Lia's shoulders slump, and guilt crosses over her features. "I know," she says. "I just overreacted."

"I know. You usually do," Kyle retorts.

Lia throws a fry at him, and he throws it back at her.

"I thought you were supposed to be the Peacekeeper," I say to Hunter.

He raises his hands in surrender. "I am, but he's got all the insight on Ren," he says, motioning to Kyle, who just shrugs. "I'm his best friend. I know him better than anyone else."

I just nod. It all makes sense.

"Speak of the devil, and he shall appear," Lia says with a smile.

I look up towards the front door of the cafeteria, where Ren walks through the doors. Most turn to look at him, and he's got a lazy smirk on his face.

Within seconds Ren is at the table, taking a seat next to Kyle, sitting in front of me. He reaches over and takes a grape out of my fruit salad, and pops it into his mouth.

"Fruit, huh? Is that all you're going to eat?" He asks.

I shrug. "I like fruit."

"That's fine. It just means that you're going to have a bigger dinner."

"Whatever you say," I say, my tone full of sarcasm.

His smirk grows, stretching across his face.

"Good," he says, turning to look at Kyle. "I like it when they say that," he says.

My eyes roll so far back in my head as Kyle laughs. Without thinking, I reach into the bowl, grab another grape, and throw it at Ren. It hit's him in the side of the face. He turns his head and just looks at me.

I shrug. "I don't really like grapes."

Suddenly his smile fades, and he looks down at the table. "I'm sorry," he says. "About earlier."

My eyes cast down over the table.

"I'm just... jumpy about things."

He nods.

"Whoa, whoa, whoa. Did I just hear the great Doren Edward Blackheart apologize?" Lia asks, in mock shock. She puts a hand to her heart, feigning terror. "I feel faint. I do believe hell has frozen over."

Ren rolls his eyes, while the other two boys chuckle.

"Yeah, yeah, whatever," Ren says.

Then Lia turns serious, no longer her bubbly self. "Dory... I'm sorry about earlier," she says, her voice... suddenly smaller.

He waves his hand through the air, dismissing it. "It's fine. You were just being protective, right?"

They look at each other, and they're still for a moment. Then Lia's bubbly behavior returns as if nothing happened.

A thought occurs to me. "Dory?" I ask, looking between the twins.

Everyone but Ren laughs. He lets out a groan.

"She's called me that ever since she watched 'Finding Nemo' for the first time," Ren replies.

I laugh out loud. "You're named after the girl?" I ask.

Something... well, actually, everything about Ren screams true genuine masculinity. He doesn't seem like the kind of guy who would be compared to a girl.

Ren glares at his twin, but it's not serious. "You're lucky you're my sister."

We all just laugh louder, and I grin at Doren. "It's okay. It's cute," I say.

He crosses his arms, and leans back in his chair. "I'm not cute," he grumbles.

"Fine, you're scruffy. Is that better?" I ask, in a teasing tone.

He just grunts in response, making me just grin even more.

Feeling like there are eyes on me, I look around the room. At the table left of ours, there is a group of girls, staring at me. I *hate* people staring at me.

"Take a picture," I snap.

They all fluster, and look back at each other pretending to be in an immensely intriguing conversation with each other. Turning back, I find the wolves at the table looking at me quizzically.

"What?" I ask, sheepishly. "I don't like being stared at."

The four look at each other, and then they all stare at me.

"Okay, stop it," I say, but they all continue staring at me, trying to hold in their laughs.

"You can stop now," I say, growing uncomfortable.

When they don't stop I lean my head on my arms, on the table.

"You guys suck," I groan.

It only makes them laugh harder.

## Chapter Eleven

When the last class is over, Ren decides to take Lia and I to the clothing store, where we will be working together. I am not going to start today, but this way she can walk me through what she does after class.

The car ride to the shop is full of laughter, and it makes me wonder if this is what every day is like for them. Are they this comfortable every day? Is every moment with each other is like this? A small pang shoots through me. I'll admit, I am a little green with envy. How lucky are they that they were able to grow up with each other?

The car stops in front of a small boutique on Main Street. People are milling about, walking down the street, and two of them stop to stare as Lia and I get out of the car. Ren just smiles at the people.

*La Louve*. That is the name of the shop. The curtains are a dark red, and a neon sign hangs in the window with the name of the shop. There is an 'open' sign on the door.

With a wave to the boys, we walk into the store.

There is an older woman who sits behind the counter, reading a magazine. She looks up when we walk in, and she smiles at us.

"Hello, Ladies. How was class?"

"Same as always. Boring," Lia says, making the older woman laugh. "Marian, this is Rory."

Marian turns to me, holding out a hand with a big smile on her face. "I've heard good things about you," she says. "Nice to meet you."

"You too," I say with a polite smile, and a handshake.

"Well, the store is empty for now. We sold a couple things this morning, and at noon. I'm going to head out. Have a good night, ladies."

Then she is out the door.

I take a look around the shop. It is a small shop, with fitting rooms in the back left corner, and a stock room in the back right. There are mannequins throughout the room with pretty little tops and dresses. In the front of the store, there are two mannequins that face the window. Behind them are two chairs that look like thrones. They are outlined in wood, and have a dark red velvety material that covers the seat.

"So, your father owns this store?" I ask, Lia who walks around the counter and starts fiddling with the cash register.

The register sits on a glass counter that holds a large expanse of old Victorian jewelry.

"Yeah. It was my mothers dream to have her own clothing store. Raina Blackheart got anything she wanted when it came to my dad. So, he made it happen for her. The name of the store is 'She Wolf' in French." She laughs when she see's my shocked expression. "I know, it's like Mom was just trying to reveal our identity. Mom always said that the female wolf was the strongest in the pack, because what would the Alpha be without his Luna? So, she named the store 'The She Wolf' because everyone should aspire to be the badass she wolf."

"I like that," I say. After a moment I ask, "Can I – Can I ask what happened to her? Why she is not around?"

"She died. When Ren and I were twelve. She and Ren were walking through the woods… Mom never made it back."

Pain fills my body. Pain for her and her brother for going through that. For Damen for losing his mate. I have heard the loss of a mate be compared to death twice over. It is losing a part of yourself.

"I'm sorry."

She gives me a faint smile. "Thank you."

Because she shared her loss, I feel the need to share with her. "My, uh, my mother and my brother died about ten years ago. They went out to go shopping and they never came back."

"Hunters?" She asks, and I nod.

She grabs my hand, and I squeeze it.

There is a shake of a head, and then she smiles brightly. "So, since my father owns the store, you and I have permission to take whatever we want."

"No, I couldn't -"

"Yes, you can and you will."

"No, really. I don't want to be a mooch. I want to pay my way."

"Well, you would not be mooching, but if it means that much to you, you can pay for it with your paycheck. We get a pretty good discount."

After a moment, a thought occurs to me. This pack... these wolves... they know what they are doing. They know what to do with their wolf senses.

"Do you... do you think you could train me?"

She glances over at me with eyebrows raised.

"Like... how to use our senses and stuff like that."

A grin appears across her mouth. "Of course. There is a make-shift gym on the floor beneath you. Start there. Work out in there. Don't over do it but start small. Run on the treadmill. Lift some weights. Build up your strength and then we will work on you senses."

"Thank you."

Lia shows me the stock room, and explains how to stock things, and how to know when to stock things. She shows me all of the newest clothes that they received recently, and tells me about how she is dying to try on one of the dresses.

Meanwhile she asks me questions.

"How was today for you? Was it overwhelming?"

I stop for a moment, from helping her take boxes out from the back room. I never really thought about it. I haven't really had anyone care enough to ask.

"I, uh, it was fine."

"That sounds reassuring," she smirks.

I let out a nervous laugh. "At least I expected it this time." At her odd look, I elaborate. "When your father stopped for gas on the way here, I bolted to a bus station across the way, and I... I couldn't make it all the way in the building."

"Yeah, he told me about that. Was it a panic attack?"

"No, I think, just being around that many people was... intense. I wasn't used to being around big crowds like that but at least today, I was able to accept it."

"Think you'll be able to do it again?"

I nod. "I think I can handle it."

"Good. 'Cause I'm going to need someone else to help me piss off Tess Bailey."

"It would be my pleasure," I reply, and she laughs.

After a while, a customer comes in and Lia is whisked away for a moment. When she returns to me, she continues talking like nothing had happened.

"During the week one of the pack members, my fathers age, works while we are in class. Alice and Marian switch off during the week, and you and I will work after school Monday through Friday. Saturdays we have off, and then everything in town is pretty much closed on Sundays. Also, we are only open until seven during the week."

For hours we talk about everything and nothing. Lia fills me in on things from her pack, and then just things from the town. When we are closing up the shop, I ask her, "Do you have a boyfriend?"

I'd be surprised if she didn't. She is gorgeous.

A snort is the response I get.

"What?" I ask.

"My brother won't let me close enough to talk to a guy, let alone date one," she says as she puts her keys in the front door, locking up the shop.

"Seriously?"

She nods. "He is very protective."

"What about when you go to the parties or to the mall?"

"Having Kyle and Hunter as best friends is very beneficial for Ren. They are practically my bodyguards."

"Oh. So you haven't had a first kiss?"

Her cheeks pink up a little. "I know, pretty sad for a twenty-one year old."

"No," I say, nudging her shoulder with mine. "I haven't either."

"Really?"

"There weren't many options besides old men in my fathers pack."

"Ew."

"Yeah."

"I think we are going to get along," Lia says, smiling. "And we should really do something about this whole kissing thing. Say, there's a party this Friday night. Wanna go?"

"Hell yeah," is my reply.

"We should go shopping for outfits. Which reminds me, we need to get you some clothes. We can go on Friday, and since you're probably not going to let me pay, we can get your paycheck, and then go. We just need to let my father know that we're taking off on Friday afternoon."

"Sounds good," I say with a smile.

We walk out of the store, and she locks up behind us. Then we go up to the curb and wait for Ren. She looks over at me.

"So, Colin Spacey seemed pretty interested in you today," She says.

I try to remember who that is. Oh, the jock from this morning.

I laugh. "Actually, he seemed more interested in pissing off your brother."

"That's true," she says with a laugh.

The jeep comes barreling down the street, and pulls to the curb right in front of us. Ren looks over at us with a smirk. We pile into the car, Lia in the back and me in front.

Lia brings up Colin again, and it is hard not to notice Ren's fingers tightening on the steering wheel. I need to remember to ask Lia what exactly Ren's problem with Colin is. During our last class of the day, I had everyone in class. And I mean *everyone.* Hunter, Kyle, Ren, Lia, Tess, and Colin. I ended up sitting in the back of the class with Ren and Lia on either side of me. Hunter sat in front of me and Kyle sat in back. It was really odd, until Colin and Tess walked in. It made sense that they were protecting me from them, I just don't really know why. Tess glared at me, but it didn't come near us, taking a seat in the front. Colin tried to come near us, but all three guys stood up, blocking his path. Colin and Ren had a stare off, and in the end Colin just smirked and backed away. I wonder what happened between them.

By the time we get to the pack house, Dahlia is complaining about being hungry so she practically runs into the house.

I jump down from the car, and when Ren begins walking towards the house, I stop him before he can open the door.

"Hey, Ren?"

He turns around and looks at me expectantly.

"I just... there is something I'd like to say."
"Shoot."
"I don't like to be pitied. Things have happened to me, yes, but things happen to everyone. I'm not weak, and I don't want to be seen as weak either."

"I don't-"

I put my hand up to stop him. "I saw the way you looked at me when you found out about my father. I saw it on the faces on some of the others, too. Maybe that's why you don't want me as your mate. Either way, I just want you to know, I don't want it and don't need it."

For a moment he seems stunned. I take that as an opportunity, nearly running inside. I just had to get that out.

There's a sigh, it sounds like out of frustration, and then the sounds of footsteps behind me, but I don't really want to hear what he might have to say. Not right now.

In my rush, I don't notice the person coming out of the dining hall, and I run head first into them. When the force propels my body away, warm hands grip my forearms, stilling me. I rub my forehead as I look up to find... Colin smiling down at me.

"Well, hey there. Just the person I was looking for," he says.

A low growl fills the air and I flinch, but Colin ignores it.

"What... how... what?" I'm at a loss for words. He's a biped - as the Blackhearts call them - in a werewolf pack house. What?

"I live here," he says simply, smiling down at me.

"What?" I ask again, even more shocked now then I was before.

"I'll explain later," he chuckles. "It's dinner time though. Lia asked me to come get you."

"Okay," I say. He turns and walks back into the dining room. I follow him but stop at the doorway, twisting my head around. Ren stands by the front door with his arm crossed, glaring over my head at Colin.

"You coming?" I ask him.

His gaze flicks to me, and the anger on his face… fades a little. He nods stiffly, but follows me anyway. Inside the dining room, the table is full except for three empty seats. Two of them are in between Lia and Hunter. I sit next to Lia, and Ren sits next to me. There's an empty seat across the table from me, and Colin slides into it.

Lying in between us on the table is bowls of mashed potatoes, salads, strawberries, and pork chops. My wolf growls at the sight of the food. It smells delicious.

Before I can react, a big piece of meat is dropped onto my plate.

I look at Ren. "I was getting to that."

He grins. "Well, you were just staring. I thought I would help you out."

I laugh. "I was deciding what to grab first, but thank you," I say, rolling my eyes.

"No problem," he says, while shoving a piece of meat into his mouth. "Make sure you fill up."

"Aye, aye, Captain," I say, with a salute, my voice full of sarcasm.

"Actually, the correct saying is 'Yes, Alpha'." He smirks.

"Not yet," I say in a sing-songy voice.

I bring a strawberry to my mouth and bite into it while Lia starts cracking up next to me. His smile doesn't fade. He watches me bite into the fruit, and I see his eyes darken a little, a hint of gold peaking out. He leans in close, his lips nearly touching my ear. I resist a shiver.

"Just wait," he says, his voice deep.

"I'm shaking in my flip flops," is my reply, but it's shakier than I'd prefer.

"Just wait, Darlin'. When I'm done with you, you'll be saying 'Yes, Alpha' to every damn thing I say."

I gulp. Oh shit.

What the fuck is that supposed to mean?

Oh, god, what do I say? What do I do?

I stare at my plate, trying to figure out what to say.

A throat is cleared. "Can you, um, pass the mashed potatoes?" Lia asks, the amusement clear in her voice. I snap out of my trance, and grab the bowl with shaky hands, and give it to her. My cheeks are probably burning red right now. How does his words have that much of an affect on me? What the hell is he doing to me?

Like the mature person I am, I just stick my tongue out at him, and return to my food. He just chuckles next to me, and the sound is something I could get used too. I'm not used to laughter in general, and the sound of his is just… wonderful.

I start eating and the taste of mashes potatoes almost has me moaning in my seat. It's just *so* good. This whole place… it's something different than I've ever experienced. Here, it actually feels like it could be a home. Everyone is happy here. Kind, loving. It's better here. And I am getting very comfortable, very fast.

## Chapter Twelve

After dinner, Ren goes upstairs to give Jasper a bath. Lia, Kyle, and some others decide to put a movie in. While they bicker over what movie to watch, I decide to wander outside.

"Just stay within the walls," Lia says.

"I will," I assure her.

I leave through the front door, and walk around the left side of the house. I'll save the hedge maze for another day. I follow along the pathway until I reach a stone bench under a huge tree. It has a huge trunk, as most trees do, but its branches are long, full of light green leaves, and they are all drooping downwards. It is a breathtaking sight. I take my phone out a snap a few photos, trying to capture the scenery. The wind blows, making the air cool, and the sky is only a dark blue, the beginning sign of nightfall, making everything serene. I lift my hand, touching the branches.

This is where Colin finds me.

"Hey," he says.

"Hi," is my reply. I still play with the branches.

"I wonder what kind of tree this is," I say, more to myself.

"It's a weeping willow," Colin replies softly. "You're probably wondering what I'm doing here."

"A little," I say. A lot, actually.

He runs a hand through his hair. "Well, I don't really know where to start."

"Let me guess, it's a long story?"

"Actually, it's probably not that long. My mother died during childbirth and when I was about six, my father met Lucy who turned out to be his mate. He died when I was ten... and then around the age of fifteen, Lucy met Damen. I've lived with Lucy ever since my father died."

"Okay," I say. "But your father... are you completely human?"

He chuckles. "Yeah, and so was my dad. It's unique for a werewolf to have a human mate but not impossible. There are some that also think I might have a little of werewolf blood in my genes. A little is all it takes, I guess."

"How... how did he..."

"Die? Hunters. They were aiming at Lucy but he jumped in the way."

"I'm sorry," I say, placing a hand on his arm, and he covers it with his own.

He simply shrugs. "It was a long time ago." He looks of into the distance, and I can feel myself hurting for him as if someone has cut me open. I feel tears trying to breach my eyes, but I won't let them pass. So much death in his life, in all their lives. I feel the need to tell him something about my past, considering how much he shared with me.

"I-"

A growl pierces through the air. Both of us turn to find Ren, glaring at Colin. Well at his arm actually, where our arms are touching. I yank my hand away, as if I've been burned. As if I were doing something wrong.

I don't know what I'm going to say but it doesn't matter. He cuts me off.

"Ren-"

"Lucy is looking for you," he says to Colin.

Colin nods, and gives me one last glance before walking away. Ren turns to go, but throws some words over his shoulder. "Dahlia's looking for you," he says.

"Ren?" I call hesitantly. He halts.

"I... I..." I attempt to find words, but I can't. Come on, Rory, pull yourself together.

"If you have something to ask, just ask," he says, a little shortly, might I add.

"I... Lia told me about your mother. I-"

"I don't talk about that," he says, and then he's gone. Poof. Damn werewolf speed.

My thoughts go back to when I first arrived at the house, and Ren told me that he wasn't going to be with me. He hates when Colin is around me, but he hasn't rejected me as his mate. Something in me, feels hopeful... but I don't even know if I want that. If I want Ren. If I am with him, I want to be sure that it is because of who he is, and not who my wolf wants it to be.

Shaking my head to clear my head, I go back into the house, and find Lia in the front room with the others, the movie playing on the big flat screen. I tap Lia's shoulder, and when she sees me, she drags me into the hallway.

"Hey, Ren said you wanted me?"

She grins. "Oh, I didn't really want you. I just wanted Ren to go find you."

"I was with Colin…"

Her grin grows. "I know."

I shake my head. "You sly devil."

"I know," she says proudly.

I yawn, and she taps my shoulder. "Go to bed. I'll see you in the morning."

Nodding, I go upstairs to do as she says. When I reach the top of the third-floor landing, I see Jasper sneaking in Ren's room. I smile at that.

Going into my room, I change quickly, and then I set an alarm for five thirty in the morning, so I can get up early and work out. I rest my head on my pillows, and curl into a ball underneath my blankets. Then I fade away.

When my alarm goes off, I pull myself up and out of bed even though it kills me to leave my cushiony haven. Lia told me about a gym in the floor below me, and I have every intention on working on this whole 'weak' body thing. I don't want that word to be associated with me in any way.

I change into a pair of shorts, and put on a sports bra and a tank top, then pull my hair into a ponytail, and then I leave my room. I go down to the floor below me, and find the door that belongs to the gym. Then I get on the treadmill and I start running. I run until I can't anymore. I make it about two miles before I have to stop. I go the weight set next. I can only do two sets of ten with twenty pound weights. Then I do thirty squats, and thirty crunches. Then, I do a few rounds of planks.

By the time I am done, I am completely sore. I leave the gym, and go back to my room, and into the bathroom. I take a long hot shower, and then get ready for class. Walking down the stairs has me wincing with every step. Ren meets me at the bottom of the steps in a flash.

"What's wrong?" He asks me, his hand reaching out to gently grab my forearm.

"Nothing, just not used to working out," I say.

He nods. "Let me know if you need anything for the pain," he says.

I give him a grateful smile, then follow him into the dining room where we sit, and eat our morning meal, talking and laughing among the pack mates.

For a few weeks, this is how life around the pack house is. I get up, work out, and then have breakfast with the other wolves.

We pass a full moon within the first few weeks of my being at the manor, at the end of September, but I don't change. I stay in my room, locking Colin out, who was instructed to check on me.

Wolves can change from human form to were form and back, whenever they want, but on the full moon, our bodies forcefully change. The power and energy running through our bodies needs a chance to be let out. So, every since we were created, we shift on the nights of the full moon. Because of this, the Blackheart pack all runs together, leaving me by my lonesome in the manor. In between the days and the nights, Lucy checks on me, and I can sometimes feel Ren outside my door, but he never comes in. I ask if food can be brought to me, rather than me having to go get it, which they agree. I do it more from shame than anything else. I'm tired of being the werewolf that can't actually shift, and the looks that I've gotten from the other wolves. I don't need nor want to be pitied.

    As much as the full moon was discouraging, it didn't stop me from working out. Actually, it made me even more motivated. Slowly, I can feel my body changing. Eventually I find a scale, and weigh myself every few weeks, happy to find that I am gaining on the pounds. When I look in the mirror, I can no longer see my ribs now, I can see actual definition.

    After breakfast, I go to class, and then go to work with Lia. Then back to the house, and we all have dinner together. The first couple of weekends, Lia and I watch movies when she isn't making me do my classwork. Ren is not around. He is there but he isn't. It is like he's around enough to know what is going on, but then he's gone, too busy to worry about anything else. Life is good. And it gets better every day.

"Ready?" Lia asks from behind me.

I turn around to look at her, dropping my phone, startling me away from looking at some of the photos on my phone that I have taken recently. Lia had texted me about ten minutes ago telling me to meet her in the front of the house. It is Saturday, and most of the wolves are out of the house. Ren is visiting his grandfather. Kyle and Hunter are out shopping.

"What are we doing?" I ask, looking at her outfit in the process.

Black tennis shoes, black workout pants, and a hot pink tank top. She looks ready to run. She is also holding a black garbage bag in her hand.

"You'll see," she says with a grin. She leads me around the house.

"You didn't want to go visit with your grandfather?"

Lia looks away from me. "Uh… no. I don't really talk to him."

"Really?"

She nods. "My dad doesn't either. Not really. Ren does because he wants help with becoming the Alpha. He wants to be the best so he is getting information from both him and my dad. He never stays long, though."

"Is he really that bad?"

Lia just shrugs. "He is just a cranky old man who is set in his ways."

She stops, and when I look up we are standing at the entrance of the hedge maze.

"Remember when you asked me to help with your senses?" She asks. "Today we are going to start."

I look up at the tall mass of bushes in front of us, and take a deep breath.

"So, one of our most important senses is the sense of smell. It just takes a small inhale and you can track anything. We use the hedge maze as a way to learn how to track a scent. To get ourselves trained in using the sense. Most of us know the routes in the maze inside and out now, so we don't use it that much. But, for you, it will work perfectly."

"Okay," I say.

"When tracking, you have to want to do it. If you don't want to find whatever you are looking for then you are not going to. So, you're going to smell what I have inside this bag, and when you inhale the scent, have it fill you completely. Your mind, your body. Let it run through you. Then take a step back, and smell the air. Let your senses search for you, and find it. They will lead you, tell you where to go."

I nod as she pulls open the garbage bag and holds it out to me.

"Go ahead. Take a sniff," she says.

Leaning towards the bag, a little wearily I might add, I take a sniff of the bag, and almost start dry heaving.

"Oh my god, what is that?" I ask, jerking away from the bag.

"You don't want to know," she says, chuckling.

I stare at her with wide eyes, surprised by her laughing. Straightening out, I give my body a shake and take another step towards the bag. I close my eyes, and inhale the scent, and do as Lia said. I let it float through my body, and it is almost as if my wolf grabs at it, latching on to it, like she knows what we are trying to do. The smell fills my body, and I open my eyes, nodding to Lia.

She grins. "Count to ten." Then she takes off running into the maze.

Slowly, I count in my head, and then I begin walking the path that Lia took.

The hedges are over ten feet tall, and right within the entrance, I can either go left or right. Directly in front of me is a wall of green. I smell the air, and something in me tells me left. For what seems like hours, I wonder through the maze, my body telling me which ways to go, and suddenly, I turn a corner to see Lia smiling at me. She leans against a stone bench, arms crossed, her phone in the palm of her hand. She taps the screen of her phone.

"Thirty-five minutes. Not bad for someone who has never used her senses before. Ready to try again?"

She leads me through a path that I did not take, back to the front entrance.

"What was in the bag?" I ask her as we walk.

"A dead rat. We found it in the woods a few days ago."

A shiver runs through my body. Ew.

We run through it three more times, and each time I shave off five minutes from my original time. Each time Lia finds a different unique smell for me to find. I'm feeling confident about doing it again, until Lia pulls me back away from the opening of the maze by about ten feet, and then steps up behind me wrapping a piece if material over my eyes.

"Now that you have gotten used to using your senses, I want you to try without the eyes. This way you really must rely on your sense of smell to lead you. Smell."

I can sense her holding something up in front of my face, and I smell something sweet smelling this time. It is soft like a flower, but almost too sweet like cotton candy. Once again, I inhale deeply.

"Again, count to ten, then go." I nod.

After ten Mississippi's, I begin slowly walking. The fresh scent of the hedges hits me, and I know that I am close to the opening. I spread my arms out, and the tops of all ten fingertips touch against the rough leafy greens. I smile to myself. So far so good. Filling my lungs with air again, I carefully choose which way to go.

For minutes, I walk slowly but soundly, feeling like I'm making it at a good pace, but then suddenly, everything that I've been working towards, the smell that I've been fixing to find, disappears, and another smell fills me. It overloads my senses, and I stop still, completely frozen. I inhale the smell greedily, a shower of gooseflesh forming over my skin as something coils deep inside of me.

"Ren!"

Lia's voice cuts through the air, her voice filled with a laugh.

His throaty laugh follows, and I can tell that they are not far from me. Not far at all. I take a couple dozen more steps and a few more turns. I'm no longer searching for the original smell, but the new wonderful scent. The one that I have smelled before. The one that I smell all the time around Ren. I take off the blindfold, and there they are, standing in front of me.

Lia hits Ren in the arm. "You distracted her," she says.

Ren chuckles. "I didn't mean to. I was trying to scare you."

He turns to me, his eyes meeting mine, and something makes me look away. I feel like my face is burning. Does he know how his smell affected me?

"How did she do?" He asks, looking back at his sister. A small part of me bristles that he acts like I am not here,

"The first time just over a half-hour, but I got it down to just under fifteen minutes," I say, answering for Lia.

They both look to me, and Lia has a grin on her face. Ren has a small smile of appraisal.

"Good. Kyle got called away by my dad, and I need someone to run through the south part of the territory. Are you okay with doing it, Lia?"

She nods. "Yeah. Can I go in my wolf form? My wolf is getting restless."

Ren hesitates. He turns to me. "Want to go with her?"

I nod enthusiastically.

"Fine. Don't go all the way down, just a few miles from the mansion. Be her eyes and ears, Rory. Anything seems strange or you see someone who is not a part of this pack, you hop on Lia's back and you both run? Got it?"

"Yes, Ren," we reply.

## Chapter Thirteen

Lia practically drags me out of the maze, and towards the south side of the territory.

"Be back in two hours for dinner," Ren yells after us.

Neither of us replies.

Once we get to the wall, Lia shows me a secret doorway, hidden in the big stonewall. It is shrouded in shrubs and is almost hidden, except if you know where to look.

I turn around while Lia sheds out of her clothes and shifts. She brushes against my leg and then I face her again. Her wolf is a light brown wolf, her vibrant green eyes the only thing I recognize on her. Her wolf stands almost to my height, near six feet tall. Her tail swings back and forth behind her as she gazes at me, waiting patiently. Before we go anywhere, I pull out my phone and take a picture. I've become addicted to this it seems. After putting it back in my pocket. I open the door, and she walks out ahead of me, and then I close it behind me.

We walk for a while in silence, and then she brushes against my leg. I smile down at her, but don't say anything. She pushes against me this time.

"What?" I ask, with a chuckle.

Of course, she doesn't say anything. But she turns her head to me, and I see something in her eye. I don't know what it is about exactly, but she wants me to speak.

"So, this whole school thing, is it supposed to be an actual thing? Like, I am expected to get very good grades? Because I am kind of worried about how that is going to play out. I haven't been in an actual class in a long time, and I don't even know how to really focus heavily on something like that. So, how can I be sure that I am actually going to be able to learn and turn homework in and take tests? I don't know, Lia."

Rambling seems to be my specialty, and I go on for so long that I'm surprised that Lia hasn't taken off running away from me yet. We've been walking now for what seems like forever, mainly because my legs are burning.

The path that we have taken leads past the beach that Ren had once told me about. It's a small beach, but it has a large span of water. We stop, and Lia goes to the water to take a drink. I walk and look around at the trees.

The forest is thick with trees. So thick that one can't see too far ahead of them. Shrubs, and thick branches cover pathways, and the trees are so thick and bushy with leaves.

Something snaps in the air, and I whirl around to look, my eyes scanning up and down through the trees. I look back at Lia but she is a few feet away, still drinking water.

A bird squawks, and I look up to see a canary land on a branch. It stands out against the green background.

As I'm just turning back to Lia, a piece of metal catches my eyes. My eyes widen.

"Lia," I say quietly.

Out of the corner of my eye, I can see her look at me.

The metal is a long, thin, rounded shaft that connects to the butt of the gun, which is in the hands of a man. He stands at about five and a half feet tall, in his late fifties, with a camo hat on, and a matching vest. He lifts his head from the eyepiece on top of the gun, and his eyes meet mine. He makes a shushing motion, before looking back at Lia.

"Lia, run," I yell-whisper.

But she stands frozen.

The hunter begins lifting the gun high, and I do the only thing I can think of. I run to Lia, stepping in front of her. I hold my hands out.

"No!" I yell.

"Move out of the way," the hunter yells back, moving the end of the rifle, trying to find a shot to Lia. There is no doubt that Lia has called Ren. I just have to stall until they get here.

"No, you can't shoot her."

"Move, girl," he says gruffly.

"No, you are going to have to shoot me first if you want her." Stupid thing to do, I know, but he is not hunting a biped. I've really grown to start using that word.

"You are not what I want, now move!" He shouts.

Loud growling begins behind me, and I can imagine that Lia's head is bowing, and she is getting ready to attack. She tries to brush past my leg, but I push forward ahead of her again. I am not going to let her stand in the way of this guy. I am not going to let her risk her life.

"Move, girl. Now!" The hunter yells again.

A loud roar echoes through the woods not far behind the hunter, making him look over his shoulder nervously.

The delicious scent of trees and rain begins to fill the air.

Ren. He's almost here.

Lia steps out from behind me once more as I'm distracted, and the hunter turns back in time to see that. He lifts his gun, aims, and pulls the trigger. Before I can think, I push Lia and something hits my arm. Pain radiates through me, but I don't think about it.

I let out a loud growl, and turn back to the hunter. I can feel my teeth lengthening as my chest rises and falls heavily.

The hunter lowers the gun slowly as fear falls across his face.

"You're going to pay for that," a low voice says, as a shadow steps through the forest. The hunter spins around just as Ren comes walking into view, his face a canvas of fire and rage. His eyes are dark, and like me, his teeth are lengthened. His chest heaves with heavy breaths. He reaches a hand down to the man's throat, and lifts him inches off the ground. The gun drops to the earthy floor.

Liquid drips down my arm, and I look at it. Blood has been splattered across my body, and it drips down my right arm. There is a gaping hole in my arm where the bullet is. I should probably do something about that. I lift my left arm and cover the hole with my hand.

Next to me, Lia shifts back to human form and comes over to me, removing my hand to look at the wound.

Ren sets the man's body harshly back on the ground, and he rushes over, copying his sister.

"Get home," he says to Lia. "Now."

She nods, and with a last lingering look at me, she takes of running, and shifts back into her wolf form mid run. Another wolf follows her. Kyle and four other wolves I cannot recognize at the moment stand near the still living man, making sure that he doesn't run. I know he is alive because I can hear his fast heart beat from where I stand.

Pain shoots through my arm, making me jerk, and look at Ren.

"Sorry," he says, gruffly, and produces a shirt from I don't know where, and he wraps it around my arm. He stands for a minute, thinking.

"Can you hold on to me? If I shift?" He asks.

I nod. "Yeah, I can with my other arm."

"Okay, if you can't, just tell me and I'll shift back to my human form, okay?"

He turns to the other wolves. "Take care of him."

I cast a glance at the hunter once more and I see the fear on his face. Guilt forms in my body because if it wasn't for us, wasn't for me, this man would live. He would go home to his family, and have a good night. But now, he will never go home again. It is another one of those rules that we have – humans cannot find out about us. They cannot see us shift, if they do – they will be killed.

There is movement in front of me, and I look back in front of me to see that Ren is no longer standing in front of me. Now, a six-foot-tall black wolf stands where he stood. He has certain imperfections to him. Like in certain places he has missing patches of fur. He lays down on all fours and I remember the urgency of the situation and where we are. I climb onto his back and wrap my arm around his neck.

"I'm good," I say, and then he takes off. Branches whip by us, and wind rushes in my ears as he picks up speed, running faster than I ever thought possible.

I don't know the distance, but it has to be a lot. Part of me is too distracted by the feel of his body against mine.

After running for a sizeable distance, I see lights coming from the tops of walls that surround the mansion, miles away. All the lights in the house must be on. When we reach the walls, there is someone standing by the trap door, holding it open.

Ren brushes past, and rushes through the big yard, and into the back of the house. Up a flight of stairs, and finally into the make shift hospital room. Lucy and Damen already stand waiting for us and once we are in the room, I am traded from Ren's arms to Damen's. Damen sets me down on a cot while Ren collapses onto the one next to me. An arm thrown over his face as his chest heaves up and down. His… hot… naked… muscular chest. My eyes travel farther down. Holy crap he is completely naked. Heat floods my face.

Pants are thrown at Ren, and Lucy steps in front of me, blocking my view. Lucy places an IV into my arm. When she moves, Ren has pulled on a pair of pants, and is laying in his original position.

"We are going to give you a blood transfusion because you probably already lost a lot. Then I will numb your arm and get that bullet out, okay?" Lucy explains, and I just nod.

"Little pinch, okay?" She says, and then she slides the needle into my arm.

Colin, Hunter, and Lia walk into the room. All eyes are fixed on mine. I meet Lia's eyes first, because she looks like she is about to burst into tears. I give her a smile to show that I am okay, and then Damen comes up to her and wraps an arm around her shoulder.

Colin steps forward reaching an arm out to me, but then a growl cuts through the air. I take a quick peek at Ren, but he stills has an arm thrown over his face, shielding his eyes, even though everyone in the room knows the growl came from him. Lucy looks between the two boys.

"Maybe we should give her some space. Everyone clear out of the room please."

Colin stares at Ren's body for a minute, before looking at me, giving me a smile, and then walking out of the room. Hunter gives me a thumb's up before following Colin. Lia smiles at me, and then she and her father walk out of the room. Ren doesn't make any move to leave, and I wonder if Lucy knew he wasn't going to budge when she cleared the room.

Once the IV and blood bag are securely placed where they should be, Lucy reaches for a tray with supplies on it.

"How are you feeling, Rory?" She asks, as she begins covering my arm with lidocaine.

"Fine. It really doesn't hurt that much."

She appraises me with raised eyebrows. I don't know why this surprises her so much. I have a high tolerance for pain.

"Are you sure it's still in there?" I ask.

Lucy smiles. "Yes, I'm sure."

She pulls a kind of forceps off the tray.

"Now I need you to stay still," Lucy says, and then she thinks for a minute. "Ren, climb up behind Rory and hold her still for me."

Ren heaves himself up onto his feet, and then comes over, and swings a leg over the cot I'm on. My body stiffens as his legs rest up against my outer thighs, and his arms come around my arms, holding them in place. I try to relax, but honestly, like that is even possible when he is this close to me.

Lucy pokes around my arm.

"Can you feel that?"

I shake my head stiffly.

"Alright, I'm going in."

My hands clench into fists in apprehension, and I take a deep breath. At first poke, I don't feel much, but then I can feel her digging through my arm. I let out a choked gasp, and Ren's body snuggles closer to mine. His chest is now fully pressed against my back. He readjusts his hands, so that now his arms are still over mine, but my palms rest against his, allowing me to squeeze as hard as I need.

Lucy begins digging again, and I cringe. Pain shoots up and down my arm, and I squeeze Ren's hands as tight as I can. My eyes drift shut, I breathe slowly through my mouth to try and soothe the pain.

"Got it," Lucy says, and removes the forceps from my arm. She puts them on the metal tray with a clang.

"Now, we just need to clean out the wound and stitch you up."

The cleaning makes me cringe more than anything else. I don't know why, but it almost hurts worse than the bullet itself. When Lucy does the stitches, I barely even feel it because of the lidocaine. Then finally, she is wrapping up my arm with a white bandage, and Ren is moving away from me.

"If there is any sever pain, or bleeding, let me know immediately, okay? I'll be staying here tonight, so I won't be far if you have any problems. Don't overuse your arm."

"Thank you."

"No need to thank me. We should be thanking you."

I look away at that. She pats my good arm, and then she leaves the room, leaving Ren and I alone. I inspect the white bandage as he watches me.

"What you did… It won't be forgotten," he says, his voice low.

"I didn't do anything."

"You saved my sister."

Something in his voice makes me look at him.

"Thank you."

I nod. What am I to say? Of course, I did, and I would do it again. For her, for them, I would do it again.

"Are you hungry?"

My eyes meet his again.

"What? You're thinking about food? Now?" I chuckle.

His mouth tips up. "No. I'm not hungry. It's just, we missed dinner by hours, but if you were hungry I would go get you something."

"No, thank you, though. I have to go get the blood off me, and then go to sleep, I think."

I start walking towards the door, but he stops me with the clearing of his throat. Turning back, I look at him, waiting.

"Can I – can I do something?"

It shocks me. Ren, he never seemed to have trouble forming words, and he never seems to ask for things either.

"Yes."

He steps closer. Close enough so that he can reach his arms out, rest them on my shoulders, and look me up and down. His hands squeeze my shoulders.

"I'm okay," I say.

His head lifts and his eyes meet mine.

"She's okay. We're both fine."

Then, he pulls my shoulders and engulfs me in a hug. His mouth rests by my ear, and I hear his heavy breaths.

"She called to me, and I swear, Rory, I've never run so fast in my life. I saw both of you in my head, dying. It doesn't... I don't-"

"Shhh," I say to him, reaching my arms up over his back, running my hands up and down. "Sh. We're both fine now. We're okay."

The door opens, but we don't pull away. We turn our heads, and Lia stands in the doorway, tears in her eyes. I hold out an arm, and she comes flying into the mix, wrapping her arms around us both. I feel Ren place a kiss on top of her head.

We stand like that for a while, arms wrapped around each other, thankful that we are all okay. That we can live another day with one another. Thankful that I moved and the bullet only hit my arm.

We're all okay.

## Chapter Fourteen

The next day, there is an article in the local newspaper about a body being found on the boundaries in town. It looks to be a wolf attack. The article warns people to stay in doors when possible, and not to go out alone. The man that was killed, his name is Carl Hansen, and he didn't have a family. He did have a group of hunting buddies that will miss him dearly.

I throw the guilt deep down inside me because I know that there is nothing I can do about it. What's done is done.

We go to class, like normal, and the day is totally unsuccessful. It is a Monday, so everyone really seems dead. Then there is the pain in my arm, so I don't really feel like writing, which causes me to doze off. Also Lia and I stayed up late talking last night, a lot about the hunter, and some of what I was talking about when Lia was in wolf form. So, yeah, I'm pretty tired, so I fall asleep in class. Sue me.

The fun really begins when Lia and I get to work after class. It is honestly one of my favorite things to do. I get to work with my best friend and she pretty much runs the store. We get to be loud and gossip and not have to worry about any nosy werewolves. After the hunter incident, Ren made sure to have someone following Lia and I at all times. Since Lia and I are usually together, that made it easier for him. Now Victor, one of the

Hunters, is sitting in the coffee shop across the street. He's giving us space, and still watching.

Lia and I have been here at the shop for over a half an hour, sorting through some older clothes to put on the discount rack. She is not letting me lift *anything*, and I mean absolutely nothing. I tried to grab my bookbag off the floor in class, and she nearly yanked my arm out of my socket, trying to grab the bag from me. Now I'm sitting on the floor stickering the tags of clothing that Lia scans through.

The bell rings as the door opens, and we both turn to look at as Colin walks in.

"Hey," We all say in greeting to each other.

"What are you doing here?" I ask, curiously.

"What, I can't shop here?" He asks, feigning offense, as he sits down on the floor a foot from me.

Lia laughs. "Not that you can't shop here, but it is intended for girls. But, hey, whatever floats your boat."

We all laugh.

"You got me. I'm not here to shop, but I am here to talk to Rory."

"What's up?" I ask, giving him a warm smile.

"Well, I was thinking that if it was slow we could talk. I thought since I told you about my past, you could tell me something about yours. Since Ren won't let me anywhere near you at the Packhouse, I assumed this would be the best place for us to become friends. Plus, Lia probably knows everything about you, already."

Colin is right, I never really see him at the Manor. It seems it is not just because of Ren, but a lot of the time he is just never there. It makes me wonder if he doesn't actually like being there.

"Sure, though, I haven't told Lia much, either. I really haven't had time and its not something I like thinking about let alone talk about."

"You don't have to say anything you don't want to," Lia says quickly, but even then I can tell she is interested.

"It's fine. Easier that I tell you both at the same time rather than on two separate occasions. So, what do you want to know?"

Colin and Lia share a look. "Well, I guess, what made your dad so mean?" Lia asks.

I shrug. "You are asking me something that I've asked myself for years. I never really noticed it when I was younger. I think I was just oblivious. My mother and brother... they were still alive, and I think he was mean to them. And even when he was mean to Austin, you could tell that he still loved him. He wanted him to be better. Marcus didn't go about it the right way, obviously, and I still hate him for it all, but I think that's what it was, essentially. See, he loved my brother, Austin. And I mean *loved* him. So when he was around, I was never really paid attention too. But after he died, that changed. At first, he had this great son, someone to be proud of, and then he was stuck with me. He couldn't leave his pack to me. He didn't even want me. That's when the beatings really started. Sure, I'd get hit when I was a kid for doing something wrong, but later on it was all about how his luck must have been so bad to lose this great son and end up with just me. And he has something against woman. He's sexist, thinking that they are only good for things like sex, and cleaning. There are only men in his pack because he doesn't think that woman deserve to hold rank. And all the men in his pack are just like him. Power hungry, sexist, and mean. The only thing I can thank Marcus for is that he kept me locked in my room. He never let any of the dogs sniff around me. That was always my fear that one day he would make me…" I can't even say the words. "His Beta is even worse. The only reason why he never took it upon himself to beat me whenever I had to go shopping with his was because he didn't dare take the privilege away from Marcus. I never understood why that man hated me. It seems he hates me more than Marcus does. "

We're all quiet and I can see the two of them taking in what was said.

"Did you ever tried to run away?" Colin asks.

I take a deep breath. "Yeah, I tried. Often. After a while it seemed like it was a game to him. Like he would purposely give me options to run away. One time it was leaving my door unlocked. Like he was trying to see if I would actually do it, and when I did the punishment was always worse than the time before. One time I actually made it to the end of his territory before they caught up to me and then-"

The memory cuts me off, and I realize I don't want them to have that image in their minds. Of its own accord a tear slips from my eyes, but I wipe it away quickly. Both of them watch me with woeful eyes.

"And then I tried to run away from Damen, but I didn't make it that far either," I force a chuckle out.

Colin lets out a choked laugh. "What? I did not hear about this."

Lia watches me for a second and then she gives me the smallest nod. The nod of 'I know what you went through and I am not going to force you into talking about it, but you can'. It is the kind of nod I am grateful for.

"Yeah, she was supposed to be going to the bathroom, and she snuck out on them and ran across the street to the bus stop. They found her a few minutes later," Lia says, finishing the story so I can have a moment without being forced to talk.

Colin looks over at me in disbelief. "I can't believe you did that. That you got away from him. I remember like a year ago, Lia tried sneaking out of the house. Damen heard her from two stories above. Caught her before she even left her room."

"I think Ren might have tipped him off on that one," Lia laughs.

"What can I say? I got skills," I chuckle to them.

They burst out laughing.

This is how we spend the next few hours, with breaks when some customers came in to buy things. Colin decides to hang around while we close the shop up, but when Ren walks in, it gets awkward.

We all freeze in the middle of our conversation thinking that it was another customer. He had a small smile playing on his lips, but when he sees Colin it fades away.

"Hey, Ren," Colin says, but Ren doesn't reply.

Colin turns to me. "Well, I guess I should be going. I'll see you guys back at the house."

"Bye," I say, giving him a small wave as he leaves out the door.

Then the three of us kind of stand around awkwardly.

"Well, we've just got to finish closing up. We'll meet you outside, Ren," Lia, says, thankfully.

Out of the corner of my eye, I see Ren glance at me before nodding and walking out.

Once the door is closed Lia turns to look at me. "So, tomorrow, you and I are going to go to a mall," She says with a grin.

"Why are you grinning like that?" I ask, curious.

"Don't worry, just don't tell anyone, okay? But there is a party this weekend, and you and I are going. I don't want Ren to know because he will not let us go. He'll make up some excuse that we don't need to do that or even go to the party, so don't tell him, okay?"

"Okay. Plus, a party sounds fun."

"Yes, and you Ms. Bullet in the Arm, need some fun."

"I'll be honest, I'm a little excited."

Electricity flies through my body just at the thought.

"It is going to be great," Lia replies.

Then we lock up shop, and go home. Ren and I don't share a word other than 'goodnight'.

The next day, I am counting down the minutes until classes are over.

I'm sitting in my last class of the day. Lia and Ren are both in class with me, and I am currently sitting in between the two of them. My eyes are glued to the clock on the wall above the teacher, and out of the corner of my eye I see Ren keep glancing at me.

The class is some sort of movie class, so most of the time we watch movies but not today. Vaguely, I hear the teacher say that we are going to working with partners to write a paper. She starts listing of pairs she has set up. Her voice is so low and dead like and it almost puts me to sleep.

Then she says, "Ren and Rory," and I snap my head up.

What?!

Everyone in the class gets up and moves to sit near the partners, and even Lia has to move across the room. She casts me a sympathetic glance as she goes. I, on the other hand, don't move and am content with not working with him. Ren seems to have other ideas because he literally reaches over and grabs the legs of my desk and pulls me to him.

"So what was this movie about?" I ask him, finally turning to look at him.

He sits, leaning comfortably against the back of his chair, his legs stretched out in front of him. One stretches out close to me, our feet inches from touching. His hands are folded in his lap, and his eyes are focused solely on me. He appraises me for a just a moment short of it becoming uncomfortable, and he finally speaks.

"You weren't watching?" He asks with a chuckle.

I didn't read the story either. It was about twenty pages too long. I mean, I like to read – interesting things. I was going to do it, honestly, but then I thought nah.

"No, it was boring. I zoned out," I say, shaking my head.

"Oh, yeah? What were you thinking about?"

My eyebrows raise and I give him an odd look.

"Nothing."

Ren just smiles, and then says, "Well, I didn't watch it either, so we're at a loss."

"Did you read the story?"

He shakes his head no.

"We're a crack team," I say, making him chuckle.

"We can just watch the movie this weekend, and then do the essay afterwards. Want to do it after school?" He asks.

"I've got plans with Lia," I say, with a shake of my head.

"What are you two doing?"

Oh, shit. Don't react. Don't react. I'm a terrible liar. Remembering what Lia said about not wanting him to know, I try to look normal.

"Uh, I don't really know. Hanging out. We might go through Lia's closet and look for outfits for the party."

This surprises him. His head snaps to me. "You're going to the party this weekend?" And let me tell you, his voice is not really full of approval. Not that I need it, but still, it's just a party.

I just nod my head.

"Why?"

"Why not?"

There's a moment of silence.

"You're really quiet," Ren says suddenly.

Again, I look at him with a confused expression. "Okay?"

"But, I don't think it's because you don't have anything to say."

Where is he going with this?

"I just think it's because you spent so long without anyone to talk to, and now you're just so used to it."

My eyebrows come together. "And your point?"

"Well, my point is that you can talk to me. I would... like to hear what you have to say."

My jaw almost drops. The man who has spent weeks purposely avoiding me, not wants me to talk to him. Maybe... things between he and I could be changing. Not that I am holding my breath for it or anything, but still, it would be nice to know that things for us could be different.

Something about my expression must not please him, because his eyes harden a little. "What?"

"Nothing, it's just surprising is all. Mr. Brooding and not so talkative wants to talk."

He's scoffs.

"I don't brood," he says in total and complete denial.

"Well, you certainly don't talk," I quip back.

"First," he says in annoyance. "I didn't say that I would talk, just that you could."

"So I get to tell you all my secrets, but you won't tell me anything? Yeah, that is not the way it works, dude."

"Is that why you talk to Colin? Because he told you all of his secrets?"

I flinch. Ah, so this isn't about us growing closer at all. It is just about him having to one up the biped he is jealous of.

"That's what this is about? Me talking to Colin?"

He scoffs again, rolling his eyes. "Of course not."

Yeah, because that's so absurd.

"Then what?" I ask, crossing my arms over my chest, trying to prove him wrong.

He just shakes his head.

The bell rings, and I stand up, shoving my unused notebook into my book bag.

"Fine. When you want to talk to *me,* just let me know," I say before walking out of the class, anger suddenly filling my body.

Every I think we are making progress, that we are moving forward, something happens, and it stops. We got three feet forward, and ten steps back. Every time a bit of hope springs, he squashes it.

God, he is so infuriating.

## Chapter Fifteen

Walking out of the classroom, I take a deep breath and run a hand through my hair to calm myself from the anger he has roaring through me. Something about him just bothers me. How can he bother me so much in a five-minute conversation? He's talented, that's for sure.

The path to from the building to the parking lot is short, and by the time I reach the entrance, I can spot Lia standing next to Ren's jeep. She is bouncing up and down on the balls of her feet, and she tosses the keys of the car back and forth between her hands.

When she spots me she shoots me a forced smile showing teeth.

"Whoa, you okay?" She asks.

There must be a tell on my face.

"I could ask you the same," I say, chuckling.

"Heh," she responds, and walks around the car towards the driver's side.

"What are you doing?"

"Well," she says, turning around. "I stole my brothers key, and we are going to the mall. But, we need to go fast, because right now he is talking to Kyle, and we have to go before he comes out here."

We share a look, and then I bolt to the passenger's side as she hops into the driver's seat. Lia starts the car, and throws it into gear, before bolting out of the parking lot. I cast a look over my shoulder, and see Ren standing at the entrance of the parking lot. Pissed is an understatement.

"He is really pissed," I say.

"Oh, trust me, I know," she replies, tapping her head indicating the mind link that she shares with the pack.

"You didn't have to do this for me."

She laughs. "This wasn't just for you. If I didn't do this, I wouldn't be able to have time with another girl. We would have had Hunter and Kyle, and who knows whom else traveling with us. Knowing Ren, he already has Kyle coming after us, but for now at least we get to talk, without any prying ears."

"Ren is not going to understand that. He is going to kill us when we get back."

"True. So, in that case, we might as well have some fun, huh?" She throws a grin over at me.

She pushes on the gas pedal, making the car speed at a high rate. I play with the buttons on the radio, finding a good song, and turning the volume up high. It is a song with both know, so we sing out loud to our hearts content, as we fly down the old dusty roads, letting the wind whip through our hair.

I take pictures of us, especially Lia, with the wind in her hair, smiling like crazy, and singing to the music.

When we reach the mall a half an hour later, I ask her, "Whose territory is the mall in?"

"Its uncharted territory," Lia replies. "No one owns it. It's kind of mutual place for packs to go." After a second, she says. "You can drive back if you want."

I shake my head, chuckling. "That wouldn't be a good idea."

She throws me a questioning glance before turning back to the road.

"I don't know how to drive," I explain.

"Really?! Well you're gonna learn today!" She says, seeming more excited than I am for it. "Just don't crash the car, otherwise my brother will really kill us."

We both laugh at that, because I think we both know it's more than a little true.

The mall is set up in a circle, with an indoor pathway. On one end is a Target and on the other is a Carson's. Lia decides to drag me into the Target.

"First we are going to get you essentials. You need some yoga pants. Trust me when I say they are like the most comfortable thing ever. Then we'll get some hoodies, and shirts for you."

"I'm not going to have enough for all this," I say once I've tried everything on and have it all in a cart.

"Sure, you will," she says while reaching into her bag and pulling out a wad of cash. I look at it with an eyebrow up. There must be almost a thousand dollars all in twenties.

"There is no way that I made all of that," I say in disbelief.

"You sure did."

"What, am I making almost a hundred dollars an hour?"

She just shrugs. "What? You do good work."

Then she walks away before I can say more on the matter. I give an exasperated eye roll and follow her.

After I've paid, we go to Victoria's Secret.

I raise an eyebrow at her.

"What? Hey, I've seen those things you call bras and trust me, you definitely need new ones."

My cheeks burn, and she pats me on the shoulder, lovingly.

"Don't worry. I don't blame you, I blame your father," her voice is filled with humor rather than pity and I'm thankful.

We smile at each other and then she drags me into the store. Lia puts me into the hands of a sales associates, who immediately pull out measuring tape and starts wrapping it around my body. She yells out numbers to the other one who goes around the store grabbing things. Then they push me into a fitting room with tons of bras and underwear to try on.

"I want to see how they look!" Lia yells to me as I start changing.

"Seriously?" I call to her.

"Seriously. This is what girls do. Who else is going to tell you which ones look best?"

Laughing, I begin pulling the first bra on. It's a pinkish beige color. Really plain. I open the door to find Lia leaning against the wall waiting patiently. I cross my arms around my bony midsection and let her see the bra.

"Ahh, that one's kind of cute. It goes with your skin tone well. Put that one on the keep pile. Next."

I close the door and try on the next one.

"Don't buy too many though, we're going to be coming back soon," Lia says through the door.

"Why?" I ask.

"This might sound weird, but your boobs are pretty big. If you keep working out, and gaining more weight, they're going to get bigger. So we're going to be coming back again."

Oh. Well.

"I never thought of that," I reply.

For the next half an hour, I try on so many bras, all different styles and colors. Some rainbow, some singular colors. Lia told me that I need to have a color for every kind of dress, so she gets a black one, a tan one, and a white one, amongst many more. Then I try on ones that are strapless and meant to push up, and ones that cross down the back, and ones that hook in front. The ones in the take pile are mainly blue, pink, and reds. I save the one I like the most for last. It's a blue floral color with flowers on it.

There's a tingle at the back of my neck, and a warmth feeling spreads across my skin. I ignore and continue putting on the next undergarment.

As I'm clasping the bra, there's an impatient knock on the door.

"Hold on, Lia. Almost done." I fit the bra correctly, and then I pull open the door.

I stumble back as someone walks in and closes the door behind them. He leans his back against the door, and looks at me.

"Not expecting me?" Ren asks, his voice deep, and disapproving.

"I was expecting you earlier," I say.

He smirks, and his gaze wanders lower. "Looks like I came at the right time." I look down and realize that I'm only wearing a bra from the chest up. Throughout my time here, I have worked hard for my body, and I'm glad for how it looks now, compared to those months ago when I first came to the manor. So, I don't shy away, or try to hide. Instead, I stand proud. I do roll my eyes, and cross my arms, to show that I am annoyed for his barging in. My blood is boiling underneath my skin. He's less than a foot away, causing so much trouble underneath my skin, and not just because I am annoyed. Damn mate bond.

"You shouldn't be opening the door dressed like that." Before I can reply he adds, looking down at where my arms are crossed, "You shouldn't have to cover up. Not in front of me."

"And who are you supposed to be?" I ask, glaring up at him.

There's something in his eyes, but I can't read it through his guarded expression.

"I'm *supposed* to be your mate," his voice monotone. I don't reply, just look at a spot over his shoulder.

"You shouldn't have run away, just because we had a fight," he says, catching my eye again.

"First, I wouldn't call that a fight. Second, you wish you had that kind of effect on me, and third, I didn't run away."

"Ren," Lia's voice floats through the door. "I stole your keys, she had no idea about it."

Ren growls in response, and she quiets. He looks back at me. "Get ready. We're leaving."

He opens the door, and walks out.

I take the bra off, and put my clothes back on. I grab the undergarments that I want to buy, and take them out of the dressing room.

"We are not leaving," I hear Lia saying, as I walk past her and an angry Ren to get to the cashier.

While I'm handing over the cash, Lia slides up next to me.

"We're not leaving," she says again, this time sure, and smiling.

"Does he know that?" I ask, gesturing to Ren.

"Yeah, he can't say no to either of us," she says.

I turn around to see Ren and Kyle leaving the store.

"He thought you left him," Lia says. I swing my gaze to her.

"What?" I ask her, incredulously.

She shrugs. "I don't know. You know that Alphas have like strong impulses, and sometimes it's hard to control themselves. I guess when we left, his wolf just kind of reacted. Kyle says he almost shifted on the school grounds."

"What? No way," I say in disbelief, because somehow I just can't see that happening. I just can't see me, affecting Ren in that kind of way.

"Seriously," Lia says. "He cares about you, Rory."

We walk out of the store, and the boys are sitting on a bench nearby.

"Alright, we just have to find outfits for tonight, and then we're done."

Kyle groans. "You haven't done that already? You've already been here for two hours."

"She had to get other stuff too, dimwit."

He rolls his eyes in response. "Whatever, hurry up."

"We will take our sweet time, thank you," Lia says, and then she drags me to another store. I didn't catch the name of this one, because I'm too busy looking over my shoulder at Ren whose eyes follow me the whole way.

"Alright, now the first thing you definitely have to have is an LBD," Lia says, going up to a rack. She starts mumbling to herself. "Size 8, size 10…" Then she grabs what she thinks is the right one and throws it at me, along with four others. Then she grabs some for herself.

"Uh, LBD?" I ask.

"Little black dress," she replies, before going to another rack.

Lia turns to me, and huffs, then she looks at the women behind the cash register.

"We're going to need a dressing room."

The woman rushes from the counter, and opens a room for me, and then one for Lia. We both twirl into the rooms, and step out of our clothes.

"Got the first one on?" Lia calls a few seconds later.

"Just about," I call back. "I'm going to need your help zipping it up, though."

"I got you, girl."

I open my door just as Lia is stepping out of hers, and she runs around me to zip up the dress.

"This is cute," she says, walking back around me, admiring the dress.

This dress is a deep plum lace skater dress.

There is a mirror right next to Lia's room, and I take a look in.

"It makes your hair really stand out," she says.

"Yeah, more than it already does," I say with a chuckle, and she laughs.

"Really though," she laughs, stepping up next to me.

"Oh wow, red is really your color," I say. "That dress looks great on you."

It is a simple dress; sleeveless with a full skirt, and a crew neck. It is a vibrant red, but it clings to her body in all the right places, and the red goes so well with her skin and hair.

"Eh, it is not my favorite, and I feel like I do red *all the time*."

"Try on a different one. It is not like you can't pull of any color."

She flips her hair. "True." Then we both laugh, and go to try on another dress.

The next one I try on is black, a similar version to the red one that Lia just tried on. The only difference is this one has a deep v-neckline.

"We are definitely buying that one," Lia says the moment I step out of the room.

Now, she is wearing a blue strapless dress, with a deep blue satin skirt.

"God, Lia, that dress. Get that one, definitely, but promise me you have to wear that to somewhere fancy, not just a house party."

"You think?" Lia asks, twirling.

"Yes, that dress deserves wine and fancy dining, not dirty dancing, and stale beer."

She raises an eye brow at me. "For a girl who hasn't been to a house party, you sure know a lot about them."

I shrug. "I read a lot, and have seen lots of movies. Is it going to be like *Project X*?"

Lia chuckles. "No, it'll be more a *Ten Things I Hate About You*, Bogie Lowenstein kind of party."

My eyebrows raise, a grin on my face. "You've got good taste."

"Like you ever doubted that."

We try on three more dresses each, and in the end, I get two and Lia gets three. She decides on the blue satin, an off-white lace, and a red skater dress. I choose the black dress, and a light blue strapless one. When I had the blue one on Lia told me that it was Ren's favorite color. I'm not buying it because of that, not at all. The blue one is simple, but cute. At the same store I also find a couple of cute tops, and a pair of faux leather pants. I buy them all.

When we walk out of the store, Kyle jumps up from his seat next to Ren, and claps.

"Thank God. I thought you two would be in there forever," he says, looking up at the sky, sending up a mock prayer.

"Oh, shut up, Kyle," Lia says, handing over her bags to him. "It is not like you had anything better to do."

"Hurtful, woman. Trust me, there are… things I could have been doing."

Ren comes up behind him, knocking him in the shoulder. "The only things you would have been doing was yourself, dude."

Kyle turns to Ren, a look of shock on his face. "I can show you the texts, bro. She's real."

"People consider blow up dolls real?" I ask, and all three of them turn to me. Ren with raised eyebrows, and the others with dropped jaws.

Lia starts laughing, deep belly laughter.

"I really thought you were the nice one," Kyle says, looking at me in disbelief. "You two…" he points a finger between Lia and me. "You two should not hang around each other."

I smile sheepishly, and take a peek at Ren. He looks at me, appraisingly.

"That was good," he says, nodding.

"Oh, god, why is she here?" Lia asks, and we all turn to look about fifteen feet to the left is fire-crotch Tess, and two girls standing behind her. Tess' hand is clenched tightly around the bags in her hand, and she is glaring over at us. I can't really tell who she is looking at, but I am pretty sure it is me.

Ren doesn't say anything. Instead, he turns, takes my bags from my hands, and begins walking towards the entrance of the mall, completely ignoring Tess. We all stare at Ren shocked, and he turns around to look at us.

"You guys coming or not?" He asks, and then starts walking again.

I catch up to Ren, smiling to myself.

"How did you guys get here anyways?" I ask, as we walk out towards Ren's car.

"We ran, duh. No point in taking two cars," Kyle says.

Lia falls into place next to me, smiling.

"You're just full of surprises, aren't you?" She asks with a smile on her face.

I just grin and shrug, which makes her smile grow. She links her arm with mine as we continue towards the jeep.

Ren gets in the driver's seat, and Kyle motions for me to sit front.

"Oh, my feet hurt," I complain as I climb into the passenger seat.

Ren chuckles. "That's the world's way of saying that you spent too much money."

"A girl can never have too much clothes," Lia says from the back seat.

"But you're not just any girl," Kyle says snidely. "Your special."

Lia sticks her tongue out at him as Ren starts the car, pulling it onto the road. He turns the radio on, and we listen to it for a while, until Ren suddenly turns it down.

"No more running away, both of you. Next time, just ask," he says.

Lia leans forward in between the seats, and peers at her brother.

"Are you… are you going soft?"

He scoffs, and casts a quick glance at me. "Of course not. I've just… been rethinking things."

"Mmhm," Lia says, and I look to see her crossing her arms over her chest. She makes eye contact with me, and raises one eyebrow. I know what she is thinking, that he is doing it for me, but that thought just brings about hope. Hope that maybe he is changing his mind about us, about mates. Then I remember the conversation from earlier today when he made me so angry and frustrated, and I think that hope is just another four-letter word.

## Chapter Sixteen

On Friday, Lia surprises me when we get back to the manor after class, by leading me into a room below the left staircase. It is a sizeable room, with lots of computer screens.

"What is this?" I ask Lia, looking over the room. It was stupid question. Looking at the screens, they are security camera's. This is their security room. Each screen holds a different piece of the land that is the Blackhearts territory. There have to be at least ten screens, all split into six's. Each camera moves like a panorama, moving ten feet to the left, then ten feet to the right and back again.

"There is a light above the door. It's a soft green light. When someone passes the border of the territory, the light flashes red, alerting us. The Alpha's get an alert automatically, but if someone is watching it here, and they see someone they don't know, they press this button," she says, pointing to a red button on the control panel below the computers. "It sounds the alarm, which blares through the house, and turns all the lights on. It also sends alerts to the Alphas and Betas phones. You can also use these controls to zoom in and focus on something."

There are two cushioned chairs within the room, and I take a seat at one of them, marveling at the room.

Lia continues, "We try to have someone always watching but that just doesn't happen. People get sidetracked or fall asleep. Sometimes, it just seems a little excessive. Paranoid even. That is what happened the night the hunter… found us. There wasn't anyone watching. Ren didn't see the alert until it was too late, and by then I had already mind linked him. We don't want something to happen like that again. Ren wants to make sure that there is at least one person watching at night. He even talked to some of the older folks and they agreed to come in, and each take a shift. I talked to Ren and my father and they agreed with me that you have proven that you can be trusted. We want you to be a part of making this place safer."

Pride blooms in my chest.

Trust is hard to come by, especially when the Beaumont name follows me around. I never blamed the Blackhearts for not trusting me. I mean, in the beginning, I didn't trust them either. But now, even though it has only been a few short months that I have been here, I feel that we have come a long way. They have accepted me into their home and have trusted me with their lives. They care about me, and I them.

"Thank you," I say to Lia.

She pats my hand.

"We're only going to be doing this for a couple of hours and then we can get ready for the par-tay," she says the last part in a sing-songy voice, making me grin.

For a few hours, we talk about anything and everything. We laugh for most of it. That is, until an alarm starts going off, causing both of us to jolt. We look up at the monitors and focus on an animal running across the border on the southwest side.

Lia lets out a deep breath. "Oh, good."

"Huh?" I say, as she turns off the alarms.

"It's just Ren," she replies, and without even thinking, I use the controls to zoom in on his wolf.

"Where is he coming from?"

"He had a meeting with Tess' father. I don't know what about."

Ren moves at a fast speed so it is hard for me to get an accurate image of him, but I can see that his wolf is a large mass of black fur.

"He'll be here soon," Lia says, "Which means..."

Suddenly the door to the room opens, and a large figure stands in the doorway.

"Darius is here," she finishes.

Darius smiles down at us.

"Dahlia. Rory, good to see you again."

"You too," I reply.

"Well, you two can go, I've got it covered now."

We stand up and exit the room, leaving it to Darius. Then, we walk upstairs.

"Alright go and shower, and I will meet you later to do your makeup."

Nodding, I head up the stairs to the floor my room is on, and I look out the window on my way up. It is completely dark out now. I pull my phone from my pocket and check the time. Nine o'clock. It will take us about an hour to get to the party from what Lia told me. If we leave about ten, we should get there when the party is in full swing.

I walk into my room, and then into the bathroom, and turn on the water to warm up the shower before undressing. While naked, I catch a glimpse of myself in the mirror, and turn to face it fully. I remember when I first got here; I was basically just a pile of bones. I looked in the mirror the morning after arriving and I could see my bones through my skin. Now, physically, I see my body as almost completely transformed. I am no longer skin and bones but actually fit. My body has a tone to it. My bones have meat on them. My skin is no longer ashy and stretched thin. My hair is longer and even seems thicker and full of life. Now my appearance is healthy, and dare I say it, happy. I grin.

Grabbing my phone, I open the music app, and play music before stepping in the shower. I've never actually sang to music in the shower before but something about it is freeing. I sing as I shave, and wash my body, and run shampoo and conditioner through my hair. I sing as I step out of the shower, and dry off my body, and even when I blow dry my hair. Fun thing about being a wolf is that I can still hear the music even when the hair dryer is on.

When I go into my room, I take the phone with me, and toss it on the bed, still singing and dancing as I walk into my closet. I put lotion and deodorant on, and then I pull out the clothes I bought the other day. Deciding against the dress, I pull on the faux leather pants, and a black mesh t shirt crop top, with a solid black bandeau underneath.

A knock sounds through the air, and then Lia's voice.

"Rory, you dressed?"

"Yeah, I'm in the closet," I reply and then seconds later she in here with me, holding a big carrier bag.

She smiles at me. "You look amazing. Totally badass. Ren is going to freak."

I ignore the comment about her brother.

"Oh, lord, so do you. Men are going to be lining up tonight."

She has me sit down, and opens the bag, before painting my face. She only applies stuff around my eyes, and when I look in the mirror, I see what would be described as a smoky eye. Somehow, Lia was able to really make my eyes pop, more then they already do, and the eyeliner is so straight, some people would probably kill for that steady of a hand. When she pulls out a black bandana I look at her oddly.

"For the bullet hole," She says, and rolls it up before wrapping it around my arm. I still have stiches in my arm, but Lucy is confident that they are almost healed, and the stitches can probably come out tomorrow. That is good on many levels. My body is healing at a quicker speed then before, and soon I will be in tiptop shape.

Lia hands me a blood red lipstick, which I apply, and it becomes the cherry on top of the perfect outfit.

Lia's makeup is done just like mine, but her dress is blood red. It is an A-line dress with thin spaghetti straps, and a low neckline. She has a thick black choker necklace around her neck, with a small werewolf charm hanging at the center.

"You really do look great," I say to her.

She blows me a kiss. "You too, darling."

Then she grabs my arm, linking it with hers, and pulling me to the door. But she stops. "Wait, don't you want to take a picture?"

I feel my cheeks redden. "Don't be shy about it. I've seen some of the photos. You really do have an eye. Now, come on, give me your phone."

Pulling my phone out of my pocket, I hand it over, and she wraps an arm around my neck, her cheek resting against mine. She holds the phone above us, angling it down and then snaps a couple shots.

After she hands the phone back, I inspect the photos. I look… happy.

"Come on, the boys are waiting for us," she says.

I slip on a pair of black flats, and we head down the stairs. Once at the bottom, we walk outside to where the boys stand near the car. It is not Ren's car but instead it is the Escalade that Damen brought me to the pack house in.

Kyle, Hunter, and Ren stand talking to each other, Ren with his back to us.

"Is your car in the shop or something?" I ask, catching their attention.

"Holy shit," I hear Hunter mutter when he looks at us. Kyle's head snaps up to us as Ren turns around. Kyle hits Hunter in the arm, and they both look at each other. Ren just looks at me, his mouth set in a grim line. I falter for a semi second, looking him up and down. His hair is ruffled in an I-just-rolled-out-of-bed-and-I-don't-care-what-I-look-like manner, which makes me want to run my hands through it. He has blue jeans on, a white t-shirt, and a blue buttoned down shirt, over that. It is so casual yet so... delicious.

Lia and I step down the steps.

"The Escalade is more comfortable," Kyle says, finally answering my question. I see him glance at Ren, who still stands looking at me.

He finally speaks, but it is not something I want to hear. "Go change."

Or what I am expecting him to say.

"Excuse me?" I ask him, stepping back.

"You heard me. Go change."

"No," I say, shaking my head, holding my ground. I know he is Alpha and is used to getting his way, but no.

"Do as I say, Rory. Go change. Now."

"I will not. There is nothing wrong with my outfit."

Ren lets out a loud sigh and drags a hand over his face. Then he shrugs out of his jacket and lays it over my shoulders.

"Fine, then you're wearing this," he says.

"But-" The look he gives me tells me that if I don't wear this, then I'm not going at all. I shrug the jacket off of my shoulder and lay it over my forearm. For a second I think that he could just use his Alpha voice on me, and then I remember that it only works in your own pack. He can't use an Alpha command on me because technically I am not a part of his pack. If that is not the equivalent to a stupid cold shower on a really great day, then I don't know what is.

"I'll think about it," I say, and walk to the car.

Let me tell you, if looks could kill, I would be dead.

I open the back door on the driver's side and let Lia slide in, so she is in the middle, and then I slide in next to her. Kyle sits on the other side of her, and Hunter climbs into the front. Ren still stand outside the car.

"You really know how to push his buttons," Kyle says in a hushed tone, and I just shrug.

"I'm not his to order around," I whisper back.

Looking over my shoulder, I see Ren give himself a shake and run a hand through his hair.

Then he walks around to the driver's side and yanks the door open with a little more force then necessary, and then he climbs into the car.

The ride is silent for the most part until I get sent a meme. It is one of those Kermit the frog ones where he is sipping tea, and it makes me laugh out loud. All the guys in the car look at me strangely, and then I cover my mouth, but still chuckle. Then I find one and send it to Lia in response, making her chuckle as well.

"Girls," Kyle scoffs. "Texting when they are right next to each other. I will never understand it."

"That is because you don't understand women, pea brain. And it is a meme war," Lia says. "Urban dictionary it if you don't know what it is."

"Oh, I know what it is. I'm just not odd like you two, feeling the need to do it."

"Get with the times, Kyle. Memes are taking over," Lia says, and we share a look before bursting out laughing.

Suddenly, I hear loud music, and I look up to see a large house, lights on, people everywhere. It is a large Victorian style house, colored a dark grey, almost black. It is only a quarter of the size of Blackheart Manor, but it is still a decent size. It has a wrap-around porch that has string lights attached that are currently lit up, twinkling in the nighttime.

Ren pulls the car up alongside a row of others, and throws the car into park.

"Stay together," he says, his voice low, speaking over his shoulder. "Neither of you go off on your own."

Lia and I nod, because after all, we are outside of the Blackheart territory. Then we climb out of the car, walking towards the house, the boys following slowly behind us.

People crowd the porch, talking together, all with red solo cups in their hands. We push past people, and walk into the house. There is a stairway to the right of the door, along the wall, and a large living room to the left. There is a large group – mainly girls – dancing in the center of the room, there is a couple leaning against the wall on the staircase, making out. The music is loud, vibrating through the house. Lia and I push past people, finding our way to the kitchen where there is alcohol set up on the table.

Lia goes straight to the table, and grabs a red solo cup and a bottle, and dumps some of the contents into the cup. She sets down the bottle, and reaches for another one, dumping more into the cup.

"Here, try this," she says, handing the cup to me.

I take a sip, and nearly choke. The taste is so strong, burning like fire going down my throat. I've never had liquor before, so I let out a cough after the first sip.

She takes the cup from me, and looks around the table.

"Aha," she says, grabbing another bottle, and dumps something else into the cup. She hands it back to me. I try it again, and smile. This one being better, I nod and take another sip. I think I like alcohol.

She grins, and then makes herself a cup of the sweet concoction.

We mill around for a bit, peering around at the people, talking to a few, sipping on our cups. When we finish our first cups, Lia goes and makes seconds. Lia hands me a cup, and then Colin comes up to me.

"Hey," I say. "I didn't know you were here."

"Yeah, I rode in with Mary, and Victor. I wasn't expecting you to be here."

"Why?" I ask him, curiously.

"Honestly, because I didn't think Ren would let you come," he replies.

"He doesn't own me," I scoff.

He looks at me with raised eyebrows, as if to say 'really?'.

"Does she honestly strike you as the type to take orders?" Lia asks Colin as she brushes past him to stand next to me. "And believe me, I love watching her tell Ren 'no'."

"I just can't let him push me around. I can't let anyone. After Marcus, it cannot happen."

"Good on you," Lia says, raising her cup. I knock it with hers. "To being badasses."

I laugh. "To being badasses."

Colin knocks his cup against ours.

Kyle sidles up between Lia and I.

"What are we drinking, ladies?" He asks, taking Lia's cup out of her hand and taking a sip. He makes a face.

"What is that? Way too sweet."

"Then don't drink it," Lia says snidely as she takes her cup back.

"What do you say we have some actual alcohol?" He says, placing an arm around my shoulders and Lia's.

"Sure," Lia chuckles. "It will actually put some hair on your chest."

He just laughs and leads us into the kitchen.

Colin follows us and we all circle around the kitchen table while Kyle grabs a bottle of some kind of alcohol, and four shot glasses.

"Ever had a shot, Rory?" Kyle asks, and they all look at me, even though they probably already know the answer.

I shake my head.

He slides a glass full of amber liquid across the table to me.

"Don't tell Ren I gave it to you," he says, and I resist the urge to roll my eyes.

When we all have a shot glass in our hands, we raise them and clink them together.

"Cheers," we say, and then knock them back.

The liquid burns as it goes down but somehow in a good way. My eyes squeeze shut and I resist the urge to cough. After a few seconds, I open my eyes, but tears form and I have to blink them away.

"Good?" Lia asks me.

I nod.

"Use your words," Kyle says, peering at me.

"I'm fine," I say, and my voice comes out a little raspier then I would like.

I push the glass back towards him.

"Another."

He smiles, and pours another round of shots. From my spot I can see Ren across the room talking to someone. Stealthily I take out my phone and take a snap of him. Something about him… he just looks so handsome tonight. I want to remember it.

A few shots later, Kyle and Colin have disappeared, and a cute guy comes up to Lia. We are still in the kitchen, and I lean against the kitchen counter, giving my head a break, and giving Lia a chance to talk to the *really* cute guy. He has blonde hair, and a very muscular body under those jeans and plaid shirt. A picture-perfect cowboy, who is clearly entranced by the beauty that is Dahlia Blackheart. She laughs at something that he says, and I smile, happy for her. Finally, a moment without her brother cock blocking her.

Sliding against the counter, I make my way to the door, eyes on Lia and the boy, ready to give them space without me watching like a creep. As I turn to go out the door, I knock into something hard, almost wiping out completely.

Nice, Rory, way to run into a door.

Hands grab my upper arms, and a shiver runs through my body.

Nope, not a door.

I look up the long, hard body and up into Ren's face.

"I'm sorry. I didn't know that you were there," I say.

He watches my face, his own stoic. His eyes move past my shoulder, to where he must see his sister, then he looks back to me. And he does not look happy.

"You don't know what you are doing to her," he says.

I glance at her to see if she heard, but she is too engrossed in the conversation. Turning back to Ren, I place my hands on his chest, and push him backwards. Surprisingly, he lets me. We move out of the doorway, and away from the kitchen so that hopefully she cannot hear us.

"I am not doing anything," I say, crossing my arms over my chest, pinning him with a glare.

Clearly the alcohol has made me feel even more courageous to stand up to him.

He shakes his head. "She falls for this guy, and then what happens? What happens when her mate comes around and she is already in love with someone else?"

"How do you know she is going to fall in love with him?" I ask, raising an eyebrow. "He said hi, not ask her to marry him."

"First, she will because she is a girl."

I roll my eyes. "Oh, shut up. You and all of your alpha male bullshit."

"It's not alpha male, just Alpha. Something you seem to need to remember."

"First," I say, placing my hands on my hips. "Talking to a guy doesn't mean that she is going to fall in love with him. Second, she deserves to have fun, not live her life to please you. And three, how do you know her mate would even want her?"

I rub my eyes with the palms of my hands, and let out a sigh. When I pull my hands away, I see makeup smudged on them. Shit, I forgot I was wearing makeup.

"Dammit, I messed up my makeup. And, of course he would want her. Who wouldn't? It is just *my* luck that I end up with a mate who doesn't want me."

"I never said I didn't-"

Cutting him off, I continue ranting. "And do you know what the funny thing is? You were supposed to be my – what's that stupid Disney thing? – my knight in shining armor? Yeah, that's what you were supposed to be. I mean, I never thought I'd be lucky enough to find my mate, but a small part of me thought that if I did, he'd change everything. Make everything better. Like, just being with him would make everything better." Oh, my god, Rory shut up.

Werewolves usually have to drink a lot in order to get drunk. Since we naturally have a high body temperature, our bodies burn the alcohol off easily. Guess, I'm a little late in that department too. I'm totally sloshed.

The look on his face is completely priceless, so I, drunk Rory, decide to continue.

"And then I meet you a couple hours later after *finally* escaping from my father, and I could literally see the pity on your face. Then you say you don't want me. Then you-"

I'm silenced. By his lips on mine.

Holy shit, Ren. Is. Kissing. Me.

Holy. Shit. Ren is *kissing me*.

My body is buzzing, but somehow I am able to think through the haze that he causes in my mind, and pull away. My brain catches up to my body, and I shove him away from me, wiping my lips, trying to get rid of the feeling of his lips there. Like that is ever going to happen. I glare daggers at him.

"I told you *not* to pity me, and then you go and do that?!"

A growl follows my words, and something fills me body. Whatever it is, it vibrates through my body making me hum.

"Rory," He growls out. His body tensing, and his eyes darkening. Why the hell is he angry? "Don't *ever* say that I don't want you, or that I pity you. And do *not* growl at me."

A louder growl comes from deep inside of me. I've never heard nor felt this before. Something is boiling beneath my skin.

Ren reaches out to me, but I back away, another growl emitting from me.

"Rory, you need to calm down," he says, his voice low and warning.

Something about his voice calms me, but there's another part, a bigger part of me that's fighting against him. Arms come around me, and Lia's scent hits my nose.

"Whoa, girl," she whispers in my ear. "Calm down. Your eyes are changing color."

I close my eyes, and take a deep breath, forcing myself to calm down.

To Ren, Lia says, "Go. I've got this. *Go.*"

When I open my eyes, I see Ren's nostrils are flared. With wild eyes, he takes a deep breath, and walks away without a glance back at me.

Lia turns to me, and places her hands on my shoulders, and looks me levelly in the eye.

"What just happened? If I didn't know better, I would say you were about to shift. What did he do to piss you off so badly?"

I cross my arms, frowning, my earlier anger, seeping out of me. "He kissed me."

Lia lets out a roar of laughter, and I glare at her in response. She tries to cover her giggles, but it doesn't work.

"I'm sorry, but someone getting mad because of Ren's kissing. God, I never thought I'd see the day."

"Hmph," I say, blowing out a breath.

She laughs again, and then wraps her arms around my shoulders.

"Come on, you could use another shot."

I silently agree with her, and we walk towards the kitchen.

There are girls standing in the doorway, staring at me. Already irritated, I just smirk, flip them the bird, and continue on my way.

## Chapter Seventeen

My feet hurt, my head is fuzzy, and my bladder is full. I would think these are the signs of a night gone well. After dancing for what feels like an hour, I look over to where Lia is dancing with another girl from the pack.

"Where's the bathroom?" I shout at Lia, trying to be heard over the music. Her senses are probably off the wall right now, so I can't guarantee she can hear me.

"What?" She yells back.

"Where is the bathroom?"

She nods, hopefully in understanding, and then yells, "I think it's upstairs!"

I clasp my hands together in the prayer sign as a thank you and then I turn and stumble towards the stairs, and then pull myself up them. I have to weave in and out of people who are standing on the steps talking, except for the one couple groping each other – I just avoid them. But seriously? On the stairs? How is that comfortable?

Once I safely make it to the top, I shuffle my feet to the first door. Nope, that is a bedroom. I close it, and then move to the next one on the other side of the hall. My head is pounding and my hair falls around my face. I open the next door. *Nope.* That one is also a bedroom, and it is currently occupied. Thank god the lights are off, otherwise I might have to invest in some bleach, or hydrogen peroxide. Quickly, I close the door, and then again move back across the hallway to the third door. My head pounds, and I wince, and run a hand through my hair, moving the hair from around my face.

Closing my hand around the doorknob, I twist and push the door open. My jaw drops, and my hand falls from my hair. Good news: I found the bathroom. Bad news: I found Ren... and Tess. He leans against the counter in a cool relaxed pose, his legs stretched out in front of him, and his hands resting on the counter behind him. Tess stands in front of him, maybe a foot away, arms crossed over her chest. They both turn to look at me.

My hand tightens on the doorknob, and I hear it creak under the pressure. He didn't pity me, huh? Yet he kissed me, and then came up here to... to... I can't even bring myself to say it. But he came up here to be with her.

Composing myself, I close my mouth, lift my head up high, and raise an eyebrow at the... couple.

"What did you do? Lose a bet?" I ask Ren, a smirk forming on my face.

Ren opens his mouth, but Tess beats him to the punch.

"What the hell are you doing here?" She asks, venom dripping through her voice, and her face turning unpleasant.

"Well, I did have to pee, but now I'm feeling the urge to puke."

A muscle in her jaw twitches. "I meant. In. My. House," she seethes.

"Your house, huh? That makes sense. I was wondering why the stank of bitch was all over."

"You need to leave! Now!" Tess yells, and then a growl escapes her.

"With pleasure."

I move to leave, pulling the door closed, but then Ren is there blocking it from closing all the way. He reaches out and grabs my forearm. I lift my eyes up to look at him.

"Rory -"

"Don't." I let go of the door, and yank my arm away from him. "No pity, right?"

Without closing the door I turn and walk away. With a quick pace, I walk down the hallway, and descend down the stairs. Behind me I hear a rush of footwork on the stairs, and know they are following me. Lia is in the middle of the room, and we make eye contact the second I reach the bottom step. I watch as her eyes dart behind me and then widen.

Once my feet hit the floor, there is a push on my shoulders, sending me forward a few feet. I regain my balance, and turn around. Tess stares at me, hate burning in her eyes, her fists curled.

"I said leave," She hisses.

Vaguely, I see that we are drawing attention, as pretty much everyone in the room turns to stare at us.

I cross my arms over my chest, and shrug.

"Oh, I'm sorry," I reply. "I thought you just wanted me to leave the bathroom so you could continue trying to fuck Ren."

Lia steps up next to me, and I hear her swear under her breath.

Looking behind Tess, I see that Ren is not behind her. Surprise, surprise.

"I don't give a shit what you thought. Just leave," she snarls.

Wanting to get out of here as soon as possible, I say with a tad bit of snarkiness, "I'm trying too, but I keep seeming to run into some… *trouble*."

I start to turn away, but then I stop as a thought occurs to me. Looking back at Tess, I make eye contact with her, and ask, "Do you have any respect at all?"

She at least has the decency to look shocked by my question.

A bitter smile falls on her face, as she puts her hands on her hips.

"I don't respect people who take my things."

Taking a few steps towards her so that I'm a foot away, I lean in close. "I feel bad for you. You are going to live your life like an unhappy child, and when you find *that person* you're supposed to spend the rest of your life with? He'll probably run the other way."

I pull back, and before I can react, she pulls a fist and hits me square in my chin. My head flings back, my hair covering my face, and liquid forming in my mouth. A hand comes to my shoulder but I shrug it off. I straighten out, shaking the hair out of my face, and I place my hand on my lip as I slowly look up at Tess. When I pull my fingers back, blood coats the tips of them. I slowly grin at her.

"I've been waiting for you to do that."

Her face matches mine, and she lets out a low chuckle. "You have no idea who you're messing with."

I roll my neck around, cracking it. I wipe the blood from my lips with my hand. "Trust me, I've been told. And, honestly, I'm not at all intimidated. You're just an ungrateful little *bitch*."

She growls and lunges at me.

We both fall as she tackles me to the ground. The impact hurts my still healing arm, and on the other side, I feel something crack as I take the brunt of the impact. She sits up, straddling my hips, and raises her arm, her hand curling into yet another fist. When she goes to strike, I raise my hand with lightning speed, and catch her fist. I throw my weight against her, sending her off of me. I jump up, with her doing the same a second later. Ignoring the pain in my shoulder, I go to charge at her, but arms catch me around my waist.

Ren's usually calming touch just aggravates me even more and causes me to fight harder to escape from his hold.

"Enough!" He bellows, causing everyone but me in the room to still.

In front of me Kyle has grabbed ahold of a squirming Tess. Without another word, Ren lifts me off the ground with arms around my waist and carries me out of the house.

"Let go of me," I growl.

"Knock it off with the growling already. I get it, you're pissed."

I kick my legs in hopes of hitting him. "You are not the boss of me."

"I think you keep forgetting that, actually, I am the boss of you."

"Ha, no," I say, because time and time again I am reminded that I am not actually apart of the Blackheart pack. Not really. I am just a guest here.

He growls, angry, setting me on my feet next to the car. He throws his hands up in frustration "I did not want you to come here! I *knew* this was going to happen."

I flinch at his yelling.

"I'm sorry, what are you exactly? Some magician who can see into the future? Because you seem to know everything that's going to happen. We're never going to be together, I'm going to beat Tess' ass. Blah, blah, blah." I walk closer to him, and he lifts an eyebrow. "Tell me, Mr. Know It All, what am I going to do now?"

He smirks, and crosses his arms over his chest. "You're going to hit me."

"Close. But I'm not that violent."

He raises both eyebrows.

"Okay, maybe I'm a little violent. But only when I find my *mate* in the bathroom with other girls," I say, glaring at him. I turn away, looking into the deep forest that surrounds the house. I've already said too much, given away too much. I think it's the first time I actually referred to him, while talking to him, as my mate. I cover my face with my hands, and let out a deep sigh. I just need to sleep.

A few seconds tick by.

Vaguely, I'm aware of Kyle as he steps out of the house and assesses the situation in front of him.

"It's not what you think," Ren says on a deep exhale, ignoring Kyle's presence.

Chuckling, I turn around. "It never is."

"She asked to talk," he shrugs.

"And you believed that's all she wanted?" I ask, throwing my arms out wide. I let out an exasperated sigh. "Are you really that daft or do you just like playing stupid?"

He smirks like it's a joke. "A little bit of both."

I roll my eyes. "I don't even know why I'm upset. You don't owe me anything."

Something about that comment makes him flinch, but maybe I imagined it.

"I didn't do what you think I did. I wouldn't. You are still my mate."

This time his words make me flinch. It's the first time he's really referred to *me* as his mate, his actual mate to my face. Looking away from him, I shake my head and wrap my arms around myself. "I don't think that means what it should anymore."

The door opens and Kyle walks out, looking at us both, quizzically.

The movement of my arm, causes pain to shoot through my shoulder, and then I realize what happened. I run my right hand over the odd large bump in my left shoulder.

"I need someone to help me pop my shoulder back in."

"No," Ren says firmly, pointing a finger at me. "You're waiting until we get back so you can talk to Lucy. I have to find Lia. I'll be right back."

I roll my eyes at his back as he walks back inside the house. Getting to Lucy is going to take over an hour, and I am not going to wait that long. Does he not understand that this hurts?

I turn to Kyle. "Are you going to help me?"

He gives me an amused smile – like why would I even ask. "No."

"Fine," I reply. I reach my right hand around, and find my left shoulder. I cup it in my hand, getting a good grip on it, and then I take a deep breath. On the exhale, I apply pressure to my shoulder and pop it back into its socket.

"Oh, god! Gross! Why did you just do that?" Kyle yells.

I let out a slow deep breath trying to wait for the pain to lessen.

"Really, that's what freaks you out?" I ask through clenched teeth.

"Did you just pop your shoulder back in?" Ren asks, emerging from the house.

I don't look at him or answer him. I roll my shoulder trying to alleviate the pressure.

He growls in response.

"I need your help finding Lia," Ren says to Kyle and then they both go into the house again.

Really? He couldn't just have used his super smell to find her? Way to go, Alpha.

Taking a deep breath, breathing away the pain in my shoulder, I lean against the side of the car, and run a hand through my hair.

Colin emerges from the house seconds later, and walks down the steps, heading straight for me. He sidles up next to me, leaning on the car as well.

"Hey."

"Hi," I reply.

"You okay?" He asks.

"Just peachy," I say, making him chuckle.

"So what were you guys fighting about? Ren?"

I scoff. "No. It was bound to happen. Two Alpha females in the same place. Not a good mix." Though we are not technically Alpha females we are the daughters of Alphas, which still makes us strong.

What I tell him, is a half lie, but Colin nods along like he understands.

We're quiet for a moment.

Colin lets out a deep breath that he sounds like he has been holding in for ages.

"Look. Rory there's something I need to tell you," he says.

I turn to look at him, waiting.

"Oh, screw it," he mumbles and then presses his lips against mine.

I push him away by his shoulders not a second later.

"What the hell are you doing!" I yell, pushing away from the car, away from him.

"Look, I like you," he says it so simply as if it's no big deal.

"I'm with Ren," I reply, running my hands through my hair.

"No, you're not."

Suddenly, I feel small, which is ridiculous because I am almost six feet tall, but somehow I do. I feel like a tiny slug.

"Okay," I say, nodding, because yes that may technically be true but still. "But we're-"

"Mates? He doesn't want to be with you. If he did, he would."

I don't know what hurts worse, the words, or the way he says them. Like a condescending adult, talking to a child who did something stupid. It makes me flinch.

"Even if that's true, I can't just turn away from him." I close my eyes and shake my head. "You wouldn't understand."

"Why? Because I'm human? Or a biped as

you all like to call us."

It takes me a second to respond. I open my eyes and watch him for a second. "Yes."

He stalks towards me, angrily.

"That's bullshit and you know it. You know I hear all of you *animals* complain about your mates and none of you realize you really don't have it bad. When you meet the person you're meant to be with, you know automatically. It is literally like a switch is flipped. Bam! There they are!

But for us humans? We don't know. We could spend so much time on one person, thinking they are the one we are meant to spend our lives with, and then we find out they're the complete opposite." He says the last part sadly. "It's fine though. Go spend your time with the non-humans and the mate that doesn't want you."

He gets up and walks away.

There is nothing that I can say, nothing that I even want to say to him. His words hit me hard, and I feel my eyes begin to water. I take a deep breath and dig my nails into my hands, trying to stop the tears, and focus on a different kind of pain.

Despite my efforts, Colin's words echo in my head again and again. Of course he's right, and that is what hurts the most. Ren doesn't want me. He has told me that and shown me that time and time again. Yet, somehow he keeps getting in my head, making me believe that we might actually have a chance.

"What's wrong?" Ren's voice echoes

through the air, angry and concerned.

I whip around, facing the opposite direction so that I can try and wipe my eyes without him noticing. I hear his footsteps as he comes closer to me." Taking a deep breath, I calm myself, and then I turn back to him, saying, "I'm fine. Why?"

He is closer than I thought, and it makes me stumble back. I look up at him, our eyes meeting, and I watch as his nostrils flare.

"Why do I smell Colin all over you?" He takes another step towards me.

I shove him away, when he gets too close. I try to turn away.

"Nothing, okay? Where's Lia? I want to go home."

"No. His scent is all over you and you're crying." He turns me around, and forces me to look at him, with hands on my shoulders, and his thumbs forcing my chin up. "What. Is. Wrong."

"Nothing." I say in a hard voice, forcing my eyes away from his.

"Don't push me, Rory. If he's laid a hand on you, I *will* kill him."

This conversation, his threatening Colin, it all makes me angrier, and I throw the anger at him.

"Then don't push me, Doren! Maybe you should take a look in the mirror before you judge anyone for hurting me. I've said twice now that it's nothing, but you won't listen. Now, take me home!"

He walks towards the car, muttering. I catch 'never' and 'listen'.

"Let's go," he barks out.

Lia appears, wrapping her arms around my shoulders. "I had fun tonight," she slurs, nuzzling my hair. Normally, it takes a werewolf a lot of alcohol to get really, really drunk. She had to have a shit ton.

I laugh, and help her get into the backseat of the car.

"That's good. Did you do what we had planned?" Meaning getting her first kiss. She was talking to the cute cowboy for a long time.

She nods vigorously. "Yes, and so. Did. You." She says, tapping my nose with each word.

I force out a laugh. "Yeah, I certainly did."

Kyle climbs into the back with Lia, and as I'm pulling the passenger door closed, Colin runs out of the house.

"Hey, can I catch a ride with you guys?" He asks a little, breathlessly.

I turn away from him as he looks between Ren and I. I look to Ren to find him clenching his hands around the steering wheel. He looks at me, then after a second, he rolls his eyes. "Get in."

Colin shrugs, and climbs into the back with the others, which leaves me to sit in the front with Ren. Silently, I climb in, and buckle up.

Ren starts the car, throws it in reverse, and backs out of our make shift parking spot. After we've been on the road for about five minutes, when I blow out a huff of air.

"What?" Ren asks, gruffly.

I hesitate. "I still have to go to the bathroom."

Ren looks over at me, and then lets out a laugh, followed by Hunter and Kyle.

When they quiet down, Ren says, "I'll make a stop. We have to get gas, anyways."

I settle in as best I can, and Ren relaxes into his seat. I feel a warm sensation on my arm that makes my hair stand up. I look down to see his forearm and mine resting next to each other, less than an inch apart. I peak a glance at him, but he just stares ahead, eyes on the road.

We go on for a while, the road completely dark except for the headlights of the car. The road, enshrouded by trees. About halfway home, we finally see a gas station in the middle of the woods. Wordlessly, Ren pulls into the shop, pulling alongside a pump. The station is empty save for the cashier inside. The lights are all on, but the place still has an eerie feel to it.

Kyle and Ren get out of the car first, Kyle going to the pump. Ren walks around the car and opens the door for me. I climb out, and he wordlessly closes the door, before following me into the building.

The cashier is a young, skinny guy who looks to be about seventeen. He gives me a nod when I walk in. There is a rest room sign at the back of the building, and make a beeline for the door. I empty my bladder in a matter of seconds and feel instantly better.

I step out of the room a minute later, and find Ren looking at drinks.

"Want something?" He asks, as I come up to him.

"Sure," I say, scanning the fridge.

After a few short seconds, Ren clears his throat. "I'm sorry," he says. "For yelling at you."

My anger from earlier and has since dissipated. Now, I'm... calm, to say the least.

"Which time?" I ask, in a playful tone while smirking at him.

He looks over at me, sees me smirking and the corners of his lips rise.

"All the times. But more specifically, this last time," he says.

"Oh, okay," I say, nodding. That's good, I think.

"Are you okay?" When I look at him, he adds quickly. "I'm not trying to pity you, I'm just – she threw you pretty hard."

He's acting odd...

"No, I'm fine. She hits like a wuss."

He nods but the smile still plays on his lips.

Suddenly the front door dings and Kyle comes through the door. He strides up to us.

"You guys ready?" He asks.

Ren nods. "Just about. Do you want anything?"

In response, Kyle grabs a bottle of pop through the door, and goes to the snack aisle. Ren grabs a chocolate milk, and I grab an ice tea/lemonade bottled drink. Kyle tosses two bags of chips onto the counter, and Ren grabs the bottle in my hands. He pays for it all and then we walk out the door. Kyle circles around the car, and Ren walks ahead of me, opening the passenger door for me before going to the driver's side.

Inside the car, Colin is passed out, spread out in the far back bench seat. Lia and Hunter are fast asleep in the middle seat. Hunter is against the glass, and Lia has her head on Hunters shoulder. Kyle slides into the seat next to Lia, and opens his bag of chips as Ren pulls out of the gas station. I'm taking a sip of my drink when Kyle hands me a bag of chips.

"For Ren," he says.

Without being asked, I open the chips and hold it out to Ren. He smiles at me, and reaches into the bag.

"Cheese puffs and chocolate milk? That is an odd combination," I say and he chuckles.

"Yeah, I didn't think about that when I bought them."

"Here," I say, and give him my tea. "It's not a great combination but it is better than milk."

He takes the bottle, tipping it in a 'thanks'. He unscrews the cap and takes a sip of the tea. I can't help but think of his lips touching where mine did. Or his lips touching mine. I go back to that blissful moment at the party. Yes, it was short lived but it was still a noteworthy occasion. Something I am definitely going to think about it for a while.

When we pull through the gates of the mansion, I stretch. My eyes are starting to feel heavy. I check my phone. It is just past two in the morning. It's not long before we are pulling up to the front of the mansion, and everyone is waking up.

"Colin, can you go get Lucy, please?" Ren asks, rather civilly, which surprises me. I think this is the first time I've heard him say please. I get out to help Kyle with Lia, who is now passed out in the back seat. Kyle shakes his head at me.

"We've got it," he says.

Kyle lifts her out of the car and carry her into the house. Ren follows them inside.

I look around. I could go inside, up to my room, but as much as I am tired, I do not want to go to bed. My gaze transfixes onto the sky, and I find myself, without even thinking about it, wandering to the garden around the side of the house. I sit down on the stone bench underneath the willow tree, pulling my knee to my chest, and wrap my arms around my legs. Then, I just stare up at the sky.

I'm here for what feels like only be a few minutes, before I feel *his* presence. It is just a sort of shiver that breaks out across my skin, making the hair on my arms stand up. It is so small, one might think it's from a breeze blowing past, but I know that it's him. It's so odd, that for so long my wolf has been dormant, but all of a sudden when I meet *him* she's back, and I can feel her every time he's around. Maybe it's because I'm his mate, the fact that he's so powerful. There are stories about what happens when two powerful Alpha's mate, about how strong they become. I wonder what would happen if we did mate. How powerful we would be? Would we be unstoppable?

"What are you doing?" He asks softly, as he sits down next to me.

"I'm staring up at the sky," I say in a dreamy voice.

My eyes are beginning to drift shut of their own accord. I guess I'm more tired than I thought.

"Well, I got that," he chuckles. "Why?

"It's so pretty. So dark. So… calming," my voice coming out slow and languid.

"You find the dark calming?" He asks, surprise coloring his voice.

"Is there anything better?" I ask, turning my head to look at him. He smiles down at me.

He chuckles. "No, I guess you're right."

"I know," I say, before letting out a loud yawn. Without thinking, I continue on, telling him more than I normally would. "My father kept me in my room most of the time. I spent a lot of my time in the dark."

I don't look at him, not wanting to see the look on his face when he realizes just how damaged I really am. I mean, who wants to mate with a girl who hasn't even seen the world? And I don't mean anything like traveling the world but a girl that has barely seen the world around her. I wouldn't know about phones or computers, or anything about todays generations if it wasn't for the books I've read and the movies I've seen.

Ren is quiet for a moment, but when he speaks, his voice is soft, maybe even loving if I didn't know any better.

"You sound like one of those princesses... the one in the tower? What's her name? Sleeping beauty?"

I close my eyes at the thought. "No, that's Rapunzel you're thinking about. Plus, I'm not a princess."

He looks over at me with a grin on his face. "Whatever you say, Princess."

I roll my eyes, that nickname bringing back unwanted memories.

"You shouldn't call me that," I say to him.

A grin forms on his face in response. I can see the wheels turning in his head. Him thinking that he is going to forever call me this, just so that he can push my buttons.

When it has been a few moments, and Ren hasn't look away, I roll my eyes.

"What?" I ask, annoyance coloring my voice.

"Nothing, it's just... something you said earlier."

"What?" I rack my brain, ready to kick myself for whatever stupid thing came out of my mouth.

"You called this place home."

"Sorry," I say instantly, visibly flinching. Turning my head away from him fast, my cheeks beginning to burn.

Ren takes a deep breath to say something, but then stops. Three seconds passes by – I count them - and then he clears his throat. "Lucy wants to see you, and check out your shoulder."

Shaking my head, I yawn. "My shoulder's fine."

I lift my arm and move it around as proof. The movement throws me off balance and I begin to fall backwards, off the bench. Two strong arms catch me before I even come close to the ground.

Ren chuckles again but this time it's much closer to me. His breath hits my forehead.

"Yeah," he says. "You're perfectly fine."

"Hey, I'm just tired." I end the statement with yet again, another yawn.

"Yeah, I can see that," he says. I look up at him to find his gaze already on me. He smiles at me. Not a smirk, but a warm smile.

"You're smiling," I say. "That's odd. Maybe *you're* not okay." Without a thought about it, I nuzzle close to him in his embrace, his warmth surrounding me. His arms tighten around me, pulling me closer. His chuckle pulls me in, and my eyes slowly begin to close.

"Come on, Princess, it's time for bed," he says. I smile against his shirt, one of my hands clenching the material and he lifts me bridal style. I inhale his scent, and eventually I being to fade, but not before I hear, "And this *is* your home. Don't be sorry about that."

## Chapter Eighteen

Sleeping like the dead. I've never really thought about that saying until now. I never thought I slept like the dead, but then someone tries to wake me up, and it is so hard to make my body move. It is so hard to wake myself and comprehend what is going on around me. It is so hard not to punch the person waking me, right. In. The. Face.

I let out a loud, noisy groan, and pull my arm away from whoever is shaking me. They reach right back for my arm.

"Stop," I say, and it stops.

Turning my head, I look over at my right side to see who is trying to wake me from my wonderful dream. Ren gave me a house of chocolate, and I desperately want to get back to it.

Jasper stands at the edge of my bed, a fearful expression on his face.

"Jas, what's wrong?" I ask instantly alert, looking over the scared little boy in batman pj's to make sure he's not hurt in anyway.

"Rory," He whines, fear written all over his face. "Please, I need your help."

"What? What is it?"

He grabs at my hand. "It's Ren, please, Rory." His voice pleads.

My heart lurches. "Where-"

That's when I hear the moans. Groans, actually. Then a whine sounds, coming from Ren's room. I crawl fast out of bed, and run to the bathroom, the sounds getting louder. Once I get to the door, I stop, turn around and look at Jas.

"Stay here, okay?" I say to him and he nods in response, instantly sitting down on the edge of my bed.

He nods, and I close the door behind me, then cross the distance of the bathroom, into Ren's room. Ren lies on the bed, in only a pair of pajama pants, the covers thrown off of his body. His arms lay straight away from his body, his hands are curled into fists, and his hands struggle against the bed as if they were tied down.

"No," he moans. "No."

From hear I can see the sweat on his forehead and chest.

"Ren," I say, moving swiftly to the left side of the bed, sitting down next to him. I touch his shoulder gently, shaking it, attempting to wake him. "Ren, wake up."

He flinches from my touch. Looking closer at his face I see…are those tears? What the hell could he be dreaming about?

I grab both his shoulders, and shake him.

"Ren!" I nearly yell.

His heartbeat begins to dramatically slow, and he seems to calm, but he doesn't wake up. I climb onto his body, my knees at either side of his hips. I place my hands on either side of his face, and I use the pad of my thumbs to wipe away his tears.

"Doren?" I call softly.

He sighs and his eyes slowly open. He stares at me in what almost seems like awe.

"What happened?" He asks, his voice deeper, harsher than normal.

"You had a bad dream," I say, thinking about my own nightmares. I don't have them as often anymore but they still come back here and then. It's another thing in common that I did not expect us to have. Both of us have demons.

He clears his throat.

"Not unusual," he replies calmly as if nothing happened.

I open my mouth to respond when I hear a voice coming from my room, and then a second later, Lia flies in from the bathroom, coming to an abrupt stop when she see's us. Well, more like, when she see's me on top of Ren. Then her father follows her.

I let out a shocked yell, and jump off the bed.

Ren leans back on his forearms, a smirk appearing on his face.

Lia's gaze goes back and forth between her brother and I.

"Tomorrow, I will be asking the two of you a lot of questions, but for now…" Lia trails off and looks over at her father.

"We have an emergency," Damen finishes, his gaze starting on his son, and then landing on me. "You need to come with me."

I look to Ren, but he looks confused as well. Nodding to Damen, I follow him out of the room. Ren and Lia follow close behind. We make it down the stairs to the foyer, where... two police officers stand. One man and one woman.

"Aurora Beaumont?" The woman asks.

I flinch at my real name; it has been a long time since anyone used it.

Confused, I nod to the officers. "Yes?"

"You are under arrest for the assault of Tess Bradley."

Silence descends. We all just stare at the officer.

"What?" I ask, a laugh following it. This has to be a joke.

"You cannot be serious," Lia says. "Tess hit her first. Roary never actually hit her. Not really. Tackled her to the ground sure, but never threw a punch. And, it was all self-defense!"

"We have video proof, and Miss Bradley has decided to press charges."

"Video proof? What video proof? We have to see this video," Damen says. Lia agrees and the two of them both argue with the officers. Ren steps up close behind me, his chest almost touching my back.

"Can I go change?" I mumble, looking down to see that I'm still wearing the outfit from the party.

"No, ma'am. You need to come with us now," the male officer says, stepping forward. He reaches to his waist, and pulls out a pair of handcuffs.

"She's not going anywhere," Ren growls, moving from behind me, and stepping in front of me.

"Stand down," the female officer responds, her hand moving to her gun, out of what I assume is instinct.

There's no doubt in my mind that Ren could take the officers down, but that's not a risk I'm willing to take. It would cause even more problems then we already have.

I step around Ren, putting a hand on his still naked chest. Causing him to look down at me. Our eyes meet. He shakes his head, which causes me to shake mine in response.

"No, please," I say. "I'll go."

Turning, I place my body so that my back is facing the officers, and I put my arms out behind me.

The male officer steps up and takes my wrists, handcuffing me. The movement jostles my shoulder a little, the one that was dislocated, and pain shoots through it, making me wince.

My eyes haven't left Ren's face, and I watch as he notices the wince on my face. His features darken, and a growl emits through the air. I can see the indecision in his eyes. He wants to step up and stop what is going on, but he can't without causing more damage. Because this pack is so big there are wolves everywhere in town, working. On the police force, the fire department, the school, anywhere you can think of. We have normal lives just like the bipeds, for the most part at least. Even though there are some from the Blackheart Pack on the police force, it doesn't mean that they can just do things. They can get away with a lot, but the officers cannot just ignore an arresting report like this.

Again, I shake my head at him.

"Don't," I whisper, knowing that he can hear me.

There is a tug on my arms, and then I'm being pulled out of the house. They push me towards the car, and I'm placed into the back seat of the squad car. As we drive off, I look back through the rear window, and see the twins and their father standing on the front steps. Damen's hand is clamped down on Ren's shoulder as if holding him still. I turn back around, and lean against the seat.

I blow the hair out of my face.

"Hmph."

I guess I underestimated that bitch.

By the time the processing is over, my eyes are starting to close again. I'm slumped in a chair, with both hands handcuffed to the arms, next to an empty desk, in an almost empty police station. A young woman in her late twenties wearing a police uniform comes up to me.

"So you're the Beaumont girl, huh?" She asks.

I nod.

"Well, it's nice to meet you. My name's Mel. I'm a part of your soon to be father-in-law's pack." She holds out her hand. I try to lift mine but they're constricted.

"Oh, that," Mel says, and sticks her hand in her pocket. She pulls her hand back out with a key in her palm, and uses it to take the cuffs off.

"What are you doing?" I ask, rubbing my now free wrists.

"Oh, you're free to go. Ren got Tess to drop the charges, and Lia found a video that hadn't been tampered with to prove that it was self-defense."

"Well, thanks."

"Don't thank me, thank them. They're outside waiting for you."

"Alright, well, it was nice to meet you," I say.

She nods. "Yeah, just next time we meet, let's not let it be here, okay? Or at the very least not you in handcuffs. Otherwise we're going to have a cell dedicated just for you and your fiancé." I nod, even though I don't really understand the last part. And I pretend I didn't hear the fiancé part.

"I'll try," I say.

"And be careful with Tess, okay? Now you know the extent she'll go to, to be with Ren. Not that he even wants her."

"Thanks," I say, and then she points me to the exit.

Moving the way she told me to, I get outside, to find Ren leaning against the passenger side of the car with Lia in the passenger seat. Lia see's me first – Ren's on his phone – and she grins at me.

"Hey. How was your first night in jail? Did you get a bitch?"

Ren looks up at me, his face neutral.

I smirk at Lia.

"Sadly, no. They were fresh out of bitches."

"Ah, rats."

Ren slips his phone into his pocket, and stands up straight.

"So, how did you get her to drop the charges?" I ask him.

He shrugs. "I have a way with words."

Really? Ren good with words?

I scoff. "Yeah, right. Mr. Silent-and-Brooding."

He shrugs again. "I told you, I don't brood," he says, and reaches into the backseat, pulling out a sweatshirt.

"Thanks," I say, and pull the sweater on over my head. I go to the back and pull myself in while Ren walks around the front and gets into the drivers seat. After Ren pulls onto the road, I lean forward, sticking my head between the twins.

"So, I was told that if I was arrested again, there would be a cell dedicated to me and you... so what'd you do?" I ask Ren. "Did you beat somebody up?"

Lia laughs. "Yeah, more than once or twice."

Ren just smirks. I poke him in the shoulder. "So, what's on the rap sheet, Blackheart?"

He chuckles. "It's very long. Some of the reoccurring ones are public indecency, assault, and the wielding of a deadly weapon."

I scrunch my nose. "Public indecency?" Then I narrow my eyes. "Did you have sex with a girl in public?"

Lia lets out a bark of laughter, and Ren just looks at me in bewilderment. "No, dork, but it's nice to know what you think of me. And, although that thought has crossed my mind, no, that's not what I got arrested for." He then shrugs. "I'm a werewolf. Sometimes, when I shift into my human form outside of the pack walls... I've gotten caught."

"Uh, huh. And the assault? Who did you beat up?"

His voice is suddenly cold. "Hunters. For the most part."

I gulp, and think about the day in the woods. Ren must think about it too, because he says, "We were lucky that it was just a regular Hunter. He was probably searching for deer. If it was a Hunter, they would have been searching for us. They wouldn't have been alone, either. He probably just came across Lia and thought that he had gotten lucky."

"The Hunters... are they common around here?"

The twins look at each other.

"No," Ren says, shaking his head. "Sometimes some come sniffing around, but we lead them off the trail. We do everything carefully so that we don't attract them. Hence, the pack walls. And if we do... we handle it."

They kill them, he's basically saying. I'm not naïve. I know the threat of the Hunters. They think of werewolves as abominations, that we don't deserve to live. Thankfully, I've yet to come across one – a real one, that only hunts our kind - but they have taken family from me.

I lean back in my seat, and I stare up at the hazy light sky of early morning. It must be about five in the morning now. Behind me, the moon slowly descends. I look at it for a full moment. Goosebumps break out over my skin, and I know what is coming. The moon calls to me, stronger than it ever has before.

"The full moon is coming," I say, more to myself then the twins.

They both nod, but remain quiet. We all know what this might mean. I might shift. For the first time in my life, I might shift!

I have been hear throughout two full moons, but each time, I forced everyone to leave me alone. I locked myself into my room, and wouldn't let anyone in until the night was over. I barely remember any of it. All I do remember is that Ren would be there the next morning to check on me.

This time, with my body changing physically, I can feel everything in me changing as well. My senses are heightened. I can feel the moon. I can smell that change in the air. This time… this time I think it is going to be different.

This time, it also happens to be Halloween. I heard around school that there were going to be parties all weekend. Lia wanted to go but we will all be a little incapacitated during that time. Seeing as how we shift into furry animals during that time. Well, they shift, I just kind of writhe in pain.

When we get back to the house, Damen meets us at the front door. It is clear that he has been waiting for us. He smiles down at me when we walk through the door.

"Good to have you back, Rory," he says. "And don't worry, we all have been arrested a time or two."

"Hey! Speak for yourself," Lia says.

"Yeah, I don't really think that is something to brag about," I chuckle to Damen.

Damen smiles at me and turns to his son. "It's all been taken care of?"

Ren nods.

"Good, then let's go to bed, shall we? I think there's been enough excitement for one night."

We all bid each other goodnight, and then we go our separate ways. Damen to the second floor, Lia to the third floor, and Ren and I to the fourth. Silently, Ren follows me to my room.

"She won't bother you anymore," he says, after a moment.

"What did you do?" I ask, knowing he's talking about Tess.

"Nothing important," he replies, his face stoic, not revealing anything.

I open my door, and we both walk into find Jas, sprawled out on my bed, fast asleep.

Ren chuckles at the sight.

"Well, I guess I'm sleeping on the couch," I say, turning to walk downstairs. Ren stops me with a hand on my arm.

"No, you can sleep in my bed. I'll sleep on the couch."

"No, Ren-"

"It's fine, Rory," he says, waving a hand.

"Fine, but you sleep in the bed, too," I say, stopping him before I can really think about what I am saying.

He raises an eyebrow at me, in surprise, and honestly, I don't know who is more surprised, me or him?

"With a pillow between us, of course," I say quickly, to clarify that *that* is not going to happen. "No funny business."

He snorts. "I wouldn't dream of it."

I roll my eyes.

Ren walks into his room through the bathroom, while I go into my closet and change into my pajama's.

I go into Ren's room, right as he passes me to go to the bathroom. I climb into the bed, and pull the blankets over me. Ren comes out a few moments later, and smiles at me, before collapsing face first next to me onto the bed. He lets out a content sigh.

A thought occurs to me about the last time I was in the bed with him.

"Ren… your dreams… what are they about?"

He lifts his head, and he looks straight at me, indecision clear in his eyes.

"They're just dreams," he says. Then a slow grin begins to spread on his face. I look at him funny, and then he raises an eyebrow. I grab a pillow, and place it in between us.

Ren laughs. "Afraid of the big bad wolf?"

A sly smile forms on my face. "You're not that bad."

"Oh, Princess, you have no idea," he says, giving me a wink.

My face flushes, but I force myself to say, "Actually, I think I do. After all, you keep referencing fairly-tales. It makes me wonder about you."

"A lot of people wonder about you."

I snort. "In your dreams."

"No," he says. "But, I'll be in yours."

Suddenly, I'm so tired. My eyes start to droop, and my limbs no longer work. I don't reply to Ren. I just slowly begin to fade.

"Goodnight, Princess," I hear him say, softly.

I really have to stop imagining him saying things like this.

## Chapter Nineteen

I'm warm. Completely warm. And content.

A smile spreads across my face. I lift my arms above me, stretching. A groan sounds, and there's movement against me. I open my eyes, and peer across the bed. I lay in the center of it, with Ren's body pressed against me. Glued to me, really. Ren's head is tucked into my shoulder, his forehead against the skin of my neck. His arm is thrown across my waist, holding my body tightly to his. There's a clock on Ren's nightstand, and it reads eleven o'clock.

A picture of Ren's face flashes through my head. It is not one that I want to see. It is him when he wakes up and see's us pressed together like this. An unhappy expression when he realizes that he and his mate are too close for comfort.

I shake my head. I don't want Ren to wake up like this. I don't want to see the horrible expression on his face, so I slowly, pull his arm from around my waist, and crawl out of the bed. I don't know how I do it without waking him, but I do.

Walking into our shared bathroom, I close the door, and shower. Then I creep into my room to find Jas gone. I wander into my closet, and change.

In a fresh outfit, and feeling clean after spending the night at a dirty party, and then in a dirty police station, I leave my room and head downstairs to the dining room.

The only person in the room is Lia, and she is eating scrambled eggs while reading a magazine. She looks up when I walk in and smiles at me.

"Hey," she says, a sly smile on her face. "Want some food?"

"Sure, can I get a sandwich? And a sprite?"

She nods, and closes her eyes for a second, mind linking someone in the pack about the food. She opens her eyes, and then turns to me.

"You know I can make my own food," I say, not wanting to make anyone do anything for me.

"Oh hush." She says, and then changes the topic. "And where did you sleep last night?" She asks, a sly smile on her face.

"I have a feeling you already know, so I'm not going to answer." I say, busying myself with a napkin in front of me, purposely avoiding looking at her. One of the cooks, Ben – a tall dark haired man in his thirties – brings out my food, and sets it in front of me.

"Thank you," I say, and he smiles, and then walks back to the kitchen.

"Did anything happen?" Lia asks, going back to our conversation.

I snort. "No."

"Sooo, how did you end up in his bed, anyways?"

Between shoving bites of food into my mouth, I explain to her what happened.

"He was having a nightmare?" Her body freezing up, shock forming on her face.

I nod. "Does he have them often?"

She hesitates before shaking her head. "No, not anymore."

Something tells me that she is not going to elaborate more on his dreams. We finish our food, and Lia looks over at me.

"You want to go for a walk?" She asks.

"Sure," I say.

We go outside, to the right side of the house, into the hedge maze. High in the sky there is a faint outline of the full moon.

"So, how do you guys handle full moon? Do you all, like, run around within the walls?"

Werewolves can shift from human form to wolf and back whenever they want. We have that control. *But*, we cannot control the shift during a full moon. Once the sun sets, our bodies begin to change, and they cannot return to human form until the next morning, after the sun as risen. I know that the Blackhearts have an issue with shifting outside of the walls, and since the space within the walls goes on for miles, it would make sense that they stay in.

Lia shakes her head. "No, we have a strategy. We have guards stationed on our boarders beyond the walls twenty-four-seven. When we want to shift, we stay within the wall, but on the nights of the full moon, we have guards check the territory, and then we all run together as a pack. We can split up if we want, like a lot of mates go off on their own, and... you know. But either way, we just have to stay within the borders, and just be alert. Colin is actually a big help. He tends to be on watch, keeping an eye out on the cameras for us, since all of us will be shifted. If he see's anyone he hits an alarm that sounds throughout the territory. The Alpha's can hear it from a great distance away, and they will call everyone back to the wall before anyone gets hurt. This way things like what happen with Carl Hansen won't happen again."

*Woah* is my first thought. That is a good plan, especially with what happened to Carl. My cheeks also burn at the thought of Colin. Thoughts of him, with his lips pressed against mine.

Lia notices the burn, and raises an eyebrow. "What?"

I turn away. "Rory?" She nearly screeches, and I can actually hear the grin on her face.

"I, uh… I didn't tell you about something else that happened last night," I say, slowly.

"Yes?" She asks, stepping into my field of vision.

"So," I wring my hands together, and drop my voice an octave, in hopes that no one can hear me. "Ren isn't the only boy who kissed me last night."

Lia stops, slapping a hand over her mouth. "Oh, my God. Who was it? Colin?"

Slowly, I nod. "But he kissed me! It didn't last long at all! I pushed him away right away! And I kind of yelled at him."

"Holy shit," She says, and she actually looks kind of scared for a moment. "Does Ren know?"

I shake my head vigorously. "Of course not," I breathe out. That is the last thing that should ever happen.

"Good. That's good. Rory, he can't know. Alphas have a bad temper to begin with, and Ren... he can be a hot head. If he finds out, he'll kill Colin. Literally."

I just nod to what she is saying. It's not like I doubt any of it.

"Oh, my god," I say, covering my mouth with my hand.

"What?" She asks.

"I completely forgot... your first kiss."

"Oh," she says, turning her head away, but I can see her blushing.

"So... how was it?"

She tries to fight off a grin, but she can't. "It was good. It was definitely more than one kiss."

I hit her playfully in the arm. "Dirty girl. So, who was he?"

"Just this guy, Matt. He goes to our school."

"Did you get his number?"

She scoffs. "Of course not."

"What you're not going to talk to him again?"

Lia shakes her head. "No, I could like him. I know that, but say hypothetically, something more did happen, and then I found my mate... I would just drop Matt. That wouldn't be fair, so I'm just going to wait."

I nod. "Okay, at least you know what you want."

She looks at me quizzically. "You don't know what you want?"

"Honestly, no. Your father made a deal with me to spend a few months here and then decide if I want to leave. And, I – I don't know if I want too. I don't know if I want to stay either. It's hard to be around him. Especially, when my wolf is calling for him."

Lia places a hand on my arm. "He'll come around. Boys can just be stupid. Especially boys like my brother. And, I mean, he kissed you, didn't he? That means something."

I shake my head. "Nah. I think he just did that to make me feel better. I was drunk and rambling."

"Well, all I can say is that I know my brother well enough to know that if he doesn't like a person, he shows it. And the way he acts towards you, he definitely is not saying that he doesn't like you."

Suddenly, she's still and her eyes glaze over.

"Rory, you've been summoned," she says no less than a second later.

"Let me guess, Ren is abusing his soon to be alpha privileges?"

She laughs. "Surprisingly, no. It's actually my father. He wants to see you in the infirmary. Don't worry, it's nothing bad."

We walk back to the house, into the infirmary where we find Lucy and Damen.

Lucy comes up to me, and touches my shoulder gently.

"How's it feeling?" She asks, calmly.

I'm puzzled for a second, then I remember that Tess hit me last night. Wow, I don't even feel it anymore and I completely forgot. "It's actually fine. I haven't felt any pain at all."

"That's good. Can I take a look?" She asks.

I shrug my black cardigan down my shoulder, and she shifts the strap of the tank top I'm wearing down my shoulder. She gingerly feels around my shoulder.

"No pain? At all?"

"Nope," I say.

She pulls away, and I pull my cardigan back up.

"Well, it's completely healed which is a good thing. That means that you're getting stronger. But remember what I said? If this happens again, come to me first."

I nod, feeling sheepish. "Sorry about that."

"It's fine, just don't let it happen again, okay? We also want to talk to you about the full moon and what's going to happen."

"What do you mean?"

"Well, you've been doing exceptionally well. Your weight and your strength are looking much better, but I'm still worried that it may not be enough. So, what I am thinking is that we'll set you up in your room and make you comfortable, and when nightfall comes, Colin is going to inject you with this. It's pain medicine that will hopefully knock you out."

"Why do I need the syringe?" I ask. I've been fine without it.

Damen and Lucy share a look. Then Damen speaks. "The change is a very painful experience, and sometimes very weak wolves... don't make it. Really, it is amazing that you have survived this long, Rory. Basically, you're a miracle. But we don't want to lose you, so we're trying to help you and your wolf through this."

"We need your wolf to shift on its own, not forcibly shift on a full moon, because there is a smaller chance of surviving. By doing this, we're making sure you stay alive," Lucy cuts in.

I take a deep breath as I digest their words. "Whoa. I'm a miracle. I've never heard that one before."

Lucy gives me a reassuring smile. "We're going to take care of you, Rory."

I just nod. "Thank you."

They give me odd looks, like 'why is she saying thank you'.

"Alright, the day is coming to an end, and the time for the shift is coming closer. Rory, I suggest you go upstairs, and get comfortable. Colin will be up there shortly," Damen instructs.

I follow his orders, and go upstairs with Lia. When we walk into my room, there is a TV positioned in front of the bed.

"What's the TV for?" I ask.

"That was actually Ren's idea," Lia tells me. "He knows you like movies, so he suggested the TV and some of your favorite movies to help you be comfy. He's actually at the store now. He'll be back soon."

"Okay," I say. That was… nice of him.

Lia heads out of the room while I go into my closet. I change into a pair of comfy yoga pants, a sports bra, and tank top. When I emerge from the closet, there's a plastic grocery bag on my bed. Hmmm.

I look around, but I'm the only person in the room. I walk cautiously over to the bag, because, ya know, it could be a bomb or something. I peer into the bag, and instantly start grinning. It's from Ren.

Inside is a group of my favorite movies, and all of my favorite snacks. There are four movies. All action packed, and comical. Grinning, I grab the bag and get comfy on my bed.

My door opens, and Lia walks in, dressed in black joggers, and a black tank top.

"Hey, it's almost time. We're going to be heading out soon."

I nod. "Okay."

She gives me a sad smile. "I'm sorry you can't come with us," she says.

I simply shrug. "It's not your fault."

The bathroom door opens and Ren comes through. The twins look at each other, then Lia turns to me, smiling. "I'll see you later, alright?"

I nod. "Have fun," I say, returning her smile.

She leaves and then Ren turns to me.

"Is there anything else you need?" He asks.

I look at the food laid out on the bed. "No, I think I'm good."

"Okay, then. We'll be back in a few hours."

He begins walking towards the door that Lia left through.

"Hey, Ren?" I call out, after a second.

Ren stops and turns to me. Before either of us can react, I throw my arms around his shoulders. He stiffens under me.

"Thank you," I say into his shoulder.

He nods stiffly against me. I let go of him, and step back.

He clears his throat. "I'll see you soon, okay?"

I nod. "I'll be here."

He gives me a small smile, and then he's gone. That smile sticks in my head after he's gone. After all, a small smile from him is better than nothing.

I put one of the movies into the DVD player, and then I settle back onto the bed. After a few minutes, Colin comes into the room, carrying a chair.

"Hi," he says.

"Hi."

He sets the chair down next to the bed, and sits in in.

We're both quiet for a few moments.

"I'm sorry," he says.

"Me too."

"No, I mean it. What I said yesterday, it wasn't true. I was just… angry."

"You'll find her one day, Colin, and I promise she'll be everything you'd hoped for."

He just nods. "So… this movie, huh? Never thought of you as someone interested in *The Avengers*. There is so much action."

I laugh. "Oh, you have no idea."

"So," he says, leaning against the bed. "Who's your favorite character."

## Chapter Twenty

I'm so engrossed in the movie that I don't notice the fading of the sun. Halfway through the movie, I begin to feel it. It is a pain that shoots through my body, blanketing me. I clutch at my chest. My heart is pounding, shaking my body. I can feel it all, the moon calling to me, to my wolf, forcing it out of it's hiding place.

I jolt straight up, shaking the bed, and shocking Colin.

"Rory? What's wrong?" He asks, standing up. He comes around the bed.

I can feel my wolf wake, coming to the surface.

"I'm going to inject you with the medicine, okay?"

I nod, and he steps closer to me while pulling something out of his pocket. There is a sharp pain in my neck, from Colin pushing in the syringe, and after a moment, I feel the medicine flow through me. I wait a couple seconds, but nothing happens. The pain doesn't go away.

"Colin, I need you to go," I breathe out.

"What? No, I'm supposed to stay."

"I don't care! The medicine isn't working." I growl. "I don't know if I can control this. Please, go," I gasp, barely getting the words out.

He hesitates.

I roll off the bed, landing on all fours. My neck cranes, and I feel like I'm a puppet, being pulled by strings. Everything snaps. I can feel everything changing, my teeth elongating.

Colin still stands in front of me.

"Go!" I growl, and this times he listens.

The pain grows and grows, and I scream and scream. All I can see is red. Everything begins to grow hazy.

Then it's all dark.

My dreams aren't much different from my reality. All pain.

When I wake up, it's to the feel of a blanket being laid over me. Then hands are under me and they lift. I groan. Every piece of my body aches.

"Shhh," a voice soothes. His hands, his voice, his smell, they're all soothing.

He lays me on the bed, and when I open my eyes, I see him hovering over me. Sweaty, and... *naked.*

"Ren," I groan, and shut my eyes, trying – not very hard – to erase the images from my head.

"Oh, sorry," he says. There's movement, and when I open my eyes, he's wrapping himself in a sheet, and he sits in the chair next to the bed that Colin had occupied earlier.

He looks at me with kind, worried eyes. "Are you okay?" He asks.

I try to nod the best I can.

The door to my room opens, and Damen and Lucy walk in, fully dressed, thankfully.

"Hey, sweetie," Lucy says, in a soft tone. A tone one might use with a wounded animal. I guess that sounds about right. "Did you shift?"

I shake my head, and close my eyes, as shame consumes me. "No, I passed out before," I say, my voice hoarse, from screaming. "The medicine didn't work."

"Well, we can consider that a good thing. Wolves are naturally warm, and they usually sweat things out quickly. Alcohol, medicine, calories," she says the last one with a chuckle. "If the medicine didn't work on you, it means your closer to shifting."

Feeling uncomfortable with all of them watching me, I open my eyes, and get out of bed, clutching the blanket around my body. I stumble a little on my way to the bathroom, but I wave away their hands when they try to offer help. I make it to the bathroom without falling, and even into the shower. I turn it on full blast, letting the hot water run down all of my sore muscles, finding a pleasure in the pain.

When I get out of the shower, I find a tank top and shorts, on the counter. As I'm changing, I hear Damen say, "You'll help her heal. Your touch, it'll be soothing to her."

I exit the bathroom, and find Damen gone, and Ren in a pair of sweatpants. He holds something in his hand.

"I have this cream that Lucy gave me. She said it should help soothe the muscles."

I nod. He steps closer. I hold out my hand, but he shakes his head. "I've got it," his voice hard. Determined.

My hand falls away, and I stare at the wall beyond him.

He steps even closer. "I'm going to touch you, okay?" he says, his voice low.

Another nod.

He puts some of the lotion on his hands, and begins sliding it slowly over my shoulders, my arms, my neck. He slowly lifts my tank top up, ending right below my breasts. He kneels, and begins rubbing it on my stomach, and my back. Then he rubs up and down my legs. I close my eyes to his touch, relishing in it. The feeling of his skin on mine, I absolutely adore it.

When he stands, and pulls away, I open my eyes, heat burning in my cheeks. Our eyes connect, and he nods towards the bed, and I take that as him telling me to get in. I walk over and slowly – carefully, crawl in, and lay down. I leave the blankets off of me because between the sore muscles and the heat of Ren, my skin is practically on fire.

Ren comes over and begins to lie next to me.

"What are you doing?" I ask.

He doesn't stop moving. "Laying with you."

It is the tone of his voice that makes me concede. Makes me think that this is okay. He speaks the words so softly, quietly, like he is bearing the truth and doesn't want anyone to hear it.

I put my hand against his chest, stopping him. "I don't want you to, just because you feel like you need to. Like you're supposed to."

He shakes his head. "I want to."

Lying on his back, he throws his arm across the bed by my head. I lean on my left elbow looking at him. He just stares at me, waiting. I look over his chest. Scars, and burn marks cover it. He doesn't shy away or hide them under his clothes like most might. Instead, he wears them proudly, like the warrior he is. I touch a burn mark with my fingertip. He tenses underneath my hand.

"Wolfsbane?" I ask, looking up at his face. He watches me carefully.

Wolfsbane is sort of like werewolf kryptonite. When it touches our skin, it burns like a bitch.

He nods.

Slowly, I lean in and lay my head on his chest, curling against his side. He wraps his arm around my back and shoulders.

"I'm sorry," I murmur against his warm skin, wishing I could take away his pain – even though the pain is long gone. Or at least, physically it is.

"*Sleep*," he commands, and for once, I do as he says.

This is my life for the next three nights. I sleep during the day, my body knocked out from exhaustion. My body heals itself, with Ren's help, and when I wake up, I'm no longer in pain. But then the shift begins, and the pain starts all over again. Each night I would wake up after the shift, and find Ren resting on the bed, waiting.

The others go back to school on Wednesday, but I stay in bed, sleeping. When I wake up around noon, there is a body next to mine in my bed. I smile to myself, thinking its Ren. I pull the cover off of my head, and see long dark brown hair. Nope, not him.

"Morning, Lia," I say.

She rolls over and smiles at me. "Morning, sleepy dead. How are you feeling?"

I shrug, the best I can, considering I'm lying down. "Definitely better. I guess that's a good thing. I'm healing faster."

"Yeah, your body is definitely in better shape. Maybe your wolf will come out and play soon. And on top of that, I've got exciting news. Ren says you're a white wolf."

Woah. White wolves are... well, I don't know much about them, but I do know that they are extremely rare. I certainly don't think *I* am a white wolf. There is no freaking way. It must have been a trick of the eye or something like that. There is no way that I am a white wolf. There is just no way.

"Wait, how-"

"He stayed with you while you shifted. You don't remember?"

I shake my head.

"Yeah, after the first night, he stayed with you. He shifted, of course, but stayed on your bed to watch over you. His presence helped, my dad said. Then he was there when you woke up."

I just stare at her, shocked. I wasn't expecting to hear that.

"I told you," she says with a sly smile. "He *does* care about you. I just wanted to stop by before I went to class. Make sure you are feeling okay."

"I am," I say, nodding. "I'm just a little tired."

She smiles at me. "Okay, I'll come by to get you for dinner, okay?"

I nod, and then she is out the door. I lie in bed for a few minutes, but her words echo through my mind. 'Ren says you're a white wolf'. A white wolf. Would could that possibly mean? Obviously, it makes sense, considering the thick mane of white hair on top of my head, but I've never actually seen a white wolf. Only heard of them. Then, I think of the small library that is here in the manor.

Pulling myself out of bed, I force myself up and into a pair of yoga pants and a t-shirt. Then I slowly, make my way down the stairs.

The house is quiet, except for the noise that I am making. When I walk into the library, I don't really know where to look. So, I go to the nearest corner, and start looking through the books, but I don't see any titles that might help me.

"What are you looking for?" A voice says, and I turn around.

Damen leans against the doorway, looking at me with a curious face.

"I, uh, want to know about white wolves."

He nods, as if he was expecting that from me. "You won't find anything in here. There hasn't been a sighting of a white wolf in a long time. But... white wolves, they represent hope."

He walks into the room and takes a seat underneath the window.

"The colors of our fur, the represent a part of us. For example, wolves with a burnt orange fur, like your dear friend Tess Bailey, are attention-grabbing. They are meant to steal the focus, to distract. They have a hunger for attention."

I smirk at that.

"Brown wolves are warm creatures. They represent earth and nature. Full of confidence, much like my daughter. Colors like theirs are the most common among wolves, but yours... it's unique. Special. White is the purest thing in our world. It represents purity, newness, and innocence. It represents life. Your wolf is a beacon of hope for our kind. It shows that there will always be life. Always be innocence. Something to look forward to beyond the darkness. I've never seen a white wolf in my existence."

Me. A beacon of hope. I give a dismissive shake of my head. There is no way this is true. No way. This is not me. I've never been something that people look up to, and I never will be. Nothing has ever felt farther from the truth than this. As this sinks in, another question forms into my mind.

"Then how do you know it is so special? A white wolf? How do you know that Ren wasn't wrong in what he saw, and that I really am not a white wolf? Maybe they are just a myth that doesn't really exist." Somehow, I just cannot believe any of this. Me, being a mythical creature, and still this seems far-fetched.

"You are right. Ren could be wrong. But, he also could be right. And yes, white wolves are a myth. But werewolves are a myth to humans, and we are real. So, what's to say that white wolves aren't? There is a little truth in every story. Tell me, have you heard of the King?" Damien inquires.

"You mean, the wolf who was so powerful he was considered the king of the wolves? Sure, I heard the stories when I was a child." I reply, confused by the sudden change of topic.

"Then you are familiar with what happened to his son?"

I nod, still not understanding where this is going. "Yes, his son fell in love with a human. Back then that wasn't approved of."

"You are half right. He fell in love with what he thought was a human. They kept their love a secret for a long time, but secrets always come out. They were found out, and the King punished his son. In front of his subjects, he fought his son. It wasn't a fight though, not really. His son, knowing that he disobeyed his father, and as a loyal follower of the King, he took his punishment, without retaliation. His love, the young human, knew something was wrong, and took off running. Not even knowing where to go, she ran. She ran through miles of woods, as fast as she could. She wasn't tired, even though she should have been. She wasn't even breathless. She somehow found the Kings home, and found he lover, beaten. The King was about to strike his son again, and she let out a roar. Everyone froze and turned to look at her. Though she wasn't there anymore. In her place stood a white wolf."

A deep frown forms on my face. This was never part of the story I was told as a child.

"How did none of them know she was a wolf?" I ask. We can smell wolves in their human form. We can tell from miles away when a wolf is near.

"Legend says that she was half human, half wolf. She was adopted, and didn't know of her past. Her shift was triggered by her mate almost dying. She was protecting him."

"What did the King do when he found out she was a wolf?"

"Well, his son wasn't necessarily forgiven because he did go behind the King's back, but their love wasn't against the rules anymore. They mated, becoming even more powerful then the King himself."

"This wasn't that long ago. Maybe like what fifty years? What happened to them?"

"It was more like twenty years, and they were killed. Slaughtered, by an unknown party."

"No one knows who did it?"

Suddenly solemn, Damen shakes his head. "The whole pack was demolished save for a few who were able to get away."

I take a deep breath, taking in everything. I shake my head again. What does all of this have to do with me? There is no way I am a white wolf. I know who my parents are. They are nothing like that girl. The white wolf. I'm not like her. My parents are cowards. My father a power hungry man who hates everything that doesn't help him in some way. He hates woman, thinks there beneath them. And my mother let a man treat her the way that Marcus did. She didn't run. She didn't try to stop him from doing the worse to my brother and I. They resemble nothing that the white wolf represents. She went up against an Alpha, *the* Alpha and all because she thought her mate was in trouble. She didn't care that she was human, and that everyone in that pack would have ripped her to shreds. She was courageous, strong. A fighter.

Not like me. No. Nothing like me.

"What about Ren's wolf? What does he represent?" I ask, thinking back to the original conversation Damen and I were having just moments ago.

He lets out a deep breath. "Well his is a black and that is why it would make sense for you to be a white wolf. Mates are like a yin and yang.

One fits the other. You – your wolf represents life, and his represents death. You are the black and the white of our world. The strongest pieces. The most powerful. You were right, Rory. You are the farthest thing from weak. If you and Ren were to mate… you would be the most powerful wolves in our land."

No, I know that this is not true. He is talking about someone else. I'm not destined for greatness. I'm a small-town girl who has spent most of her teenage life left locked in a room, and I haven't been able to shift for at all in my life. I am not supposed to be this great and powerful being. This is not in my cards. "You – you've got the wrong girl. This person that you are talking about, this white wolf, it isn't me."

Damen stands up, pulling me from my thoughts, and with a hand on my arm, brings me to the wall with the pictures lining it. He points to a photo, obviously from a long time ago. It's a picture of a young man, in slacks, and no shirt, dancing with a girl in a white dress and a flower crown. The man is facing her, and only half of his face is shown. Her face is on display, as they seem to be dancing.

"That was Raina. It was our wedding day. She was the yin to my yang. Everything that I ever wanted in life. I love Lucy, but Raina was it for me. I would give anything to have her back. But I have accepted that things happen for a reason. Ren and Lia they are going to be the best they can because of what they have been through. And you, my dear, will have the same fate. Don't over think it. Just let things fall into place." He places a hand on my shoulder and gives me a reassuring squeeze. "I'm glad you're feeling better."

Then he leaves me to my thoughts. I stand at the wall for some time, looking at the photo of Raina and Damen, and then I search for her in other photos. Marveling at the beauty that was the Blackheart Queen. Later, I replace him on the bench below the window, and stare out at the trees for a while. How did I end up being in this place with him? Destiny? Is that what this is? Is this the way it is supposed to go? I mean, Ren and I are mates, but we avoid each other. We are not together, and yet we supposedly represent something so great.

Eventually, I make my way upstairs, and back into my bed. I spend most of my time not sleeping and staring at the wall doubting everything that Damen has just told me. I let out a deep sigh. What in the world could possibly happen next?

The next morning, Lia wakes me up again. "I wanted to see if you're up for going to school today. You kind of have to go. It's been three days. Some people might get suspicious."

"Yeah," I say with a yawn. "I mean, I don't want to go, but I'm feeling better, so I guess I have to. Plus, if I stay here, I am alone with my thoughts, which is never good."

She laughs, and gets off the bed. "That's the spirit. Now get your little fit butt up."

"Fit butt?" I laugh.

"Yeah, have you not felt your butt? Someone's been doing squats."

I don't remember her ever touching my butt. "Did you touch me while I was sleeping?" I ask.

"Oh, calm down. It was just the butt." She starts giggling manically. "'I touched the butt.'"

"What's up with you and 'Finding Nemo'?" I ask, laughing with her.

"Um, only that it's like one of the best movies ever."

"Alright, whatever you say."

"That's right, it is. Now get dressed."

"Yes, ma'am," I say, giving her a salute, before I drag my 'fit' butt out of bed.

"I'll meet you downstairs," she says, and then she's gone.

I change into something comfortable, and meet up with Lia and the others downstairs. Ren's nowhere to be seen.

"Where's Ren?" I ask his sister.

Lia looks at Kyle expectantly. "He's um," he clears his throat. "On a run. Blowing off some steam."

Lia and I just look at each other, and then we shrug.

## Chapter Twenty-One

After the full moon, life goes back to normal. At least, it goes back to my normal. I start working out again, this time with Lia, and after, we go to school. I haven't talked to Ren. Literally, not one word. Whenever I am at the manor, he is nowhere to be found. I am pretty sure he is avoiding me, though I have no idea why. It is probably because he was only helping during the full moon since he felt like he had too, and now he is worried that I think he wants something different. Trust me, I have no doubt about what that was. There is no question as to whether or not he changed his mind. I know he didn't.

It's Monday morning of the week following the full moon, the first week in November, and I'm walking into school with Lia and Colin. Colin and I have gotten better, back to being friends, which I am grateful for.

"So did you and Ren ever do that project for film class?" Lia asks.

I laugh. "No."

We walk past Tess who's staring – glaring at us.

"Can I help you?" I snap, without even thinking.

Ever since she got me arrested, she's stayed away from me. Except for the occasional glare of course, but today for some reason, it bothers me more than usual. Anger and irritation consumes my body.

Lia and Colin look over at me with the same expression that Tess has on her face. Shock. None of them, including myself, were expecting that.

"Excuse me?" She asks.

"You heard me. You got *me* arrested, and then you spend the whole week glaring at me, like I've killed your cat. So, is there something I can help you with? Because *obviously* you have a problem."

The shock slides off her face, and anger appears as she steps closer to me.

"I actually do have a problem. Considering you can't seem to stay away from things that don't belong to you."

"Are you talking about Ren, again? God, get over it. I think it's about time that you changed your tune because this talking about the same thing over and over again is starting to make you sound like a broken record."

"I wouldn't have to keep repeating myself if you would just stay the hell away. And I'm not just talking about Ren."

"Then who are you talking about?" I say, throwing up my hands in frustration.

"None of your business," she snarls.

"Seriously?" I ask. "It's none of my business who I'm supposed to stay away from, but I'm supposed to stay away from them even though I have no idea who it is that I'm supposed to stay away from."

Out of the corner of my eye, I see Colin looking confused. "What?" He asks, with a hesitant chuckle.

Tess' eyes glance over at him and her eyes soften for a second. She closes her eyes and shakes her head. When she reopens her eyes and looks at me, they're full of anger again. What the hell?

"I don't like you."

"The feeling is mutual," is my reply.

"Ever since you got here, you've put your nose where it doesn't belong," she says taking a step closer to me.

I roll my eyes. "Actually, ever since I got here, you've pulled me into your petty drama that I don't want any part of."

Tess' hands clench. "I swear to God, Aurora." I think that's the first time she's ever said my name, and that makes me even angrier because she has no right to use it in that tone.

"What? Are you going to hit me? Or are you going to try and get me arrested again because you couldn't hold up in a fight. I prefer the first option. Try it, I dare you."

We've attracted attention now, and Lia tries to pull me away, but I won't budge. Somewhere deep down I know that I shouldn't do this. That I should walk away, but I can't. I am just so overwhelmed with an anger and I can't seem to walk away.

Tess just stares at me, and I can tell she's debating her options right now.

"Do it," I say, trying to agitate her, wanting her to throw the first fist. My body itching for a fight. What the hell is wrong with me?

Tess raises her hand, but it never connects with me. A body pushes in front of mine, and catches her fist in his palm. His scent fills me up, and I resist a moan. I step forward, placing my hands on his hips and leaning my forehead on his back. I inhale deeply. Oh, god, he smells delicious.

"I told you to leave her alone," I hear Ren tell Tess. His body is tense against me. His voice rough.

"She came at me," Tess says, in a childlike voice. God, she is such a baby.

"I heard what she did, but I know you've also been antagonizing her this whole time. I told you what I would do if you messed with her again. You should know by now not to mess with me, Tess."

There's silence for a moment.

"I'm sorry," She says quietly.

"Don't do it again," he says quietly. Threateningly.

There's shuffling, but I don't bother to look.

Ren looks over his shoulder. "Are you going to let me go anytime soon?" He asks, humor in his voice.

My eyes shoot open – I didn't even realize I'd closed them – and I realize what I'm doing. I'm touching Ren. Practically pressed completely up against him. I push away from him, and take a couple steps back.

"I don't need you to come to my rescue," I say. "I was handling it."

He chuckles. "Oh, yeah. Handling it like you did last time where you ended up in jail?"

"Whatever." I turn to go to class, Lia still in step with me.

"What the hell was all that about?" she asks, when we are a few feet away.

I shrug. "I have no idea."

What is going on with me?

At lunch, I sit down in the cafeteria in front of Kyle, and Lia sits next to me, in front of Ren. For a couple days Mary and her mate Trevor had been sitting with us. Mary is a warrior and Trevor is the Lead Hunter.

"Where's Mary?" I ask Lia, when I realize that neither she nor Trevor is with us today.

Ren and Kyle are currently in the middle of their own conversation, and they don't pay any attention to me.

Lia looks over at them before turning to me, and whispering, "She's in heat."

"What is that?" I ask, with a confused glance. "That sounds painful."

She shrugs. "It can be." In a hushed voice she explains, "It happens once a year, and it's supposed to help you have pups. Your body gets hot, and you get really turned on to the point where it can be painful, and your mate is the only one that can soothe you. It just... it helps move things along."

"Does it have to be your mate?" I can't help but ask. What? I'm just curious.

Lia opens her mouth to respond, but a low growl cuts her off.

"No one else is going to touch you," Ren snaps, his voice low because we are in public.

I slowly turn to him, with a 'did he just' expression on my face. He is glaring at me. Literally glaring at me.

"This is a private conversation," I growl at him.

"I don't give a shit!" He hisses again.

"First of all," I snap back, trying to keep quiet, but struggling to. Who does he think he is? "It was a simple question. I'm trying to learn what I was never taught. Second, who do you think you are telling me what I can and can't do?"

"As your mate, and your Alpha-"

"You are not my Alpha!" I hiss.

We're drawing a lot of attention.

Ren's glare turns deadly. "That's right. I'm not. *Your* Alpha beat you and kept you locked in a room. Go ahead and go back to that if you're not going to listen to me."

I shake my head and let out a harsh laugh. "I don't get it. You don't want me, but no one else can have me?"

He scoffs. "I said, I can't be with you not that I don't want you."

"Isn't that the same thing when it comes to mates?"

He rolls his eyes, and I look away.

"You're just like him," I mutter, pushing my plate of food away from me, suddenly disgusted.

This angers him again. "What? Like who? Your father? I will never treat you like that asshole did. I will *never* hit you. I am nothing like him," he says filled with disgust.

I lean forward, making sure our eyes are connected, and in a low voice, I say, "Before you judge the man I'm forced to call my father, you should really look in a mirror. You may not have hit me… yet, but trust me. When it comes to causing me pain, you're just like him."

I stand up, while grabbing my bag, and I walk away. I throw my bag over my shoulders as I push through the lunchroom doors. Anger radiates through me, and I really want to punch something. I'm literally shaking. How dare he? It was just a damn question, and it didn't even involve him? Why did he have to blow a damn gasket? As I run a hand through my hair, I hear the doors open behind me.

"Ro," he calls. Ro?

I keep walking. I hear his footsteps as he comes closer to me.

"Rory," he growls this time, and then his hand is on my arm and he is pulling me around until

I am flush against his chest. He lowers his head, so it is inches from mine.

"Never compare me to that monster," he growls, his hands gripping my upper arms tightly. "And don't *ever* say I don't want you, again."

Then, his mouth meets mine. And, my back meets a wall.

His hands slide up to my shoulder, past my neck, and stop at my cheeks. He splays his fingers out in my hair, and his thumbs settle under my chin, and lift my head up. At just the touch of him, my body ignites. All the anger I was feeling washed away and was replaced with something... more.

My hands lift to his waist, sliding up his back, my hands fisting his shirt, pulling him closer. I can't explain the feeling within me or the feel of his lips on mine. I just... need them. I feel like I can't live without it. I *need* it, and then some. I pull him closer, my hands sliding along his back, and he comes willingly, a low sound coming from the back of his throat.

"Hey guys - Woah! I was not expecting to see this!" A voice says.

Ren pulls away and leans his forehead against mine breathing heavily. A low sound echoes through the hallway, and Ren pulls back a few inches, looking down at me.

"Rory, what's wrong?"

The sound echoing through the hall, is a loud growl that is... coming from me.

I look up at Ren, and the... whatever it is consumes me again. I grab Ren's shirt at the collar, and pull him to me, and this time I initiate it. I kiss him with force, and for a second he reciprocates before pulling away, blood on his lip. I nipped him. He touches the blood with a fingertip, then looks at me.

"What's going on?"

"What do you mean?" I ask, biting my lip while I look up at him. "I just want you." Oh, jeez, did I really just say that?

"Okay," he chuckles. "Now, I know something's wrong."

Lia's face comes into view, and I growl because she's too close to him. They both look at me strangely.

"Look at her eyes, Ren. I... think she's going to shift. Her teeth, they've lengthened."

His head snaps to her in shock, then he slowly turns back to me. I smile at him, and reach out to touch him, but suddenly pain radiates through my body. I cry out.

"Ren, she's going to shift, you have to get her out of here," Lia says in a rush, her voice hushed.

He jumps into action, grabbing my hand, dragging me down the hallway. At some point my backpack falls off.

"Ren? What's happening?" I ask, as another wave of pain rolls over me, my body shaking.

"The way I see it," he says while dragging me out of the building, and down a path that leads to the woods surrounding the school. "You're about twenty, right? I would say you hit puberty around what thirteen – fourteen? But, you never really experienced everything that should have happened to you. So, I think you've got a lot of pent up tension in you. Now, you're about to shift. Real deal, fully shift. Your wolf is near the surface, and being near your mate… well, you're full of need. Now, you need to shift, run, and let some of the tension out."

"Oh, okay, werewolf boy thinks he's so smart," I say with a pain filled laugh.

He chuckles. "It's Alpha to you," he says, but it's in a joking tone.

I double over from the pain this time, causing Ren to lift me into his arms. He continues on walking, and we go deep into the woods, the whole time, I'm crying out in pain.

"Is it going to be like this every time?" I ask him. "This painful?"

After what seems like hours, Ren stops walking and sinks down to his knees, placing me gently down onto the ground. He shakes his head. "No, I promise this will be the worst time. But… having your mate with you will make it easier."

"Why?" I ask, gasping out. I don't know why but just his talking seems to be helping.

"Well, you know how people say that sometimes twins can feel what the others is feeling?

It's like that. Mates – they share one soul. Ying and yang. One completes the other. I can take away your pain. Not all of it, but say you were," he gulps. "On the brink of death, if I were with you, I could help take away some of your pain. We'd share it, therefore lessening yours, and giving you a better chance at surviving. It would be easier if we were fully mated but, still, it's the same. Basically, a mate feels what the other does, but it's only to an extent. It's all about the bond between the two. The stronger the bond, the more helpful it could be... if two were mated fully, the bond could – in theory – save one mate from dying."

His phone begins to ring, and I flinch at the sound. It's more like it's right in my ear rather than a foot away. Ren digs it out of his pocket, then answers it before placing it to his ear.

"What?" He barks out.

"*How is she?*" I hear Lucy ask clearly from the other end.

"She's getting there," Ren answers. "Her eyes have already changed color, and her teeth have lengthened. She's in a lot of pain. What can I do?"

"*Well, the chances of her making it are really high. She's survived this long. You two have a bond. Even if it might not be that strong, it's still something, but there is always a chance of her not making it.*"

Oh, that's great.

Ren stands up and walks a few feet away, completely oblivious to me being able to hear what Lucy is saying.

"What can I do?" He asks again, clearly frustrated.

"*Well, you could mate with her. That's a sure thing.*"

He's quiet for a moment. "No... I can't do that to her."

I roll my eyes despite the pain raking through my body. At least *he's* sure that I'll survive.

"*I'd figured you'd say that. Just be with her. Comfort her. That will help her.*"

My body moves by an invisible force, and I roll till I'm on my hands and knees.

"Fuck," I groan. I can feel it, my body basically ripping apart to make way for the wolf trying to take over.

"Gotta go," Ren says in a rush, and then in the next instant he's crouching in front of me so that he is looking into my eyes. His eyes are changing color, fading to almost black.

"You're going to be okay," he says, and he lifts his hands to my cheeks. I clench my eyes hut and hold in a scream that tries to force its way out of my body. I gasp.

"Please, Ren, I don't want anyone to see me like this. Please, go," I say, pleading.

He smiles softly at me. "I know, Princess. It's just me, though, and I'm not going to pity you. I never have. Just let it out, let your wolf out."

It's like he said the magic words, because I can feel her breaking through, making her way to the surface.

## Chapter Twenty-Two

My skin feels like it's being ripped off, and then being scabbed over right away. My bones break, just to come back together in new positions. My face stretches and shifts around, feeling like my face got rearranged with a baseball ball bat. My nose pulls, and my ears stretch, and I can feel a tail forming out of nowhere. My fingers mold together and shrink into paws.

When the change is complete, the pain slowly begins to fade. Standing on all fours, I shake out my fur. I feel strong, vibrant, full of life. My body humming with power.

Ren stares at me with awe. I stand a foot or two under him, my head and body twice his size.

"Rory, you're – you're a white wolf. They are the rarest, the strongest. The beacon of hope to our race."

I – I can't believe it. After talking to Damen, talking so much about the white wolfs, I don't even know what to say. There was so much doubt that I couldn't be a white wolf. There is no way that it is possible, and yet here I stand.

Ren pulls his phone out of his pocket again, and shows me the screen. Me, my wolf, is reflected. I have golden eyes, and snow-white fur. My fur matches my human hair. Pieces of doubt fly through my mind. How could this possibly be? Damen's words from the other day in the library run through my mind, specifically the story about the King and his son. Maybe... Maybe I could be like her. To love someone so much that I would do anything for them? Even go against the strongest Alpha? I look up and meet Ren's eyes. What if what Damen said that day is true? What if we are meant to be something great? Ying and Yang. Maybe... maybe love, and hope -everything I doubted- is in my future after all.

"Can you walk?" Ren asks, smiling at me. He steps a few feet back, and looks at me expectantly.

Hesitantly, I lift one paw, and move it forward. It's shaky at first, but then I set in on solid ground, and go to moving my next one, and so on, and so on. It's odd to change from two legs to four, and yet it's the same. Once I do it a few times, it so feels natural, like walking on two legs. I stop when I'm standing a foot away from him again, and I let out a whine. I – my wolf and I – want to run. We *need* to run. It's like a drug that I'm itching to use.

He smirks at me. "You want to go for a run?"

I nod my head.

"Okay," he chuckles.

Then, he reaches for his belt buckle, and I let out a whine.

His smirk just grows. "What? These are my favorite pair of jeans."

I whine again, and turn my head. I can hear the ruffle of his clothing as he removes them. He lets out a loud groan, and there are little snaps as his body shifts. Then he appears in front of me, as a wolf. I've seen his wolf before but I was a little preoccupied with being shot and all, but this time I can really look at him up close. Now, the only thing on my mind is him. He has dark shiny black hair, and bright yellow eyes. There are patches of hair that are missing on certain areas of his body. The burns on his human chest are mimicked in his wolf form. There is also a piece of skin missing from the top of his left ear – something I've never noticed before. He stands only a few inches taller that I do.

I look at his fur, and then look down at mine covering my paws. White and Black. Yin and Yang.

He rubs against me, then throws his head over his shoulder, which I interpret as a 'come here' motion. He begins trotting in the direction he indicated, and me with my newfound energy, decide to run past him. He follows in the chase, and runs after me, nipping at my tail, forcing me to run faster.

It's completely exhilarating to have the wind rushing through my fur, and the trees blurring past me as I run as fast as I can, which is definitely way faster than I can run in human form. Now it all makes sense to me, how they have wolves running through the territory and the border. They run so fast, they can go miles in just minutes.

Ren charges past me, and I act on instinct. I jump and land on him, knocking us both to the ground. I get up, and jump so that I'm standing over him, with my tongue hanging out. Then, I start running again. A classic game of tag.

I hear a growl from behind me, but it's not one of his angry growls that I'm so accustomed to hearing. No, it's something… different. It's more like enjoyment. He encourages me to run faster, but it's not fast enough, because he knocks me to the ground, just like I did to him. I roll over, but before I can get my paws underneath me, he's there, locking me into place. He leans down and begins licking my fur. My body, my wolf, begins humming in contentment.

"Well, well, well, is this Ren? *My* Ren? Look at you, all grown up," says a voice dripping with malice.

Suddenly the carefree, happy Ren is gone, and is replaced with something worse than the angry Ren I have come to know. This time, he's downright scary. He growls lowly, and he bows his head, the hair at the back of his neck rising, as if he's feeling threatened. I roll onto my stomach and try to lift myself up, but Ren presses me down into the ground. The idea of him feeling threatened, makes me growl along.

A man stands in front of us, a few feet away. I don't understand how he could have found us here. We have not passed the edge of Blackheart territory, because Ren wouldn't lead us astray. But we are in the middle of the woods, with no homes nearby.

"And is this your mate? I never thought I'd see the day," the man says.

Ren's response is for his growls to grow louder and louder. I peer up at the man standing before us. He only has a little bit of hair that goes around his head. He's an older man, in his forties, possibly early fifties. He'd be pretty average looking if he didn't have three scars that down the left side of his face. The three lines are parallel to each other, and they start at the corner of his eye, and go all the way down to his chin. He smiles at me, but it's a sick, cruel smile, which he wears when he looks back to Ren. On his neck is the Celtic symbol that Ren once told me about, the one that Hunters wear.

"It's good to see that my scars have healed nicely," he says, looking over Ren's wolf.

This causes me to growl louder. The idea of him putting those scars on Ren. My mate pushes me farther down into the ground, as if he's trying to keep me covered, keep me hidden, even though we both know it is not going to work, considering how big we both are.

"I'll be seeing you soon, Doren. And your mate, as well. I can promise you that we will meet again."

Those are the man's parting words, before he turns and disappears through the trees. It's now that I notice the sky has darkened. We've been out here for hours.

Before I can think anymore, Ren grabs the fur at the back of my neck between his teeth – not hard enough to pierce the skin but enough to lift me in the air. He lifts, and turns me around to the direction that we came. When I don't move, he nudges me, and I start running. He stays behind me the whole time, nipping at my tail angrily to make me go faster.

He stops only when we reach his pile of clothes that he left just beyond the school grounds. He grabs them between his teeth, and then starts chasing me again.

It's not long before I can see the lights of the manor. There are all lit up just like the night that I was shot. Ren must have mind linked the rest of the pack, and everyone is on high alert.

Ren then charges in front of me and instead of going to the front gates, he goes along the wall, and stops near a door within the wall.

The wire door is already open, and Ren stops at it, and throws his head towards it. I go first and then he follows. Damen, Lia, and Kyle are waiting for us just within the door. The door is slammed shut, and I turn to see Hunter closing it. Lia and Kyle have ghostly expressions on their face. They are terrified. Damen... his eyes are filled with an anger, much like the anger that I saw in Ren earlier tonight.

Lia wordlessly steps forward with pieces of clothing in her hand. She holds them out to me and I take them in between my teeth. She points to a big tree to my left. I go behind it for coverage, and shift back into human form. It's painful, but not as bad as shifting into wolf form. To be honest, I kind of miss being a wolf already. I throw on the shirt and pants that Lia gave me before stepping out from beyond the tree. I cross my arms over my chest, because, ya know, I don't have a bra on.

I walk over, just as Ren steps out from beyond another tree, fully clothed as well. He has a grim expression on his face as he walks towards his father and the others.

"So, you are a white wolf?" Damen questions, though it sounds more like a statement. As if he knew all along. Like, he didn't doubt it as I did. "That's amazing," he says, and there is a sort of 'awe' in his tone.

"Thanks," I say, awkwardly, not really knowing how to feel at this point. One part of me feels like celebrating just for the sheer fact of my finally shifting, but casting a glance at Ren, I don't think that anyone is in a celebrating mood. Ren just stares at his father, his face stony.

"He knows about her," Ren says, clearly angry.

It doesn't take a genius to figure out who he's talking about. *Me*.

Damen sighs. "I know what you want to do. Believe me, I understand, and I want to do the same thing. But-"

"What you and I want don't matter. What matters is that now he knows about her, and now, she's as good as dead. There is a reason why I never wanted a mate, and he just proved it ten-fold."

I flinch at that statement. Lia, Kyle, and Hunter all shift their gaze to me, and I move around uncomfortably.

Damen closes his eyes for a moment, and exhales before opening them again. "We wait for the elders to decide," he says, his tone clear. His word is final. When an Alpha uses his Alpha voice, the command cannot be disobeyed, without utter determination. Most Alphas don't use it. Most think of it as degrading.

After that, Damen turns and walks away, and his son is left shaking with anger. I turn to him, to say I don't know what, but he's walking away before I have a chance to get a word out. Hunter follows Ren, probably to make sure he doesn't do anything bad. That is his job as Peace Keeper after all.

Lia throws her arms around me while I stare at her brother's retreating back.

"Congrats!" She says, a faint of a smile on her face, even though I can see that there is a type of sorrow in her eyes. "You've shifted!"

"I know," I say back, and she gives me a hug. "Finally!" I shout, completely excited for the fact, even though complete and total exhaustion pulls at me. With everything, shifting and running through the woods, all I want to do is sleep, but now... there are more important things.

I wrap my arms around her and hug her back before we both pull away. Kyle pats me on the shoulder as a way of saying 'congrats'.

I'm quiet as the two share a look. I can tell they're talking through the mind link.

"What?" I ask.

They look uneasy.

Kyle begins. "The man you saw in the woods... he's a Hunter. He's well known, and he-"

Lia cuts him off. "He's killed a lot of people. A lot of wolves. And his presence stirs up a lot of emotions for a lot of us here. Despite him being a known killer, we don't kill bipeds unless they attack first. But in cases like this, even though the decision may be obvious for some, it is up to the elders to decide. In this extreme case, the elders have been called and they're already here."

My eyes widen, I wasn't expecting them to be here already.

"They're preparing now. We should head in soon," Kyle says.

Suddenly, Kyle winces. "Yeah, Ren wants us back now."

We begin walking back to the mansion, and Kyle goes off to find Ren, while Lia and I go to my room. I change – put a bra on – before I follow Lia back downstairs again.

"Am I allowed to be in the meeting?" I ask. "I mean, I'm not technically a part of the pack yet."

Lia pauses. "This is a different case. If you were just his bride-to-be, you wouldn't be. But you're Ren's other half. It's one of the highest rankings you can get besides Luna. Since you are not an official pack member, I must tell you… If you speak to anyone who isn't a pack member about what is said in this meeting… you'll be subject to death."

I wince.

"Sorry!" She says, quickly. "And I'm not accusing you of being a traitor or anything, I just want you to know."

"No, no, it's fine. I understand," I reply.

"Are you ready?" She asks me.

I let out a sigh. "As ready as I'll ever be."

We continue walking again, and I don't even bother asking her what Ren meant earlier about me being as good as dead. I know I won't get an answer from her. I'm just going to wait until the next time I catch Ren alone, and then ask. I think it's about time I've found out what's going on.

Lia leads me down the stairs, and into the basement. There's a door at the bottom of the steps. She gives me a reassuring look before opening the door. I take a deep breath and follow her into the room.

Here we go.

## Chapter Twenty-Three

I feel like I'm in a room with a bunch of old professors. Seriously, the elders are a group of old hairy men. Figures it would be all men. Two of them are very round men, three of them are very skinny bean pole types, and the rest are average – not physically fit but not over weight either. The one things they all have in common is that they all have stark white hair. Some have short, and some have long, but they all have a full white beard covering their face. They have to at least be a couple hundred years old.

When Lia and I walk in, they all turn to look at us with… disgust? Or at least something close to that. The one in the very middle looks at me with a curled lip. Something about him seems to be oddly familiar. Like it is a face I have seen before. Damen leans forward in his seat, speaking quietly to him, and that is when I realize who the old man is. He is Damen's father and the twins grandfather. The one who the twins don't really talk too. I look away from him, feeling uncomfortable.

There is a long wooden table in the center of the room, about six feet wide, and twenty feet long. On one side of the table, there are five chairs. On the other side, there are fifteen. On the side with five seats, Damen sits on the far end with Kyle on his right. Ren sits in the middle next to Kyle with two empty seats on his right. Damen's Beta stands behind him, his gaze on the older men across the room.

On the other side of the table, all the other chairs are occupied with the old wolves.

Lia moves slightly on my right and places a light hand against my back pushing me towards the seated men. Kyle stands up from his chair, and pulls the chair to Ren's immediate right out for me to sit. He does the same for Lia with the last chair before returning to his own. I hesitate. Ren turns to look at me as I sit down next to him. If only I could know what he was thinking. With Marcus' pack, I was never allowed to be in the pack meetings. Even now, sitting here with all the men staring at me, I feel like I don't belong.

There's breath against my ear as Lia leans in to whisper, "Don't worry about them. If they had their way, there would never be women involved in making decisions."

I suppress an eye roll. Old men. Gotta love sexism.

A few more wolves file into the room, and then the door is closed, and the room grows dead silent.

"Well, we might as well start," one of the elders says. "Let's get on with it."

Ren nods, and he stands up.

I guess Damen is letting him take control of the meeting.

"Allister McHenry was spotted in the woods past the pack line this afternoon. I want to gather a search party to find him. I want to pay him the justice he deserves."

The elders look amongst themselves. Ren's grandfather is the one who speaks next.

"We have decided not to support this quest. Allister is one of the best Hunters our kind has ever gone up against. He never travels alone. If we track him, we have no idea what we might find. We understand what you feel-"

Ren slams his hand on the table, cutting the elder off. "No, you don't!" He yells.

I flinch.

Their grandfather, this elder, looks over at me quickly, before returning his gaze to Ren. The elder clears his throat.

"I can see that you have a lot of… stress. But, I'm going to need you to get a handle on it before you lose your head."

That felt like a slap in the face. He just… he thinks that I'm the reason why Ren has stress. Because I'm not…*relieving* him. That's what the looks were about earlier. To them, women are just there for the men to use. *Oh my god*, can we get with the times? Woman are not just for sex!

"If he needs *relieving*, he can go on right ahead and do that. I'm not stopping him,". That's not what I'm here for! And, there is nothing stopping him if that's what he needs. Lia grabs my hand under the table, squeezing it tightly, and at the same time, Ren's right-hand shoots onto my left shoulder, clamping down. Not hard, but enough to know that it's a silent warning to *shut the hell up.* I bite my tongue. Really, really hard.

"Allister deserves to die," Ren says, his voice dangerously low.

"We all agree to that, Doren, but we cannot stand by you on this decision."

Ren's jaw clenches. "If that's what you feel," he says.

Ren pushes up from the table to leave, but then the elder speaks up again.

"There is one last thing, Doren, before we depart. It is in regards to your... *mate."*

I close my eyes so that no one can see the eye roll that I can simply not hold back. I've heard that tone before. It's full of disgust, probably not only towards me but towards the fact that I am a women as well. I've heard it so many times before from Marcus. Ren stops and turns back to him. He raises his eyebrows in a silent question.

"Her father is on his way here. It seems he wants her back. He should be here within a few hours."

After dropping that bombshell, the elders make haste in leaving.

My heart drops out of my chest. I can't believe that Marcus thinks he can just come and take me back. I can't believe that Marcus even traded me in the first place. I am not cattle. I am a person. A wolf. I am one of their own, and still they treat me as if I don't mean anything to them. I am so tried of not being able to make my own decisions. No one is asking me what I want. The last thing I want is to ever go back there. Back to Marcus' Pack.

And, why? Why would Marcus want me back? Why on earth would he want me back? I don't mean anything to him. He has made that abundantly clear from all the years of cruel treatment he has shown me. Everything that has happened in the past few months flies through my mind, and the air in my lungs is suddenly sucked out. The thought of going back there, of being back with that man, back in that room, it makes me… want to die. I've finally had a taste of what life feels like. To have friends, a family, to care and be cared for. To belong. I cannot – will not – go back to that place. It is my own personal Hell.

Chatter begins throughout the room, and Lia just looks over at me, her hand instantly tightening around mine, like she won't let go.

"Enough!" Ren yells, after a minute, quieting everyone down. "Marcus Beaumont has no hold over Rory, and he has nothing to use against us. She will be staying here. That's the end of it."

Without looking back, Ren leaves the room, with Kyle and Hunter following. Well, that's good, at least. Now I know he isn't going to just hand me over like cattle. The air returns to my lungs. Part of me thought he was going to let them take me. But… what if Marcus tries to forcibly take me? Or what if he makes the Blackhearts an offer that he cannot refuse, just like they did to him?

The though makes me sick to my stomach, that once again I might be traded like a piece of meat. I shake my head. I cannot believe that would happen.

Everyone else in the room begins to file out, but I hang back. When it's just Damen, Lia, and I, I turn to Damen.

"Why would he want me back?" I ask. "What could he get from that?"

The look on Damen's face scares me a little. "I honestly have no idea. But, trust me, you are not going anywhere. We will not let anything happen to you."

That statement calms me a little, but then what might happen to them if Marcus comes ready for a fight? I shake my head, trying to get rid of the ill thoughts, when another thought occurs to me. The Blackhearts made Marcus a deal he couldn't refuse. Damen never told me what it was exactly.

"Why exactly did you make the deal with my father to have me come here?"

Damen sighs, and looks off into space. "My mate was in an arranged marriage. Did you know that?"

I shake my head.

"Yes, to a man who wasn't cruel or anything, but her father wanted the land that he owned. I met her when she came to the mall, looking for a dress. We found we were mates, and of course, naturally, we wanted to be together. She told her father about me, but he had said no at first.

But she was a daddy's girl, and he would've done anything to make her happy. Plus, my father, who was Alpha at the time, had more land, and was more powerful. I would in time inherit that, and be more beneficial to her father. Suffice to say, I despise arranged marriages, and they should have been done away with long ago."

I give him an odd look, and he chuckles.

"You're probably wondering why I would have you in an arranged marriage if I disliked them so."

I nod.

"Well, the man you saw in the woods with Ren? That is Allister Mchenry. He's killed a lot of our people. We got word one day from a friend in another pack, that your father was helping Allister. I could never figure out why Marcus was helping Allister. It goes against everything we believe in. But… years ago, I put out a… warrant is probably the easiest way to explain it. It was like a warrant for Allister's arrest. If anyone caught him, he was to be turned in to me, and I would give him the correct punishment. When we were told that he was there, we went right away, but your father had already sent him away, and he wouldn't tell us why he was helping him. So, I threatened to start a war. When, your father claimed he had no idea where Allister was, I wanted his head, but then… I said that if he gave me you, I wouldn't start the war. I had multiple intentions. I thought if I could not save you, then at least you could give us information on your father. It wasn't a secret to anyone in the neighboring packs the way he treated you. But in the end I thought that if I couldn't get Allister, I could at least save you."

"I'm sorry that I didn't have anything to tell you about him. I'm sorry I couldn't help you get him. Both Marcus and Allister," I tell him, remember the day I got here when Ren questioned me about seeing Hunters at the Beaumont Pack.

He puts a hand on my shoulder. "As long as we were able to save you."

I take a second to digest it all.

"Thank you." I say, after a few seconds.

He clearly wasn't expecting me to say that.

"You are very welcome. I hope you have found peace here."

For a moment I feel like tears might come to my eyes. "I did. I really did."

I throw my arms around his shoulders, embracing him for a moment. He reciprocates before letting me go.

"And I know that you might not believe it, but Ren wants you here. He cares about you. And, I think he might need you tonight, even though he might not say it. But for now, it seems that we are going to meet your father before he can make it across our territory. We should be leaving now. I would go get a jacket if I were you, it is rather cold tonight. Even for us."

Damen stands, and I follow him up the stairs and to the front door. We go outside, and there are three SUV's parked in front. The first one is already full with pack members. The second one has a driver and a full backseat. Kyle and Ren sit in the back, and Lia sits in the middle. I climb in next to her. I glance at Ren, but he is turned away, looking out the window. Damen walks to the passenger side, and climbs in the front. Outside, pack members begin shifting and moments later, when the cars begin to move, and the wolves run alongside of us.

The car ride is silent, and very tense. It doesn't take long. Maybe twenty minutes to get to the far side of the territory. The drivers take a back road, leading us to an entrance to town that I assume is rarely used. They are not going to want to do this where people might see.

There is a clearing in the trees, and the car's stop just past the line of trees on the side of the road. Everyone piles out of the cars, and the shifted wolves file in front of the parked cars.

We stand for a few moments, quiet, to tense to talk, and then headlights flash around the trees, and a car appears down the road. Heading north right towards us.

Ren walks to the middle of the road, his father stands next to him, flanking his right. Kyle and Hunter flank Ren's other side, and Damen's Beta, Darius, on Damen's right side. Lia and I step up behind them, while others stand around us. As I move closer to stand behind Ren, he stiffens, and turns to look at me. Our eyes meet for a moment, but then the car is in front of us, only a few feet away, and his attention is back in front of him.

The car stops on the opposite side of the clearing and parks right in the middle of the road, just a few feet from Ren. There is a moment where there is no movement from anyone, and then the doors open. Two men slide out of the car and begin walking toward us. Franklin and Marcus. Franklin shows no emotion at all. Marcus in the lead, with a sick grin plastered on his face.

"A welcoming party for me? You shouldn't have," he says with a chuckle, his tone filled with malice, causing me to grimace. It has been so long since I have heard his voice, and it sends a shiver down my spine. If I never heard it again, it still wouldn't be enough.

Lia reaches out and grabs my hand. I grab on for dear life, clenching just as hard as she is. Both of us in fear of how this might turn out.

Franklin, follows closely behind my father.

"There is no welcoming to this visit, Marcus. Do not be mistaken," Damen replies, distaste dripping from his voice.

"Well, let's get to it then," Marcus says. "I've come here for my daughter."

"Then this trip was a waste of your time," Ren says, his voice low and warning.

"Ah, Ren. It seems you've become quite fond of my daughter. I have even heard that she is your true mate. What a shame for you. But like I've said, I've come her for her, and I am not leaving without her."

"You have come here uninvited," Ren says, his body shaking with anger. He steps forward. "You've threatened my mate." With each sentence, Ren gets closer. "And after abusing her for years, you expect me to just hand her over to you." He rushes the next few steps, and slams his body into Marcus', pushing him back towards, their car. Marcus' body slams against the car, Ren's hands clasping Marcus' throat. Kyle covers Ren, standing just a foot behind him, ready to fight.

Franklin growls and steps over to Ren, but suddenly Damen and Darius are standing in front of Franklin, blocking his path.

"You came here with one other man," Ren growls out. "I could kill you, right now." I see Ren's claws extend, a sign he's close to shifting, and they dig deep into my father's throat. "You have no hold over her anymore. You have nothing that we want in exchange. You are an idiot for coming here. Whatever you thought was going to happen is not going to happen. You will *never* get her back."

Something in his words, are deep and powerful, and there is no doubt now that this boy, this man, he does care about me. Whether or not he wants to admit it. I've never felt so sure of it before.

Ren throws my father away from him, and then backs away slowly.

"Leave," he says, his voice dark.

My father just smirks. "She will come back to me."

Marcus' eyes shift to mine. "I'll see you soon, Little Princess." I flinch and look away. That's what he used to call me when I was a child.

Franklin and Marcus get back into the car, and they slowly back away on the road. They hang a U-turn and burn rubber. Nobody moves until their taillights have completely faded from view.

Ren spins around, his glare focused on me. "What did he mean?"

His voice is thunderous, causing a shiver to break out over my body. His eyes are no longer the deep green that I have come to know, but the dark gold of his wolf. His rage is coming out, showing the beast inside of him.

"I don't know," I say, shaking my head, wrapping my arms around myself, the words of Marcus making me want to hurl. Just the thought of being back there… no, I don't want to go there again. It is a dark place.

"What did he mean, Rory?" He asks again, this time his voice harsher, louder.

Everyone in the clearing is facing us, looking between Ren and me. Somehow, he seems so much taller, towering over me, wanting an answer that I don't have.

"I don't know! I never want to go back there again! I have no idea what he was talking about!"

His words hurt a small part of me, thinking he trusted me more.

Ren closes his eyes and exhales. When he opens them again, he doesn't look at me. Instead, he walks back towards the town. He doesn't go towards a car, instead walks down the road back towards town. He strips off his shirt, then his shoes, and then he shifts into a wolf, and runs. I take a step in the direction he does, but Kyle stops me with a hand on my arm.

He shakes his head, and then he takes off running in the same direction Ren went. He jumps into the air, and shifts. When his feet hit the ground, he has four paws, his ripped clothes discarded behind him.

"Alright, it's getting late everyone. Let's get back," Damen says and we begin piling into the cars again, someone picking up the clothes in the middle of the road. No one says anything, because what can they really say. I climb into the back seat of one of the cars, and lean against the window. Lia climbs in next to me and leans her head on my shoulder, and wraps a hand around mine. I squeeze her, grateful for her presence and comfort.

When we get back to the manor, I follow everyone inside but then break away. A deep feeling inside me tells me to find him. After everything tonight, Damen is right when he said that he would need me tonight. Just like I need him, but in more than one way. I need his strength, his comfort, but I also need his truth. It is about time I find out what is really going on, and who Allister McHenry is. I take a deep breath, and smell the air, searching for a familiar scent, just like Lia taught me. Once I locate what I am looking for, I follow it. All the way to the other half of me.

## Chapter Twenty-Four

The closer I get to his scent the stronger I smell him. I can hear him once I reach the top of the flight of stairs. He is in the gym, punching a heavy bag. I slowly ease the door open, and slide inside, leaning my back against the door once it is closed. I lean my head against the door, and watch him as he circles around the bag, punching rapidly, all shirtless, sweaty, and hot… Focus, Rory. He catches a glimpse of me, and turns to face me, dropping his hands, and breathing hard. He's not surprised when he looks at me. He probably smelled me coming up the stairs.

He doesn't say anything, just looks at me.

"You need to tell me what's going on," I reply.

Still, he doesn't say anything. So, I decide to be open with him. To be honest.

"I need *you*, okay?" I say in a whisper-like tone. Like I don't want anyone to hear the words, because they are too true – too honest. "I need you, because I'm scared. I'm scared for what is about to happen, for what just happened. I'm scared because I need you to tell me the truth, and I'm afraid that everything is going to change once you tell me. I don't want to ever go back there, Ren. I don't ever want to see those men again. Please believe me when I say that I don't know what Marcus was talking about."

Begging. That is something I never thought I would do with Ren.

He closes his eyes, and rests his head against the punching bag for a moment, and lets out a deep breath.

After a few moments, he reopens his eyes and steps away from the bag. He takes off his gloves, and sits down. I go to the mini fridge that rests in the corner of the room, and pull out a bottle of water. I walk to Ren and hand it to him. He takes it, and I sit next to him, about a foot away. I clasp my hands together, resting them in my lap, and then I look down at the ground.

"You said 'she's as good as dead' earlier when we got back to the manor. Out of everything, I at least want to know why you said that."

I can feel him watching me as I speak, and out of the corner of my eye, I see him open the bottle of water, and take a sip. He lowers the bottle, and while he's screwing the cap back on, says, "Fine."

"You said you were scared. Afraid. You have no idea how afraid I am, every day. I have a lot of people that it is my duty to protect. A lot of people that I look out for. If I were to have a mate, I knew that when it came down to it, if I had to protect her or my pack, I would choose her. Hands down. I would love her so much that I would throw away everything else, everything that I have spent my life working to protect, for her. So, I decided at an early age that I didn't want a mate.

That if I ever met my mate, I would reject her because I couldn't be selfish. Not when I had my pack to protect. And what if I had lost you? I saw my father when my mother had died. He was not the same person. Hell, I am certainly not the same person. And if something had happened to my mate..." He squeezes his eyes shut as if picturing it right now. A deep breath later, he opens them again. "I never want to go through that. So, I locked away the idea of you. I was never looking for you. I never thought I would have found you. I *hoped* I wouldn't. I didn't want the pain that came with you."

    I'm not really sure how to respond. Different emotions play through me. Sadness, disappointment. Hope. I knew that Ren didn't want me here when I first showed up, but I didn't think it was because he was... well, scared. I wish that he had another reason. That he loved someone else. Or he just wanted, hell, I don't even know anymore. But to be afraid. We are all afraid. Life is scary, for god's sake. But to push away the person you are meant to be with out of fear... I don't know how to feel about that.

    "Tell me more," I request, needing to hear more. Needing to know everything that he has held back. Needing to focus on his words rather than the ones in my head.

    He stands up, distancing us. He focuses on unwrapping the punching tape from his hands.

"When I was twelve, my mother and I went for a walk. I hadn't had my first shift yet. The walls weren't built yet, and Hunters weren't a big deal yet. But anyway, my mother and I went for a walk. She had shifted and was walking beside me. Then, out came Allister."

He's quiet, and I can tell that this is hard for him to talk about. A part of me knows what is going to happen.

He continues. "Allister put it together that I was her son, so he attacked me first, but mom protected me. Then more of them came. He kidnapped us, and tried to get us to tell him where the rest of the pack was. Neither of us would tell him. He… tortured me in front of her. That's what all the scars are from. Then he tortured her in front of me. He… killed her. Right before my eyes… and, I couldn't do anything to stop it. He was going to kill me next, but by then my father had found us. He was able to save me, but Allister got away. Now, he's back to finish what he started. He wants to kill me because I'm the only one that got away from him. Now that he knows you're my mate, he'll come after you. I wasn't able to protect her then. And I won't be able to protect you, now. That's why I never wanted a mate." He turns to face me, his eyes meeting mine. "That is why I *don't* want a mate."

I'm quiet for a moment. And tears form in my eyes. I stand up, and spin around, not letting him see. He doesn't get to. I take a deep breath, getting ahold of myself, before facing him again. Part of me wants to cry while the other part wants to scream. I don't do either.

"Fuck you," I say quietly.

His eyes widen in shock. "Excuse me?"

"I said fuck you. I am sorry. Truly sorry for what happened to you and your mother."

My voice breaks for a second but I swallow it down.

"I really am, and I wish I could do something to help take away from the pain from that. But that doesn't give you an excuse to do what you did to me. No one, *no one*, expected you to be able to save your mother. You were twelve years old! You were so brave for her and that is more than anyone would have asked for. And now? Did you reject your sister? Did you reject being an Alpha? Because the last time I checked, you were about to be a leader of one of the biggest and toughest packs in the country. And then you say you can't protect *me*? Did I ever once say that I needed your protection? Despite what you think, I'm not some fragile girl who needs you to protect me.

"The first thing you told me when I met you was that you can't be with me, that you can't love me. And it was all because you think you can't protect me? Did you ever think that I could take care of myself? I've taken care of myself, Doren, for a long time. I went through my own troubles. Lost people I cared about. Everyone goes through something. Everyone has his or her own stories.

Everyone is scared. I thought that when I found my mate he would be… some type of beacon of light in the shitty darkness that surrounds me, but instead, you rejected me, just like my father did, because you couldn't deal with your own insecurities. You don't want to be with me, fine. But come up with another reason."

He stares at me out of utter shock, and I just turn away, shaking my head. I leave the room, and he doesn't try to stop me. I go straight to Lia's room, finding her sitting at her desk. I enter, and sit on the bed.

She looks at me questioningly. "Sure, come on in," she says sarcastically, before grinning at me. The grin fades when she see's my expression.

"Rory … what's wrong?"

Suddenly, it all becomes too much. I haven't cried for a long time. Not since I was younger at Marcus' home. Not when I was shot, or when Ren rejected me. Besides the close call of drunken ideocracies, I haven't let tears fall. Finally, they come through.

The bed dips as Lia sits next to me, placing a hand on my shoulder, the other hand holding mine.

"Shhh," She says, soothingly. "It's okay."

I wave my hand, trying to calm down. "I'm sorry. I just… I came from a talk with your brother."

She sits up straighter. "Oh, yeah? What did he say this time?"

"Well," I say, taking a deep breath. "He told me a lot. And, I sort of… yelled at him. Kind of. But I just really wanted to tell you that I'm…" More tears fall from my eyes. "So sorry about you mother, and what happened to Ren."

The tears fall like heavy rain, and my hands move to cover my face. It feels like every emotion is just pouring out of me. Like every time that I've wanted to cry, and forced the tears down, it's all coming out ten fold. Sobs come from my throat, taking over my body, and I shake in response.

Next to me, the bed dips as Lia sits next to me. Her hand goes to me shoulder, as she gently says, with a shaky voice, "Shhh. Shhh. It's okay. It was a long time ago. And Ren? He's okay. He's fine. My mother… she sacrificed herself for him. Allister was going to kill him first, but my mother, she egged him on. She knew my father was close by so she distracted Allister, and he ended up killing her. But she saved him, and as much as I wish that my mother was still alive, because of her, I have my brother with me."

She wraps her arms around me, lying her head against mine.

"I just – what is with all the death? Why can't they leave us all alone? What did we ever do to them."

"You've read the stories," a new voice says. I clench my eyes shut, and turn away from him. I don't want him to see this. "In all those vampire stories you've read, there is always a threat towards them. People are scared of what they don't understand, and in return, they retaliate. But that's not Allister's deal. The other Hunters, maybe. But Allister, his is a worst story. His family was killed by werewolves a long time ago. You know of the Rogues, and the danger they cause. Just like you know about some packs who go against the rules, and kill other bipeds. He had no idea about us then, but afterwards, he decided to hunt down as many as he could. He wasn't the first Hunter, but he's definitely one of the most dangerous. That's why we have the rules. That's why *we* have the walls."

When I look at him, he's leaning against the door, crossing his arms. His face stoic, revealing nothing to me about what he is feeling.

"I would like to talk to you," he says. Neither his face nor his voice gives anything away. Looking at Lia, she gives me a nod so I stand up, wiping my eyes, while following him. He leads me down the hallway, not to the end with the stairs, but the other end. There is a large window on the wall overlooking the garden, and the trees beyond that. I brace my hands on the sill, and I look outside.

We are both silent for a few moments so I decide to speak.

"Do you know why I don't want to be called by my full name?"

I look at him, and he shakes his head. I turn back to the trees outside, and take a deep breath.

"Aurora... she was different. Different from the person I am now. A kid, obviously, but she didn't see the world like I do. She didn't see her parents for who they were. She had hope. Hope in finding a mate, in living a normal life – or at least, our kind of normal. She saw the good in people. Her mother called her Princess. Said she was named after Princess Aurora. When my mother died, and my father turned me into his punching bag, that girl, she died. I didn't see the good anymore. I saw the bad and the worse. I saw pain. Anger. Not hope. And I was no a princess. And every time Marcus called me that, I hated my name even more. But… being here. It gives me hope. I see the good again. I never want to go back there, Ren. I never want to be that version of me again. I was dark there. I don't want to be dark anymore."

I turn fully, to look up at him. He slides a hand into my hair, and pulls me to him, his other arm wrapping around his waist. My arms go around his back, and I rest for a few moments, my head pressed against his chest, his chin resting on my head.

"You are not going anywhere," he says, and I wrap my arms tighter. He leans down, pressing his lips against my ear, and whispering. "You are my light."

It is said so lightly and quietly, that even me with my new hearing, think I made it up. I take a deep breath before pulling away, needing space from him, and his conflicting words.

"What did you want to talk to me about?" I ask, folding my arms around my waist.

He clears his throat, and looks away.

Well, what did he expect me to do after saying that? Just ten minutes ago, he said he didn't want a mate. Now, he says that to me. I don't know what he wants. I don't think he does either.

"You were right," he says, his voice quiet as he stands next to me.

I look at him shocked, making him chuckle.

"I know, not something I say often. But, you were. And, I'm sorry, for the way I treated you when you first came here. By the way, I never actually rejected you."

He gives me a small smirk, before he turns and walks away, and I just feel more confused. I lean my head against the window and let out a chuckle. That boy is going to kill me.

The next morning, I avoid Ren. I do my morning routine, and go to the gym, but when I go downstairs for breakfast, I sit at the end of the table with Lia next to me on my left, and Kyle in front of me on the other side of the table. He raises his eyebrows at me when I ask him to sit there, but I just shrug even though I'm pretty sure he knows what I'm trying to do.

Kyle leans across the table, smiling slyly while I keep my eyes trained on the door, waiting for Ren to enter.

"Are you trying to avoid someone?" He asks.

"No. I have no idea what you're talking about."

"Well, if you by some chance are, you don't have to worry about him coming to breakfast. He's not coming."

"Why?" Lia asks for me.

"I'm not his keeper," Kyle replies with a shrug.

"You aren't?" Lia asks, making me chuckle.

Kyle throws a piece of egg at her, and Lia just laughs in return, dodging the egg. They banter back and forth until it's time for us to leave for school. When we do, Kyle drives the jeep, seeing as how Ren is nowhere to be found. The whole ride to school, I'm stuck thinking about where he could possibly be.

When we get to school, though, Ren is already there, talking to someone in the hallway. Even though he probably already knows I'm here, I bypass him and go straight into the girl's bathroom down the hall. I lean against a wall, with my head against it, and wait for class to start. When I re-enter the hallway, it is deserted, and that is when I make my way to class.

Even walking into classes I don't make eye contact with him. When it's lunchtime, I find myself in the library rather than at our lunch table in the cafeteria. That's where Lia finds me. She comes to the table where I'm sitting trying to catch up on stupid math homework, and she slams a paper down on the table. I would've been startled if I hadn't smelled her coming.

"What is this?" I ask, looking down at the paper.

She just grins. "It's a butt load of fun, is what it is."

In bright colorful letters, the paper reads: *Thrift Store Pub Dance, December 1st. Admission ticket price is $5 per person.*

"A 'Thrift Store Pub Dance?'?" I ask, Lia, completely shocked. "Aren't we in college?" I chuckle.

She grins. "Yes, and that is why it is a *Pub* Dance. It's a few weeks from now, and we are going! It is a totally lame dance in the pub next to the student center. It's 'Thrift Shop' themed because we are coming up to Christmas, so it reminds people to get Christmas gifts, and thrifting is the cheaper way to go. But it is fun, and then there are the afterparties, which are even better."

"Wanna go together?" I ask.

Her smile turns sly. "No, I don't think you're going to be able to."

"What? What do you mean?" I ask, confused.

"Oh, I just mean I don't think you're going to be able to go with me since you're probably going to have a date by then."

"What are you talking about?" Colin is the first face that flies through my head, but I shake it. I won't be going down that road.

"I think you'll figure it out," she says. She winks at me, before walking away. "I'll see you next class," she calls over her shoulder.

I shake my head and chuckle at her as she walks away. She obviously was talking about her brother, but I seriously doubt he's going to take me to the dance. Unless, of course, she makes him, which I hope she's not going to do. Plus, we are in college, do we even need dates?

I'm able to avoid Ren like the plague until he decides to drop Lia and I off at work. We get out of the car, and I have every intention on following Lia inside, but I don't. Ren grabs my hand, stopping me. I pause and look back at him. He just raises an eyebrow at me.

"Have you been avoiding me?" He asks.

I shake my head. "Of course not." Nor more than he's been avoiding me.

"Good. Because I have something to ask you, and I cannot do that with you avoiding me."

"Alright. What do you need to ask?" I ask, turning fully around, facing him.

"Do you want to go to the dance with me?" I jerk back, shocked by the question. He doesn't ask it with any sense of hesitation.

"Did Lia put you up to this?" I ask, crossing my arms.

"What makes you ask that?" He asks, raising an eyebrow.

"Oh, I don't know. You just don't peg me as the type to want to go to a dance, let alone ask *me* to go to one."

"Is this you starting with the whole 'I don't want you' thing again? Because I've got to say, Ro, if you keep saying things that aren't true, you may just have to get punished."

I ignore the last comment. "Ro?"

He shrugs. "It's my new nickname for you."

"Oh, yeah? No more 'Princess.'"

"Well, with your father calling you it, I'd prefer to call you something else."

I nod. "Agreed."

The wind blows, brushing hair over my face, and he pushes it behind my ear with his fingertips.

"What if *I* called you 'Aurora'?" He asks, quietly, his fingertips brushing back and forth against my cheek.

I look away from him, feeling my cheeks redden. Something about hearing it come from his mouth…. "It's odd. Its been a long time since someone called me it on a regular basis. Though, I do like it when you say it."

Turning back, there is a grin on his face. "I'll save it for special occasions, then."

Chuckling, I nod. "Okay."

"So, what's your answer?" He asks, when he pulls his hand away. "We could get dressed up, go eat some dinner. Then stop for the dance. Maybe a party. I would even let you beat up Tess if that is what you wanted to do."

That puts a smile on my face. "You would let me do that?"

"If that is how you wanted to spend the evening, yes."

"As wonderful as that sounds, I think I am going to have to say no."

The amount of shock on his face makes me grin. "Thought I would be that easy, huh?" I ask.

"I don't know what to say," he says in disbelief.

"Look, I don't need a guy to take me to some dance. That's what friends are for. I need you to decide what you want. If you want me then prove that you do. That you want to be with me. Taking me to a dance doesn't say much if you push me away right after. So, maybe I will see you at the dance. Maybe I won't. Just decide what you want, Ren. Decide so that we can both finally live our lives. Together or not."

He stares at me, mixed emotions drifting across his face. I lift my hand and gently stroke his cheek.

"I'll see you later, okay?"

He nods, and then I climb out of the car, walk on shaky legs into the shop to find Lia waiting patiently behind the counter to tell her everything.

"So, want to go with me to the Pub Dance?"

Her mouth drops open in shock, and I let out a laugh.

"I don't know how you think this is a laughing matter! Oh, I am going to kill-"

Through laughing, I am able to get out, "I said no."

She freezes. "Wha- what?"

"He asked. I said no."

Lia launches herself at me, wrapping me in a hug all while laughing. "You are my favorite person ever. Literally, no one says 'no' to my brother. Oh god, I wish I could have seen his face. Was it great? Amazing? Did his jaw drop?"

"Close to."

"Okay, tell me, word for word what was said."

And so I do.

## Chapter Twenty-Five

When Lia and I get home from work we eat some food and then do homework. Ren is nowhere to be found and when I ask Kyle, he just shrugs. It is odd that he just keeps disappearing. When I feel like I am going to pass out from exhaustion, I stop by Ren's room on my way to bed, just to talk. About what, I don't know. I knock, but there is no response, and when I open the door, there is no one in the room. I sniff the air. His scent is faint; he hasn't been here in a while.

Where could he be at midnight?

Shrugging, I close his door again, and go into my room, change and then climb into bed. Not long after, I am out like a light.

"Get out! Get them all out!" A rough voice yells. A scream pierces the air. What kind of dream is this?

"Where is she? Where is she!" The rough voice yells again. Then, "Rory!" Pierces through the air. I jolt upright. This isn't a dream.

My heart is beating wildly. That was Ren's voice. He sounds worried. I rub my eyes, and try to see clearly. What the hell is going on? Is that... smoke I smell? The door to my room bursts open, slamming into the wall. Ren's eyes are wild, as he stands there, looking around the room. His eyes fall on me. His nostrils are flared, and his chest is heaving. He runs to me, catching my face in his hands, smoothing my hair onto the sides.

"Are you alright?" He asks, his voice soft and soothing.

I look up at him, confused. "What do you mean? I was sleeping… Ren, what's going on?"

He opens his mouth to speak but suddenly, Kyle appears in the doorway. "Get her out of here. Now," his voice solemn.

That shocks me that Kyle is telling Ren what to do, but what's even more shocking is that Ren actually *does* what Kyle says. Kyle disappears, and Ren scoops me up in his arms. One arm is under my knees, the other curls around my shoulders. He carries me out of the room. On the way down the stairs, the air is thick, and for bipeds they wouldn't be able to see at all.

"I can walk you know," I say, looking up at him, watching him concentrate while I'm still very confused.

"I know," he says, his voice rough. "I prefer you this way. I can't lose you."

"Ren, what's happened?"

He doesn't look at me. "Someone's set a fire."

"Who?" I ask. "Is anyone hurt?" Lia? Oh, god, Jasper?

"Two men were found dead on patrol. They were some of my father's warriors." I run faces through my mind – the men that I have met throughout my time here, trying to figure out the ones Ren's talking about. There are only a few left. Damen only has a few warriors that are still up and about, helping while Ren transitions to be Alpha.

"There's a few that have been burned, but not too badly. I was – I wasn't in my room, and when everyone started running out, you weren't there. You could sleep through anything, you know that?"

I shrug the best I can in his hold.

Once we're outside, he sets me down on my feet gently. Lia walks over, hugging me as Ren takes a step back. Lia pulls away.

"Are you sure you're okay?" He asks, looking me up and down.

As I'm about to respond, I'm pushed out of the way, and I watch as arms are thrown around *my* mate. Arms that happen to be attached to a familiar looking red head.

"I'm so glad you're okay," I hear her murmur into Ren's neck.

My body radiates with anger. What the hell is she doing on our territory? My wolf struggles to come out, but, thankfully, I'm able to hold her at bay.

I look Ren straight in the eye. "Peachy," I say, in response to his question. I turn and walk away. He calls my name, but I don't stop. I really have no reason to be mad. I'm not his, and he's sure as hell not mine.

Over the next few hours, I spend my time helping the pack. The only ones that were burned from the fire were an older woman and man. They were saving the kids, going from room to room, making sure that everyone got out. They got too close to the fire, but the good news is that they're already starting to heal. Firetrucks have already come and gone, and the police are still here. Now it is only the police officers that happen to be werewolves that are left, talking with Damen, trying to figure out what happened. Mostly everyone has been taken away from the manor, and back to their own homes with their families. The fire was bad. It started from the back of the house, and it caused enough damage to make the house inhabitable for now. Lia said that once Damen is done with the police, we would go stay at Damen's house for now. I help some people climb into their cars, and make sure that there is no one left around the property.

Lia finds me and smiles at me. "You'll make a wonderful Luna. I just hope Ren makes the right decision."

I look at her oddly. "What do you mean?"

She makes an 'oh crap' face, opens and closes her mouth.

"Oh, um, I, uh, just meant that I, uh…"

Lia, at a loss for words?

"What decision does he have to make?" I ask, cutting to the chase, knowing that there is something she isn't telling me.

Her face pales.

I sigh. "Where is he?"

"In the yard behind the house," she whispers out quietly.

Rushing past, I run around the house, and find Ren and Kyle. Ren paces, his hands on his hips, and Kyle sits on the stone bench underneath the willow tree staring up at Ren.

They both turn to look at me when they hear me approach.

Kyle begins to stand. "Um, I'm going to go."

I hold up my hand, stopping him. "No, it's fine."

My eyes don't move from Ren.

"Look," Ren says. He stands up straight and runs his hands over his eyes. "If this is about Tess-"

I cut him off with a scoff, and a roll of my eyes. "No, I don't care about the childish games you insist on trying to play. Tell me what is going on. Who set the fire? What decision is there to make about me?"

He sighs into his hand, but doesn't look at me. "Look, right now, I need you to go to the front, and wait with Lia, alright? I will come find you and-"

"No! Tell me now."

"Rory, go with Lia to my dad's house! I can't deal with you-"

"Stop treating me like I'm just another problem and talk to me! If this is about me, I have a right to know."

"God, you are a problem! That's the thing!" He grabs at his hair, clearly frustrated, but then again, so am I. "Ever since you got here you have been a pain in my ass. Scratch that, even before. The idea of a mate just lingering in the back of my mind, always just there to torment me!"

I jerk back like he hit me. "What? You think I wanted this? You think I wanted to have my mate chosen for me? To find a mate that didn't want me? I never wanted any of this."

His voice is softer as he says, "I'm trying to make this right, okay? I have to make a decision, and no matter what I decide it is going to impact all of us. So, you need to let me figure it out." I flinch when he says the last part harshly.

"You need to tell her, bro," Kyle says.

"Fine. Fuck." He thrusts his hands into his hair again, and lets out a deep sigh.
"Your father insists that you are to be returned," He says.

"I thought you said it was fine. That he didn't have a hold over me," I say with a shaky voice. Tears form in my eyes, but I try hard to hold them in. Fear strikes through me. Just the thought of going back there is terrible.

Ren watches me for a second, before placing his eyes on the table. "He... he set the fire. He left a note saying that if he doesn't get you back, he's going to start a war. We've gotten word that he's working with the Hunters. I don't know why or how, but-"

"But, that's the decision you've got to make. Give me up and save your pack. Or save me and risk your pack."

He flinches. "That's not - "

I swallow. "What... what are you going to do?"

"I don't know, okay? I don't know, dammit! I told you. I told you to leave it alone, but you just couldn't. I know that I have to figure this out, and I know that I need to do it soon, but I don't need *another* person reminding me. Dammit! Why can't you just do what you're told for once?"

I don't flinch this time. Instead, I stand a little taller.

"Do you know why I don't do 'as I'm told'? Because all of my life, I was beat into submission. If I do what people tell me to, then he wins and everything I went through was for nothing. And you think this is hard for you? You're not the one being traded like cattle."

He doesn't reply. Looking at him, it looks like he's having trouble not shifting. His eyes are shut, his jaw clenched, and his hands clench so hard, his knuckles are white.

I turn around to walk back to the front of the house. I stop and give him one last look. "I can't make you love me, Doren. So, I think your decision should be pretty easy."

Rushing, I make my way back to the front of the house. If he can't make the decision, then I'll make it for him. Pictures of Lia, Jasper, Kyle, Damen, Lucy and so many others pass through my mind. Even if Ren were to choose me, I couldn't just let him start a war. I'm not the only person at risk here. There are plenty of people that I care about that might get caught in the crossfire if this turns into an all-out war, and I can't risk that.

Before I can talk myself out of it, before anyone can see me, I run into the house, up the stairs and into my room. I hold my breath as long as I can because the smell of smoke is in everything, and it is so strong. I grab my bag from inside the closet. I dump my books on the floor, and then rush around my closet, grabbing only the essentials, taking deep breaths when necessary. When that's done, I pull on my gym shoes, and then creep into Ren's room. I go into his closet, and dig through the hamper. I find a pair of his black joggers, and a black hoodie that smell completely like him. His smell is all over them. I strip off my clothes, and pull his on, then toss my clothes into my room. I slide the backpack over my shoulder, and leave Ren's room.

Since Ren's scent is so strong, it'll mask mine. That way if anyone comes looking for me it won't be that easy to trace my scent. I stand at the top of the stairs, and listen for a second to see if anyone's around. There's no sound, so I descend down them slowly. As I round the last flight of stairs, I run smack into Lia. She begins to smile at me, but then it fades when she see's my bag.

"You're – you're leaving aren't you?" She asks.

I don't say anything. I just look down at the ground.

"Please, Rory, we'll find a way-"

"He doesn't want me here," I say with a shake of my head.

"What? Who?"

"I-I can see it on his face. And any chance that he does is because of what the mate bond is making him feel. Nothing else. And all of this, a war? Over me, when he doesn't even want me here? It's not worth it. It's not worth all of you. If I just go to my father, then none of you are in danger."

"You go back there, and there's a very good chance he will kill you. And, Ren, he's struggling. But he cares for you. He loves you."

I close my eyes for a second. "If he really did, there wouldn't even be a decision. Even if he did, I couldn't let him do it. I couldn't let him risk all of you."

When I open my eyes, I can see that Lia's struggling with what to say.

"Lia, look, I have to go. I won't risk you, Ren or anyone else. Please, I'm asking you because I *love* you. And if you love them, let them go, right? Please, let me go."

Lia pulls me into a hug. "I really don't want you to leave," she says, and it sounds as if she's trying not to cry.

"I know," I say.

"I love you, too," she says, and then she pulls away. "But, you need to get going before he catches on to what you are doing."

I nod. "I'll see you around, okay?"

She gives me a weak smile, tears in her eyes. We both know we will probably never see each other again.

"You're good, Lia. You made me see the good. Thank you." I choke on the words, and the tears begin falling. She reaches out, probably to comfort me but I shake my head and back away. "Bye, Lia."

Turning my back on her, I pull the hood up over my head trying to hold in my sobs until I get out of the house. I sneak around the house, and thankfully Kyle and Ren are no longer in the garden. I run through the garden to the small door in the middle of the wall is locked but I break it open. I step through and begin running as fast as I can. Suddenly I can't take it anymore, and I stop and lean against a tree. Tears fall from my eyes, and I let out a sob. I'm leaving the only people that ever cared about me to go back to my worst nightmare. Marcus can do whatever he wants to me, as long as he doesn't harm them. But, god, does it hurt knowing I'm never going to see them again. After I finally found a place where I belong.

I take a deep breath, wipe my eyes, and then start running. I need to hold it together, at least until I get far enough away. When I reach the end of Ren's territory, I shift, shredding out of my clothes. I put the backpack in between my teeth, and run even faster than I did in my human form. My body freezes up, when a long, loud howl pierces through the air. It's so loud that I can hear it from miles away. I recognize the voice, and I think I hear longing in it, but that just cannot be. Jerking back into action, I start running again, faster this time. I have to go faster. I have to get there before he even comes close to reaching me. If that was any indication, he already knows that I'm gone, and I have no idea what he's going to do.

    It doesn't take me that long to get to my father's pack house. Not long at all. Just a few short hours, and when I get there, I take a deep breath, before shifting behind a big tree. I pull clothes out of my bag, change into them, and then I hoist the backpack onto my shoulder, and walk up to the front door. I try to knock, but it takes me about three times before I can actually do it. It's a few seconds before the door swings open, revealing Franklin, a person I hoped I'd never see again. A slow sick grin spreads across his face.

    "Come," he says, before leading me into the house, and into my father's office. My skin begins to crawl as I look around the awful place I grew up. I never thought that I would ever be back here. At least, I *hoped* I would never be back here.

My father sits at his desk, and when he looks up at me, he just stares. I feel fear run through my body, as I think about what could possibly be going through his mind. He stands up, his face neutral the whole time.

"What." He moves around his desk.

"The hell." He moves closer to me.

"Are you doing here?" His voice is hard, cold, just like I'm used too.

Oh, how I didn't miss that.

"You wanted me back," I say, my voice quiet. "So, I'm back."

He lifts his hands, and moves my hair to behind my shoulders, and looks at my neck as if he's searching for something. Before I can even react, he lifts his hand and it flies through the air, and it hits me square in that jaw. I fall to the floor, clutching my face in pain. It doesn't last long. I can instantly feel myself healing. That's definitely different.

"You. Stupid. Bitch." He spits at me. "You can never do anything right, can you?"

He kicks me in the stomach, before I can stop him. "You never listen."

Another kick. And another. And another. His leg moves so fast it begins to blur, the pain building in my stomach, and I can feel liquid forming in my mouth as his legs slams into me again and again.

"Can't even get your own mate to want you," he mutters.

Again and again he kicks, muttering about things that I can't do right the whole time. Five more kicks, and then he finally stops, leaving me to cough up blood onto the floor. He leans down, and rolls me over so that I'm lying on my back. He grabs my face in his greasy hand. Lying on my back causes the blood to pool in my mouth, and I have to cough so that I don't choke on it. It spurts up, and lands all over my face.

"You," He spits out in utter disgust. "Were supposed to mate with your precious Ren." He sneers Ren's name out. "Then, he wasn't supposed to let you go, so I could in turn cause a war. Then with the help of the Hunters, I would kill you and your *mate.* But you just couldn't live up to what little expectations I had."

My shaky breath catches. Kill Ren? My wolf whimpers at the though and I cringe.

"You wanted my power? Our power?" I let out a choked laugh. I smile up at him, blood dripping from my lips. "I'll never let you have it."

He growls, and goes to kick me again, but a voice stops him.

"Alpha?" Franklin calls from the other side of the room. "The Blackhearts have been spotted. They're coming here. And fast."

"How soon will they be here?" My father calls over his shoulder.

"It's hard to tell. Half an hour. Probably less."

"Fine. Plan B. Get Allister."

His eyes fall on me again, while footsteps fade out behind him.

"Pathetic," He says, before standing and turning his back on me. I curl into a ball on the floor, still coughing up blood.

A minute later – I'm counting – a new voice speaks into the room.

"Marcus," Allister greets.

My father growls at the greeting. He turns around. "This is my... daughter. I want you to take her to the edge of my territory facing the Blackhearts land. When she is close to death, leave her for her mate to find. If he loves her, he'll mate with her to save her. And according to you, he does."

The words, 'when she is close to death' echo through my head.

Peeking up, I can see Allister smile as he looks down at me.

"Nice to see you again," he says, before bending down and reaching for me. "I do have to say, I prefer you this way. In *human* skin."

No shit.

"No," I yell, when he begins to lift me. I struggle against him but his grip tightens as I'm pulled from the floor and placed onto Allister's shoulder. My stomach lands right on his shoulder bone, and more blood spurts out of my mouth down the back of his jacket. "No," I shout again, starting to kick.

"Careful, Honey, hurt me, and I will kill him nice and slowly like I should've done when he was twelve. This time, I'll make *you* watch."

My movements still. He chuckles. "That's what I thought."

Allister turns towards the door, and I look up at my father.

"Why? I'm your daughter."

"You were never the daughter I wanted."

That feels like another kick to my gut. "I won't let you do this. I won't let you harm him."

My father's face turns evil. "It's already done."

My body shudders. "No!" I yell, tears streaming down my face. He just laughs as Allister takes me out of the room. He pauses in the doorway.

"Oh, there's one thing I almost forgot. I have a special gift for you, Aurora."

Allister sets me on my feet so that I'm facing him. He grabs something out of his pocket, and reaches towards the side of my face. I flinch a way, but his other hand is there, grabbing my hand, keeping me still. He pushes something deep into my ear, and the moment it touches my skin, I begin to crumble, screaming out in pain. Wolfsbane. It burns the shell of my ear, and I know that if I survive this, it will leave a permanent scar. I'll be lucky if I can hear again. Allister, pleased with himself, lifts me again and places me onto his shoulder once more. He carries out of the house, and into the woods surrounding it. He's not gentle either. It's as if he's making sure that every branch hits me on the way to wherever our destination is. Two of my father's men follow us the whole way. One of them is Franklin, who has a grin on his face the whole time. Sick bastard.

"This is good enough," Franklin says, after a while.

Allister stops, and I go down like a sack of potatoes. I cry out at the impact of my body hitting the ground, and I feel more blood begin to pool in my mouth. Something's wrong. I don't think I'm healing.

The man standing with Franklin inhales deeply. When he opens his eyes, they glow. "They're close." He says. "Maybe twenty miles."

Allister turns to the two. "You two go. She's far enough. There's only one thing left to do."

Franklin is hesitant.

"Do you really think I'm going to help her?" Allister asks, clearly annoyed.

"Fine," Franklin says. "Come back to the house when you're done with her. Hurry, we need to be on our way before the get here."

Franklin and the other man turn away from us and then disappear within the green foliage, leaving me alone with Allister. I look over at Allister and find his back to me, his face tilted up to the sky. Slowly, I lift myself up – with trouble – and I begin to crabwalk backwards.

"Did you really think that would work?" He asks, without turning around.

Stopping, I reply. "No, but I thought it was worth a shot."

He chuckles. "They always think it's worth it, but they don't realize it just makes me angrier." He turns around and pounces. His speed is sort of inhuman. He's in front of me within seconds, a knife against my throat.

"I need you to tell your mate something, okay?"

When I don't respond, he presses the knife harder.

"Okay?"

"Yes," I croak out.

"Tell him that his last breath won't be taken by your father. It will be taken by me. No *thing* ever gets away from me twice. Can you tell him that for me?"

He presses the knife in, and I can feel the vital fluid at my throat.

"Yes," I say again.

"Good girl," he says, softly, and touches my cheek. "In a way, I actually feel bad for doing this. Your father is wrong about you. You're strong. You'll be hard to kill, but fun all the same."

I don't see it happen, because he moves so fast but I definitely feel it. It's only then do I realize what's happened. The knife, that previously lay at my throat, now rests inside of me. On the left side of my stomach to be exact. I gasp. He pulls the knife out slowly, before driving it in again, higher than the first one. That's when I move my hands. My left hand goes to cover the first wound, putting pressure on it, and my right hand goes to the knife handle, half covering his hand. He knocks my hand away, and lifts the knife... he doesn't pull it out, he pulls it straight up two inches, and I scream out loud at the pain coursing through my body. It's ripping me apart. I scream, and scream, and scream, and he twists the knife handle in a circle. My screams echo throughout the trees.

"Hold on," Allister whispers, his mouth against my bad ear. "He'll be here soon."

Then he pulls the knife out of me completely and disappears from my line of sight. I lay on the ground, staring up at the starry sky, blood pouring out of me and onto the ground. Voices echo through my head.

*'You're not the daughter I wanted.'*

*'Ren, he's struggling. But he cares for you. He loves you.'*

*'I need to be honest with you, I can't... be with you'.*

*'This is my son, Doren Blackheart'.*

*'Don't question me! You will do as you're told!'*

All of my life, I was never able to do the right thing. Nothing ever went right, and now I have a chance to finally do the best thing I can. Die. I pray that the others won't find me. If they do, then our fate will be sealed, and Ren will die. I can't have that. I've lost too many people and I won't let him die, too. He means too much to too many people. He said it himself he has so many people to protect.

Slowly, my body begins to fail. I can feel it, everything, as it stops working. My breathing is already so shallow, and it's hard to breath in, let alone out. I close my eyes, waiting for the Moon Goddess to take me away. Take me away to my brother and mother who are waiting for me on the other side.

That's when I hear them. Footsteps. Dozens of footsteps. My eyes shoot open, and I hold my breath as I hear the feet coming to a stop. Everything's quiet for a moment, and then a shout pierces the air.

"Over here!" The voice yells. Ren.

My heart lurches, but I'm not completely sure if that's from knowing that Ren is nearby or if it's from the fact that I'm almost completely out of blood, and there's nothing left for my heart to pump. 'Cause, it totally could be both.

No, I want to cry out. No, please I silently call out. Please! Don't find me!

I can sense the moment he sees me. It's not long, not long at all before he slides down next to me, and I look into his eyes, seeing so much pain I want to cry for a completely different reason. An anguished cry falls from his lips as he looks down at me. I've never seen him look so broken. Why? Why does he look broken? Through the dark spots that are beginning to form in my vision, I see him look over my body. He stares at my hands covering the knife wounds. He slowly reaches out, and pulls my hands away. I try to resist, and say no, but he over powers me easily.

"Oh, god," A voice says. Lia. "I'm so sorry," She sobs out, and I see her as she moves to my other side, leaning over me. She looks down, and tears stream down her face. Kyle's head appears next to her, and his look is determined as he puts his hands against my wounds, pressing hard to stop the blood flow.

Ren leans back on his haunches, and howls loud and long. It's filled with so much emotion, and it stirs me up inside. He sags in defeat when he's done, and grabs my hand. He holds it against his chest while bowing his head against it, his lips pressing to my skin in the softest caress.

"Ren," Lia calls to him, looking over at him. "You have to," she says when he looks up at her.

He looks down at me, and I instantly know what is crossing his mind. All their minds.

"No," I try to say, but I'm not sure if it really comes out.

"Shhh," he soothes and rests a hand against my cheek. His other hand still holds mine. He moves the hand at my cheek to cup my chin, but with a lot of effort, I lift my free hand and knock it away.

Gathering up all the energy I have, I open my mouth, and force the words out. "No, Ren.

Please. Let me die." At the end of it, I choke up more blood, and turn my head spitting it out. I turn my head back to face him. "Just let me go," I whisper.

His sad, sad eyes look down upon me. "I can't do that," he says simply. "You're my light."

Ren leans down, and places a soft, barely-there kiss against my lips. Then he moves his head down to my neck. He gently kisses the skin. He inhales deeply. Then his teeth pierce the sensitive skin. I cry out once more.

Words that Ren once spoke to me echo through my head, as the dark spots around my eyes grow bigger. I can feel the blood being pulled from my body. It stops. Then liquid is poured into my mouth. His blood.

*'Mates – they share one soul. Say you were on the brink of death, if I were with you, I could help take away some of your pain. We'd share it, therefore lessening yours, and giving you a better chance at surviving. Basically, a mate feels what the others does, but it's only to an extent. It's all about the bond between the two. The stronger the bond, the more helpful it could be… if two were mated fully, the bond could – in theory – save one mate from dying.'*

Our bond will only be one sided. May the Moon Goddess hear my prayers.

*The bond could save a mate from dying.*

## Epilogue

Have you ever been asleep but awake? As in, you can hear the sounds of the people around you. You can even hear them talking to you, but you can't respond. You just… physically cannot respond. You can't call out. Can't move. Can't do anything.

That's what I'm like now. It's been like this for a while, I can't tell how long.

In the beginning, I could only feel his presence. He never touched me, but I knew he was within reach. Then, I begin to feel others as time moved on. Or at least I think it's moving. I don't think I'm dead. If I am, this certainly isn't what I thought heaven would feel like. Maybe it's not heaven. Maybe, I'm somewhere else.

I think I was wrong, though.

*'I thought that when I found my mate he would be… some type of beacon of light in the shitty darkness that surrounds me, but instead, you rejected me, just like my father did'.*

That's what I said to Ren the day he told me about his mother. I was wrong. Perhaps he *is* my beacon of light in the darkness. Because here, now, when I can't move, can't talk, can't see anything but the darkness, he's the only one I can feel. I can feel him, now, when he chooses to grab my hand. I can hear him, now, when he whispers in my ear.

"Come back to me."

But like I said. Maybe I'm in heaven. Maybe I'm somewhere else. To have him so close yet so far away just like in life… Maybe, this is my hell. Or maybe the Moon Goddess decided that I have had a hard enough life, and now I could finally be happy, and this is my heaven. To live a life with Ren, where I am no longer a pawn. To have him close even if I can't be with him. I'm no longer with Marcus. I'm no longer in pain. Now, I'm happy.

In a perfect world, I would wake up from a kiss on my lips. Where I would open my eyes, and I would be staring into the green eyes of the man that I love, and he would smile his silly grin while saying, "Good morning, Sleeping Beauty."
But, this isn't a perfect world. Nor is it a fairy tale.

I dream about a life with Ren. It is a long healthy life without people trying to kill us. There are no Hunters who want revenge. There are no fathers who hate their daughters. Instead, there is a special woman. I recognize her from the pictures in the library of the manor. Raina Blackheart. She smiles down at me, showing me the beauty that is more magnificent than what I saw in the photos.
In my dream, my heaven or my hell, it is Raina, Ren, and me. I smile because this is better than nothing. Even if it isn't the real Ren, I will take what I can get.

## About the Author

Catherine was born and raised in Chicago, and still lives there with her family, which include a dog and two cats. She studied writing at Lakeland College, and at Wilbur Wright College. Currently, she writes and works as a swim instructor.

Made in the USA
Lexington, KY
05 May 2018